**'I am not** ☐ **said instant**

That was not ☐ intentions at all! But in fact that was exactly what he was doing, was it not?

'You are not offering for me, but you think I should marry you?' Timothia queried blankly.

'What I mean is,' he amended, somewhat flustered, 'I am offering for you, of course, but not in the ordinary way. I am—well, I suppose I am proposing a marriage between us.'

Timothia blinked. 'Is there a difference?'

'Don't be obtuse! I can hardly be a—a suitor to your hand. We are too well-acquainted for me to have formed...' He trailed off, aware that he was dragging himself into dangerous waters. 'In plain terms, Timma, I am looking to strike a bargain with you.'

**Elizabeth Bailey** grew up in Malawi, returning to England to plunge into the theatre. After many happy years 'tatting around the reps', she finally turned from 'dabbling' to serious writing. She finds it more satisfying for she is in control of everything: scripts, design, direction, and the portrayal of every character! Elizabeth lives in Surrey.

**Recent titles by the same author:**

MISFIT MAID

# AN ARDENT FRIENDSHIP

Elizabeth Bailey

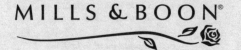

MILLS & BOON®

*First published in Great Britain 2000*
*Harlequin Mills & Boon Limited,*
*Eton House, 18-24 Paradise Road, Richmond, Surrey TW9 1SR*

© Elizabeth Bailey 2000

ISBN 0 263 82309 1

*Set in Times Roman 10½ on 12 pt.*
*04-0007-81999*

*Printed and bound in Spain*
*by Litografía Rosés S.A., Barcelona*

# Chapter One

There was some excuse for it, for the day was sultry. June had come with a vengeance, and the young lady taking her ease outside her own stables might be forgiven a somewhat indecorous proceeding. That she had recently returned from her habitual morning ride was clear to the gentleman whose affronted gaze was raking her person. He could see that Miss Dulverton must be feeling the heat. He looked, however, anything but forgiving.

At any other time, it would not have occurred to Mr Wetheral to question his cousin's right to sit about in any posture she chose. But with the object of today's visit at the forefront of his mind it struck him with unaccustomed force that this unseemly conduct ill became the lady whom he had selected for his bride.

Timothia was seated upon a rickety chair, her booted feet crossed at the ankles and tucked into a convenient slat in the kitchen fence, affording more than a glimpse of stockinged leg where the petticoats of her mustard-coloured habit fell away to the ground, gathering a quantity of dust and straw at the hem. As if this immodesty were not enough, she had discarded her jacket, which had been flung carelessly down upon the rough-hewn table to one side along with her gloves, whip and beaver hat, and her shirt was open at the neck to the tip of an embroidered waistcoat, where the swell of her bosom could be clearly discerned. Moreover, she had pushed the shirt's linen sleeves above the elbows, exposing bare arms to the sun. Last, but by no means least, Timothia's mane of flaxen locks, loosely confined in a heavy plait, was in more than usual disarray, a number of strands having come away to fall unheeded against her amber skin, which glowed with health and exercise.

It was a sight at once appealing and inappropriate, and it tugged irresistibly upon some deep-seated sensation within him that Mr Wetheral hardly recognised. It surfaced in a violent feeling of outrage.

The feeling intensified as he realised that Timothia's attention was so concentrated upon the newspaper in her lap that she remained unconscious of his presence. Then she reached out for a pewter tankard on the table, and looked up as she took a draught from its contents.

Perceiving her cousin, Timothia lowered the tankard. 'Leo! Where did you spring from?'

'What the deuce do you mean by this, Timma?' demanded Leo without preamble.

Timothia raised her brows. 'What do I mean by what?'

'This!' he repeated, tossing a gesture that encompassed the picture she presented. 'You look positively indecent.'

She glanced briefly down at herself. 'Would you call it indecent?'

'In no uncertain terms!'

With complete unconcern, Timothia took another pull from her tankard, and laid it down again. 'Well, it's hot.'

'Then go inside,' returned Leo. 'What if anyone were to see you in this state?'

'Unlikely, I think. Who else but you, Leo, would burst

in upon me unannounced? In any event, I can't see why you should suddenly take it into your head to censure me. You never used to mind how I look.'

'Well, I mind now,' Leo said trenchantly.

Timothia raised her brows again. 'Why?'

Leo found himself unable to answer this. He knew his own reasons, but he could hardly voice them without some preliminary explanation. He rather regretted having begun in this strain, for it made it difficult to know how to proceed. Moreover, Timma was right. Her appearance was typical, and, although he might deprecate them, he had hitherto found her tomboyish ways more endearing than otherwise.

She was looking at him expectantly, and he shifted his gaze from her face. Abruptly, he became aware that her habit was covered in short dark hairs. 'Do you tell me you have been grooming your horse?'

'It appears I have no need to tell you.'

A lilting smile lifted the corners of Timothia's mouth. It was a smile peculiarly her own, that never failed to arouse an answering chord in Leo. He found himself grinning at her.

'Timma, you are impossible.'

'So I have often been told. But not invariably by you, Leo. Whence this sudden change?'

He did not answer, and Timothia was surprised to see a faint tinge of colour enter his cheek. She watched him turn away and perch on the edge of the table, seeming to fall into a brown study as he eyed the toe of his boot. It was not like Leo to take her to task for being unladylike. Not that she was unused to have him ring peals over her! Four years her senior, Leo had assumed a brotherly interest in her affairs from their earliest association. Since Timothia had herself been born with considerable spirit, the resulting squabbles had echoed down the years. She was tall and strong, but Leo was taller and, inevitably as time went on, stronger, but that had never prevented Timothia from giving as good as she got. She had never allowed his strictures to weigh with her, and she did not intend to start now. Especially if he meant to turn his attention to reforming her.

She reached again for her tankard, hesitated, and then held it out to Leo. 'Would you care for some of this? It is excessively refreshing—on a hot day.'

He looked round, frowning. 'You have no need to try to provoke me, Timma. I am put out enough.'

Timothia laughed. 'I see you are.'

Leo took the tankard and sniffed at it suspiciously. 'What is this stuff?'

'A concoction of my own: ale and water, with a dash of lime juice. Try it.'

'I will do no such thing,' declared her cousin, thrusting the tankard back at her. 'Ale! Bad enough to be using that clumsy receptacle.'

'I like it. And I like ale—especially on a day like this.'

'If you did not insist upon working like a galley slave and sitting out here in the sun, you would have no need of it,' he grumbled. 'Why you must needs be grooming Faithful yourself passes my comprehension—and today of all days.'

He received a blank look. 'Today? It is Friday, is it not? What is so special about it?'

Here was his cue. Better get it over with. Leo drew a breath, and rose to face her again. 'Have you forgot that your year of mourning was up yesterday? But for that circumstance, I would have come to see you earlier.'

Timothia smiled. 'Did you suppose me to be prostrate with grief again?'

'No, I did not. I know you have long recovered from my uncle's death. But what I want to speak to you about requires your being out of mourning.'

She put up a hand to shade her eyes, and studied him. Leo had ever a lean cheek, but his aspect today was almost hawk-like as he stared at her from under dark brows. His eyes were deep-set and steel-blue, startling in features weathered to a deep tan from a life spent largely out of doors. Less startling now, Timothia reflected, the effect softened since he had left off the conventional confining queue tied at the nape of his neck and taken to wearing his dark brown hair fashionably cropped. It was swept back as it had always been, but its liberated waves tossed with a wanton abandon. Timothia approved of the alteration. It gave Leo a rakish air, at variance with the habitual neatness of his garb. He was in riding dress, top-boots highly polished, his frock-coat a sober cloth of deep blue, the waistcoat underneath darker yet, and a simple knot in his freshly laundered cravat.

'It is a matter of some moment, then?' she asked lightly.

'Very much so.' Leo hesitated. He should speak now, yet it was hard indeed to find the appropriate words. 'I suppose I might have known I should find you in such a case,' he said, prevaricating, 'and you have not answered my question.'

'Which question?'

'Why have you been grooming Faithful yourself?'

'Because Bickley is far too busy cleaning in the house to attend to his normal duties,' Timothia answered patiently.

'I should have guessed,' remarked her cousin, and bethought himself of another complaint. 'I need not ask if that means that you have been out riding by yourself.'

'But you know I always do so.'

'Don't I just! You career about the countryside with no vestige of support or chaperon. It is all of a piece!'

'Leo, you are very puzzling today,' said Timothia. 'What is all of a piece?'

'Your conduct—and this idiotic life you are leading,' pursued Leo, glad of the diversion. 'For one thing, this house is ridiculously small.'

Timothia sighed. 'Not that again.'

Upon the death of her father, she had removed from Dulverton Park, giving place to her cousin Dudley and his numerous family, to the quiet village of Fenton a few miles to the east. Fenny House, a gothic aged building full of creaking stairs and narrow passages, had been the only unentailed residence in Mr Dulverton's estate. He had bequeathed it to his daughter, with the recommendation to sell it against an increase in her dowry. Timothia had chosen rather to live in it, unearthing the elderly and widowed Mrs Hawnby, her former governess, to play propriety.

Timothia had thought it an admirable solution. Not so her friends and well-wishers. She seemed to have spent the better part of her year of mourning defending her position—an exercise which had become increasingly difficult as the inadequacies of Fenny House made themselves felt.

'It is large enough for my purposes,' she said now, as one in honour bound. 'Three parlours, bedchambers for myself and Edith, besides two additional rooms for guests, servants' quarters for six, a coach house and stabling for my horses. What more could I use?'

'Three parlours!' scoffed Leo. 'Those poky little rooms? Any one of my parlours would encompass all three. And if you have servants' quarters for six, why have you not filled them?'

'Because I have no need of six servants,' Timothia retorted. 'Three are quite adequate.'

'As we see,' he returned, gesturing significantly towards the stables. 'Surely you can afford a footman or a second maid? Why in the world Bickley continues to work for you when you oblige him to demean himself by—'

'Bickley,' interrupted Timothia with spirit, 'has been with me from my cradle, as you very well know. He put me up on my first pony, and there is nothing he would not do for me.'

'I dare say you will say the same of Padstow for allowing that gowky, giggling wench of yours to open the door while he disports himself among the cooking pots!'

'Polly is only fourteen,' Timothia said with dignity. 'You must expect country girls of fourteen to giggle when they open the door to personable young gentlemen. And as for Padstow, he is very much enjoying himself.'

'That I do not believe.'

'It's true. He is teaching me to cook.'

'That I believe even less!'

'Well, perhaps ''teaching'' is going too far,' Timothia conceded. 'But we have spent an agreeable session or two in the kitchen.'

'In cosy domesticity? You, Timma? I wish I may see it!'

'You may, if you choose to come and visit me when I am thus engaged. If you had only been here yesterday, you might have tasted some delicious tarts.'

'Of your making, no doubt,' suggested Leo derisively.

'Certainly of my making—with Padstow's help. They were blackcurrant. Or was it gooseberry?'

'Stop trying to bamboozle me!' ordered Leo. 'Do you seriously expect me to believe that you have been reduced to hobnobbing with your butler in the kitchen?'

Timothia sighed. 'If I am honest, it is a joy to hobnob with anyone. That is the worst of mourning—the lack of anything to do.'

'It has nothing to do with mourning,' said Leo irritably, 'but only with your witless determination to live here on your own.'

'I am not on my own. I have Edith, and Bickley, and Polly, and—'

'Padstow. Yes, I know, and don't quibble. You know very well what I mean. Though what possessed Padstow to leave Dulverton with you is beyond me.'

'Ask him. He will tell you that it is a great relief to him to be free of so much responsibility. The case is that he had dreamed in his youth of becoming a chef, but from one cause or another nothing came of it, and he ended up a butler.'

Leo gazed at her. He hardly knew whether to snort in derision or to laugh—if she truly believed such a fara-diddle. And if Padstow had really said such a thing it was plain that his devotion to his young mistress was of no common order. Abandoning the argument, he returned to the burden of his complaint.

'However that may be, you can hardly deny that to expect three servants to manage a household—'

'But I don't, Leo. There is Mrs Wye, who comes in daily to cook.' She added with her captivating smile, 'So you need not be sorry for Padstow. And we have a local boy to do odd jobs and attend to the garden.' She laughed suddenly. 'Though I admit to qualms about Mrs Wye, which is one reason Padstow has taken to the kitchen himself. Her cooking cannot be described as anything but mediocre, and if we are to begin to entertain—'

'Entertain!' exploded her cousin. 'In this crumbling ruin? I should hope you would not.'

'It is not a ruin!' objected Timothia indignantly. 'I grant you there are one or two repairs to be effected, but—'

'One or two repairs? Your guests might count themselves fortunate not to have the roof fall down upon their heads!'

'If you are come here merely to cast insults on my house, Leo,' warned Timothia frostily, 'you may go away again.'

'Oh, go to the devil!' exclaimed Leo, exasperated. He took a hasty turn about the table. 'How you can sit there and pass off this wreck as if you knew no better—! Deuce take it, Timma! Who is it who has jumped on myself or Valentine for the least little crack in a ceiling or wall? Who is it who delivers the sternest lectures to every landowner round about if she notices so much as a thatch out of place on a villager's cottage? Who is it—?'

'Very well, you need not go on,' Timothia snapped.

She swung her feet down from the fence and sat up, throwing aside the newspaper with a violence that spoke more clearly than any words the agitation of her spirits.

Why must Leo throw her misfortunes in her face? Could he not see that she was only trying to make the best of a situation which she had no power to remedy? She would give anything to be out of these cramped quarters! Besides, it was not quite as bad as Leo had described it, and she had already seen to some of the more urgent renovations. Indeed, in the early period of her incarceration—for so she thought of it—she had derived some small degree of relief from her sorrows in putting her considerable talent for management to work on creating a habitable environment.

The cost, in comparison to the large works undertaken at Dulverton Park over the years, had been trifling. Nevertheless, she had been obliged to request the services of the estate carpenters—a painful necessity. How she had hated going cap in hand to her cousin! Almost harder to bear had been Dudley's effusive generosity. Along with the carpenters, he had sent his agent, with strict instructions to supply Miss Dulverton with everything she needed, inclusive of materials and labour.

Crimdon, who had worked for Timothia for so long, had been far more embarrassed by the situation than was Timothia herself. But his very sympathy, and determination to go the length of his new master's orders to save Timothia expense, had served to rub salt in the wound. Throwing herself into supervision of the work had served to take her mind off the loss of her father's companionship, but it had done little to lessen the evil of losing Dulverton Park.

With some eight years' experience of running her father's estate at her back, it had been a bagatelle for Timothia to turn her hand to the improvements at Fenny House. Within a few weeks of the work having begun, there was nothing for her to get her teeth into. It had been this circumstance, as much as a dislike of being further beholden to Dudley Dulverton, that had led to her refusal to do more than the most pressing repairs.

Leo was right. It was a situation she would never have tolerated at Dulverton, nor, without adverse comment, in the estates of any of her acquaintance. But to have Leo pierce so unerringly at the core of her dissatisfaction was unbearable. She disliked those people who publicly bewailed their lot, and she would not be of their number. It was her invariable practice to make light of her troubles, even to her allies—of whom Leo must be counted the closest.

Before she could compose herself sufficiently to answer him without betraying herself, Leo spoke again.

'Timma, you cannot continue in this way.'

There was a note in his voice that she did not recognise. She looked at him, and found his intent gaze on her face, his expression full of some significance that she could not immediately fathom.

'I don't intend to,' she said, trying to speak coolly. 'Did you suppose I meant to continue living retired once my year was up? I assure you I have every intention of—'

'I don't mean that,' Leo interrupted impatiently. 'And if you were going to say that you intend to resume your former life, allow me to point out to you that without Dulverton Park you can't possibly do so.'

A choked sob escaped her, and a shadow crossed her face. Her eyes darkened with reproach and her voice roughened.

'I know that, Leo.'

Leo drew a breath. How was it Timma had always the power to make him feel brutal? Her mind was so robust that he was apt to forget she could be as vulnerable as the next female. But it was as well that she felt it this deeply. It must make her see the advantages as clearly as he did himself.

'Forgive me, Timma, but there is a reason for my being so blunt.'

'When were you ever anything else?' she said drily, recovering herself.

'That is quite unfair. We have known each other long enough, I hope, for me to be able to speak to you plainly.'

'True.' She looked up at him, leaning back in her chair

with a resumption of nonchalance. 'Well, then, your reason?'

He hesitated. There could be no more delay. What was the point in further procrastination? Yet why was it so difficult? This was Timma, whom he had known almost his life long. Had known and befriended, for they had been as close as one could ever be. Perhaps that was the trouble. They were friends. Could this truly work? Yet he had thought it all out, looked at it from every angle. There could be no denying that this was the way forward—for both of them. He took a breath, and plunged in.

'I think you ought to marry me, Timma.'

Timothia gazed at him blankly, all the earlier upset rapidly dissipating under the onslaught of amazement. His countenance darkened under the fixity of her stare, and an odd expression in his blue eyes caught her attention. It struck her that it did not fit with what she thought she had heard.

'I beg your pardon?' she said faintly.

'It's the perfect solution,' he uttered eagerly. 'Don't you see, Timma? If we were to marry, there would be an end to both our difficulties. That is why I waited until today. You could hardly have accepted me while you were still in mourning, but now there can be no barrier. Why should you stay in this skeleton of a house, when you might live at Wiggin Hall and exercise your talents on my estate? I will be only too glad to relinquish those duties, I can tell you. Do you realise I have had scarce a day's decent sport since inheriting the place? Near two years of it, Timma! I promise you, I am going mad.'

He paused for breath, and took in his cousin's expression. 'You look more astonished with every word I say,' he uttered, aggrieved.

'I am astonished,' said Timothia. 'What is more, I

cannot believe you to be in earnest. Is it some kind of joke?'

Leo threw up frustrated hands. 'Deuce take it, Timma, you must know me better than that!'

'I thought I knew you very well indeed,' she agreed, trying to fight off the hazy sensation about her head which was making it difficult to think. 'But I begin to wonder if I was mistaken. Why in the world should you suddenly take it into your head to offer for me?'

'I am not offering for you,' Leo said instantly. That was not a word that fitted with his intentions at all! But in fact that was exactly what he was doing, was it not?

'You are not offering for me, but you think I should marry you?' Timothia queried blankly.

'What I mean is,' he amended, somewhat flustered, 'I am offering for you, of course, but not in the ordinary way. I am—well, I suppose I am proposing a marriage between us.'

Timothia blinked. 'Is there a difference?'

'Don't be obtuse! I can hardly be a—a suitor to your hand. We are too well-acquainted for me to have formed…' He trailed off, aware that he was dragging himself into dangerous waters. He made an effort to pull himself together. Deuce take it, let him be coherent at least! 'In plain terms, Timma, I am looking to strike a bargain with you.'

A bargain! Timothia wanted to laugh at the absurdity of it, but at the same time she became aware of the oddest desire to weep. Torn by conflicting emotions, she found herself quite unable to speak. A bargain indeed! He meant her to understand, no doubt, that he had not formed a romantic attachment to her. Well, she knew that! How should he do so? Or she reciprocate such a feeling? The very intimacy of their close friendship precluded it. But, marriage? He was waiting. Apparently for her answer. Timothia made an effort to find her tongue.

'But it's…it's ludicrous,' she managed lamely. 'I have never heard anything to equal it. Are you sure you have not made up the whole thing for the purpose of teasing me?'

Leo met her eyes. He did not recognise what he saw there, but he acted upon it instinctively. Reaching down to find her hands, he seized them strongly and dragged her to her feet.

'Listen to me, Timma!' he uttered in a vibrant tone, his grip firm. 'Understand, once and for all, that I am not teasing you. I have not come here with some half-baked notion, but have thought the thing through most thoroughly. I have talked it over, and weighed up everything in my mind. I mean it. You are not only my cousin. I have always counted you a very dear and trusted friend. What better footing could there be for a closer relationship?'

He did mean it! A closer relationship? To Timothia's consternation, a most uncomfortable feeling of warmth began to invade her bosom. She felt her pulse pick up its pace. It thrummed unevenly, causing a disconcerting numbness in her head and a dryness at her throat. She tried to speak, and could not. Nothing came into her head. All her attention was on the unprecedented sensations within her, and the conviction that an unaccustomed flush was mounting to her cheeks.

To her relief, Leo released her hands. Timothia reached out instead to the table for support, and concentrated on steadying her suddenly unruly knees. She was glad when Leo turned, pacing a few steps away from her along the edge of the fence. By the time he returned, she had herself under better control, and was able to meet his solemn gaze without—she hoped—betraying her inner disquiet.

'That was a trifle impassioned, Leo,' she said, trying for a neutral note. 'Hardly in keeping with this marriage of convenience, do you think?'

His complexion darkened. 'It is more than that.'

'Indeed? How so?'

'Do you suppose I would marry you only for the advantages it may bring me?'

Timothia blinked. 'I thought that was what you were proposing—or have I misunderstood you?'

Leo's lips tightened. 'You are being deliberately provocative, Timma. The advantages are mutual—as I hope you may be brought to realise. I have taken you by surprise, I grant you. But if you will only give the matter some consideration—'

'Apparently I don't need to. You appear to have given it all possible consideration without my help.'

'You could hardly expect me to broach the subject without first giving it serious thought!'

'I didn't expect you to broach it at all,' Timothia pointed out. She frowned, moving slowly around the table, hardly conscious of a need to put distance between them. 'This is no doubt what prompted you to begin berating me again about my choice of dwelling.'

'I did not berate you,' he protested.

'What is more,' pursued Timothia, eyeing him with a glint of rising indignation in her fine eyes, 'it explains why you have suddenly taken it into your head to discover impropriety in my conduct.'

'I never said it was improper.'

'You said I looked indecent,' Timothia reminded him.

'I did not mean—'

'What you meant, Mr Wetheral, was that it was unfit

behaviour for the proposed wife of the master of Wiggin Hall. I wonder you could bring yourself to make this famous offer!'

Leo felt himself reddening. But the consciousness of being in the wrong—for it was exactly what he had thought!—did not act upon him as it ought. He fought down the stirrings of annoyance. 'Timma, do be reasonable. Do you suppose I would wish to marry you if I disapproved of you?'

'It doesn't seem to me that you do wish to marry me,' Timothia said bluntly. 'You have concocted this marvellous scheme—'

'I'll shake you in a minute!' he interrupted with some heat. 'If you will but *listen*.'

She was silent, but her eyes looked daggers, and Leo was obliged to admit that she had some cause. He had put it badly. He threw up his hands.

'Must we quarrel?'

'It was not of my making, Leo.'

'I know.' He smiled.

It was the old, friendly smile she knew so well, and Timothia's indignation cooled a trifle.

'I'm a clod, Timma,' he pursued. 'I've made a mull of it, haven't I? Valentine warned me how it would be.'

Timothia bridled again. A clod? Yes, indeed! Her voice became silky. 'Valentine knows of this? Famous! Why did you not simply inform the town crier, and save yourself the trouble of coming to me at all?'

There was, Leo reflected, some justice in this. He was in no wise to be censured for confiding in his best friend, but there was no denying that Valentine was a rattlepate. Yet in this instance Leo was convinced he might be trusted.

'You need have no fear. Valentine gave me his word

that he would say nothing—at least, not to anyone outside our immediate circle.'

Timothia was far from satisfied, for she knew Valentine. It might be natural that Leo should talk to him, for not only had he run tame at Wiggin as a boy, as Leo had done at Bluntisham, but he had accompanied her cousin so frequently to Dulverton Park that he was almost as well acquainted with herself as he was with Leo. But Valentine, though Lord Pentre of Bluntisham and ranking highest of the gentry hereabouts, could not be trusted to keep his tongue between his teeth. He was not malicious, merely forgetful—and he had less than common sense. If Leo had relied upon his advice—!

'Valentine encouraged you to pursue your scheme, did he?'

Leo hesitated. In truth, Valentine could not be said to have borne much part in the discussion, beyond agreeing in principle with most of what Leo said. With rare foresight, he had cautioned Leo to be careful how he put the offer to Timma, but had given it as his opinion that she would be only too glad of an opportunity to remove from that 'wretched little house' at Fenton. Leo had thought so too, but he was beginning to have doubts.

'To tell you the truth,' he said reluctantly, 'he did little more than listen to me disputing the matter with myself.'

Timothia's brows went up. 'Disputing?'

'I meant to say discussing,' he corrected hastily. 'Do come down off your high ropes, Timma! What would you? A man does not make an offer of marriage without careful thought to the consequences.'

'No, and a female does not accept one without a similar examination,' said Timothia swiftly.

'What the deuce have I been pressing you to do?' demanded Leo, annoyance breaking out again. 'I wish you will sit down, and just listen to me for a moment!'

Timothia was silent, aware that she was being driven by an irrational sensation of indignation—as though Leo had insulted her! Perhaps she should rather be flattered. It was not every day that one received such an advantageous offer. For so it undoubtedly was, considered by worldly standards. And there was nothing out of the way in the marriage of first cousins. Yet this was *Leo*, bound to Timothia by closer ties than those of their relationship or geographical location. Marriage—certainly a marriage of the kind he proposed—seemed wholly inappropriate.

Nevertheless, she moved back to the chair and sat down, looking up at him in mute question, if with a hint of wariness in her eyes.

'That's better,' approved Leo, sighing out his relief. She said nothing, and he found it difficult to begin. When he had rehearsed his speeches they had gone well. But the Timma of his imagination had looked upon their portent with approval. The real Timma was already ruffled by his admittedly hamfisted efforts—brought on, he must confess, by a wholly unpredicted nervousness. He made an effort to pull his thoughts together, so that he might present his case in as favourable a light as it had appeared to him prior to this meeting.

'Whatever you may say, Timma,' he began, 'I know that you are not happy here at Fenny House.' He looked at her, but she did not speak, and he was emboldened to continue. 'What I meant to say was that I can offer you a better home—more than a home. Though why you could not remain at Dulverton,' he added, suddenly recalling an old grievance, 'is beyond me.'

'So you have often remarked,' said Timothia.

'I told you what a deprivation it would be.'

'So you did, but I did not realise it at the time.'

'No, because you were too stubborn. If you had listened to me, you would have asked Dudley if you might stay.'

'I had no need to ask him,' countered Timothia, 'for he offered me a home there for as long as I wished.'

Leo stared. 'You never told me so before.'

'I saw no necessity to tell you. Dudley offered—out of politeness. I refused.'

'You refused? Madness!'

'Leo, pray have a little sense,' she said impatiently. 'How could I accept? Poor Dudley had enough mouths to feed without adding me. Five of them to begin with, and now augmented by Baby Harry in this last year. Heaven knows when Ella will have done with breeding!'

'You don't bamboozle me, Timma,' Leo said grimly. 'If you refused Dudley, it was not for the sake of his brood, but because you knew very well that you would continue to rule the roost.'

Timothia was betrayed into a smile. 'Just so. I had no mind to play second fiddle after years at the helm. But it is also true that I could not have endured to live with Ella's brats.'

'Could you endure your own?' he asked without thinking.

She gazed at him, the implication of his words causing a resurgence of the discomfort she had experienced earlier. Her pulsebeat was distressingly fast, and she felt distinctly hot.

Leo mistook her silence. 'I beg your pardon, Timma. I should not have said that. It is one of my reasons for marrying, it is true—I mean, I must have an heir. But I had not—it was not meant to—'

'Don't tie yourself up in knots, Leo,' advised Timothia,

suppressing her own embarrassment. Was it embarrassment? 'All landowners have that duty.'

'Yes, but it is not my most pressing concern.' The devil! Let them keep off such a subject! There was reason enough for his decision to marry her, without going into that. He harked back to one of the arguments he had discussed with Valentine.

'Timma, you know how little suited I am for the position I am obliged to occupy. Well, not quite that. But to be forced to give up far too much of my time to matters concerning my estates—! I do it because I must, my duty is clear and I could not reconcile it with my conscience to do otherwise. But it is as irksome to me as this dawdling life you lead is to you. I am as much addicted to sport, I suppose, as you are to management and business. If we married, we might both exchange dullness and duty for pleasure. Do you not see?'

'I see,' Timothia agreed, but with a marked lack of the enthusiasm Leo had hoped for. 'I am to run your estate, while you pursue foxes and go to the races.'

'Well, yes,' Leo admitted in a doubtful way, for as she put it it sounded trite. But it was true for all that. 'Come now, Timma, you know I have other interests—not that I have time for them. Do you realise that I have shot so little this season that my aim is out, and I was so busy last year that I almost missed Mendoza's final fight?'

Timothia remained unmoved. She knew very well that her cousin, despite the calls of his estate, spent the bulk of his time in a variety of sporting pursuits.

'Leo, don't try me too far. You have every opportunity to engage in sport. What you really mean is that you want to fob me off with the estate management that you still find so alarming. Yet it is not so very difficult, if you will but bend your mind to it.'

'Not difficult for you,' said her cousin bitterly. 'You have a head for business.'

'It is merely a matter of common sense.'

'You see!' he exclaimed in triumph. 'What have I been saying to you? Marry me, and you may exercise your common sense to the utmost, and let my aching head rest.'

Timothia eyed him with a calm that Leo found a trifle unnerving. That she remained unconvinced was patent. He wished he might know what she was thinking. Her next words added nothing to his comfort.

'Let me see if I have understood you correctly,' she said in a musing way. 'You require an heir, and you wish to be freed from the irksome task of running your own estate. In return for my providing these services, I barter my freedom for a larger home and—'

'Oh, go to the devil!' Leo snapped, moving sharply away. 'As if that could possibly be all! What of companionship? What of your being mistress of your own home?' He swung round again. 'Barter your freedom indeed! What freedom? Do you call this freedom?' He threw an agitated arm in an arc that encompassed her present home. 'And how dare you think so badly of me as to suggest that I would confine you in any way?'

'A wife is inevitably confined, Leo—and I am not talking of childbirth.' She added flatly, 'Not that you wish for a wife, so far as I can see.'

'I am beginning to agree with you!' He flung up exasperated hands. 'What ails you, Timma? I am offering what I believed you must greet at least with some degree of thankfulness, yet you behave as if I had offended you!'

Timothia bit her lip on a sharp rejoinder, brought up short by the thought that this was just how she felt it. Which was even more ludicrous than his offer. She sighed out a ragged breath, and gave him a wry smile.

'Yes, I ought rather to be thanking you. Yet I can't but feel that there ought to be a more cogent reason for your thinking of taking such a step.'

'But there is!' Leo burst out. 'Of course there is. Quite aside from all this, I have Babs to think of.'

For a moment it did not register. Then Timothia remembered. 'Oh, you mean your sister.'

'She is already fifteen, Timma,' said Leo, sounding faintly harassed. 'Lord, I can scarce believe it myself!'

'That is only because she is growing up away from you,' Timothia pointed out. 'You would not have noticed the passing years so much if she had been living at home.'

'Don't. It makes me guilty even to think of it, though the decision was not mine.'

Timothia was fully aware of it. On the death of Leo's mother four years ago, her uncle Wetheral had sent his only daughter to live at St Neots with his younger brother Herbert, who had two girls of his own, both much of an age with Barbara Wetheral. Mr Wetheral had preferred this solution to bringing some unknown female into his house. Seeing Leo's evident distress—for he felt it was enough for the child to have lost her mother, let alone being sent away from home—Timothia had offered to open her own doors to Babs, but her uncle had been adamant, and Barbara was sent to Uncle Herbert.

'You are going to bring her home?'

'I must,' Leo said simply. 'I cannot expect Uncle Herbert and his wife to bring her out. He will not even go to London for his own daughters. Indeed, I believe he means to marry one of our cousins to the son of a business associate.'

'Lucky Lucinda!'

'Or Maria. But you see how it is? If I don't bring Babs

home, I shall hear next that she is betrothed to some up-start of a coal merchant!'

Timothia did not waste time arguing the point, though she thought it unlikely that Uncle Herbert would sanction any such alliance, even for one of his daughters. He was not engaged in trade, merely having shares in the trans-portation of coal. And had done very well by it. Not for Herbert Wetheral the rigours of soldierly campaigning that poor Adam had to endure as a younger son. Though she had to admit that Leo's brother had not a head for busi-ness—any more than Leo had himself.

'But it is a matter of scant urgency, Leo. I collect that this marriage you propose is intended to provide Babs with a chaperon, but if she is only fifteen—'

'Yes, but it will take a year or two for me to accustom myself to being married.' Realising what he had said, he tried to retrieve the slip. 'I don't mean that. What I mean is, you—or at least my *wife*—will need to accustom her-self to the situation before we can think of bringing Babs out.'

The frost was back in Timothia's voice. 'You are too scrupulous. Not all young ladies are desirous of being brought out. Why go to the trouble of tying yourself up in matrimony?'

'It is not a question of—'

'After all, I was never brought out.'

'That was by choice, Timma. You could perfectly well have been brought out at the appropriate time. Only you did not choose to avail yourself of—as I remember it—several invitations from the ladies round about.'

'No, I did not,' Timothia agreed forcefully. 'I was far too busy at home to consider it, as well you know. Be-sides, what would Papa have done without me?'

'Well, if that is all your reason,' Leo snapped, 'there is nothing to stop you coming out now, if you choose.'

'At three-and-twenty? Have you run mad, Leo? Besides, who would undertake to present me now?'

'Lady Hurst?' offered Leo without thinking.

Timothia sat up with a jerk. 'Lady Hurst! I thank you, Leo; I had rather die an old maid!'

What had possessed him to mention the mistress of Hursting Stone? There was not a more patronising, ill-intentioned woman alive! And Leo ought to know. Dearest Susan had as much claim upon his friendship as she did upon Timothia's.

'If you imagine for one moment that I would dream of applying to her for *anything*, let alone a coming-out, after the heartless way in which she treated Susan—her own niece, mark you!—then you have very little understanding of my character. I am surprised you should suggest such a thing.'

Since he had thrown it out at random purely from irritation, this spur failed to prick. Susan was Timma's closest female friend, but Leo had also a fondness for her, and had himself been shocked at the wretched woman's failure to invite her niece to come out under her aegis. Even if it had proved a waste of time, which he strongly believed. As she had been infatuated from childhood with his friend Valentine, he doubted that the Hurst chit would have settled for anyone else. But his cousin had a more lively goad.

'If you are so ready to espouse the cause of Lady Hurst,' she said waspishly, 'why do you not ask her to bring out Barbara?'

'How the deuce could I possibly do so?' Leo said testily. 'Quite aside from my loathing of the woman—'

'Oh, you loathe her, do you?'

'—I have more pride than to sue to her for help on such a matter.'

'Whereas I should not have any such pride?'

'No, I don't mean that. I spoke without thinking.' He threw up one hand. 'Let us not argue, Timma, for this is nothing to the purpose. We both know you are not going to look for a husband in that way. For myself, there is no other solution. Marry I must, and I had as lief marry you as anyone.'

Timothia gazed at him. 'Indeed? Then I have only to thank you, sir, for an extremely flattering sentiment.'

'Oh, the devil!' uttered Leo, in a flurry of confusion. 'I did not mean that either—not in the way it came out. You have put me in such a case that I no longer know what I am saying. But think, deuce take it! Your situation is almost as desperate as mine. You clearly cannot continue as you are. You must marry someone, if you are not to remain permanently on the shelf. And who else will you find but me?'

Suppressing an inclination to box his ears, Timothia spoke with an edge to her voice, her tone silky smooth. 'Do you think you should say any more, Leo? You are only sinking yourself deeper into the mire. I must request you to warn me now if you have any further remarks to make calculated to depress my pretensions, for I would like first to send for a bottle of smelling salts.'

Leo stared for a moment. The infelicitous import of his own words struck him with stunning force, and he burst out laughing. 'Lord, I think I have run mad!' he gasped. 'Timma, forgive me! I had no idea of offending you. Pray accept my apologies. But does it not show how well-suited we are, that I can speak to you so?' He grinned at her, and held out his hand. 'Come, cry friends again, and forgive me!'

Unable to resist this frank apology, Timothia gave him her hand. Much to her surprise, Leo bent his head and kissed her fingers. As he released them, she felt them quiver, and rather hastily stuffed them into the other hand in her lap.

'Apology accepted, Mr Wetheral.'

'You are too kind, Miss Dulverton.'

For a moment or two there was silence between them, but a much more natural one than there had been so far this morning. Timothia got up, and, picking up her belongings from the table, made as if to move towards the house. Leo's hand on her arm detained her. She looked round.

'You have not answered me.'

A slight frown creased her brow, and then she smiled. 'I will give your offer serious consideration.'

Leo withdrew his hand, conscious of a strong feeling of chagrin. 'Is that all?'

'What more should there be? You have evidently given the matter a great deal of thought. Am I expected to do less?'

'No! That is— well, you might at least give me some indication of— I mean, you have said nothing to the purpose.'

'I have no need, Leo,' she said sweetly, 'when you have already said everything to the purpose.'

'My purpose, yes. But what of yours?'

'Oh, is that to be taken into account?'

Leo was silenced. His eyes narrowed in suspicion, and he eyed her with a heightened colour. 'I see what it is. I have put it all so badly that you mean to score off me for my lapse of manners by making me wait for a decision.'

A laugh was surprised out of Timothia. 'You cannot

seriously think that I would treat so lightly a decision affecting my whole future!'

His face cleared. 'No, of course not. That was stupid of me.' He smiled. 'After all, I dare say I would not wish to marry you if you were so foolhardy.'

Timothia did not return his smile. Instead she searched his face. 'Do you wish to marry me, Leo? Truly—in spite of all that has passed between us this morning?'

He was taken aback. 'Why, yes. Nothing has changed. I believe it to be the best thing for both of us.'

For a moment longer, Timothia continued to stare at him. Then her provocative smile dawned, and she swept a mock curtsy. 'I thank you for your kind offer, Mr Wetheral, and you may be sure that I will communicate my answer to you as soon as ever I have finished *disputing* the matter with myself.'

Leo regarded her speechlessly, a fulminating glare in the steel-blue eyes. Then he turned from her and strode off towards the house without another word.

## Chapter Two

Instead of going directly back into the house, Timothia remained just where she was for a few moments. She was glad Leo had chosen to walk off in a huff. He might count himself fortunate that she had such a command over herself as to enable her to conceal the real perturbation of her spirits.

She could laugh at the manner of his making this offer, if only she might set aside her own feelings upon receipt of it. Who would have thought that Leo could be such a fool? Had anyone else seen fit to enumerate all the evils of her situation only in order to set the position he might offer at an advantage, she would only laugh at it. But that Leo should do so—! That Leo should offer at all—!

And were his arguments supposed to weigh with her? They might, had they come from anyone else. Oh, she could bargain with fate easily enough for another man. Easier, surely, to make an exchange of the kind with a gentleman for whom one felt no particular affection. Marriages based on a business arrangement were not so uncommon—even among cousins. But with a dear friend? Leo had appeared to think it acceptable. For herself, it felt a very mockery of their relationship.

Worse yet, she suspected that he had gone over his arguments with Valentine in rather more alarming detail than he claimed. Naturally reserved as she was, this went very much against the grain with Timothia. And the thought that Leo had to *determine* whether or not to offer for her was galling in the extreme. Why it should be so she could not fathom. Unless, in his inmost heart, he recognised the dreadful incongruity of which she was conscious—and had fought against it? Well, if he had, then the fight had been lost. And Leo Wetheral was not the man she had thought him!

Upon this lowering thought, Timothia left the stables, and made her way through the back entrance and up a narrow stairway to her bedchamber.

After Leo's disparaging remarks about Fenny House, she seemed to see the place anew—and with not a little resentment towards her cousin. A wreck indeed! What if the panelled walls were crumbling with woodworm here and there? In the dim light of the constricted, airless little passages, one could barely notice it. True, the rooms were smaller than she had been used to, her bedchamber dwarfed by the big four-poster brought from Dulverton Park. What with the chest that contained her gowns, the dresser, and the rather unnecessary window seat built into the wooden surround at the bay, there was only just room to move. In this heat, moreover, she could have wished that the windows were not casements, which let in so little air, unlike the huge sash windows at the Park which kept the air circulating and fresh. But this was a small matter, Timothia decided defiantly, when one considered the beauty of the ancient leaded glass at Fenny House.

In a mood of turbulent unease, Timothia ripped off her habit and threw it on the bed for Polly to brush and put away, forgetting in her agitation that the lanky country maid had more than enough to do without that added burden. She had arrayed herself in a simple blue-dyed muslin gown with half-sleeves, and was placing the customary black shawl across her shoulders, before she recalled that her mourning was over.

Cursing Leo for causing her to become absent-minded, Timothia removed the shawl and instead looked among her jewels for a pearl brooch that had come to her from her mother, long deceased. The flaxen locks brushed and re-plaited, she looked at the effect in the long glass that had been put behind the door for want of anywhere else in the room where it might fit.

Did that look more like Mrs Leo Wetheral? A frisson shot through her at the thought of the name, and she drew an unsteady breath. Madness! She was not going to marry Leo. To her annoyance, she caught herself wondering if he might approve of the alteration from the 'indecent' earlier spectacle, and thrust hastily away from her own image. Let him keep his opinions to himself! If she were to accept his 'bargain', she would certainly demand on her side that he refrain from criticising her conduct. Except that Leo would never agree to that restriction—any more than she was likely to agree to the terms of his hateful offer.

Mrs Hawnby was awake by the time Timothia went down to the front parlour. A venerable dame, with something more than seventy years in her dish, Edith Hawnby was apt to doze intermittently throughout the day. It was a practice which suited Timothia, who had all the propriety of a companion with none of the nuisance of being obliged to keep her company. But she did not credit her old governess with less sharpness of mind than had been her portion in the days when she had presided over the schoolroom at Dulverton Park.

'What did *he* want?' she asked forthrightly, the moment Timothia had seated herself on a sofa a trifle too large for the room.

'To tell me that these parlours are poky,' replied Timothia, without going through the unnecessary preliminary of enquiring whom her companion meant by 'he'. Edith was well acquainted with Leo from the old days.

'You knew that,' said the elderly dame.

'Yes,' agreed Timothia, looking about. But although this particular parlour was set directly below her own bed-chamber, and was of exactly the same dimensions, she observed with satisfaction that it seemed the bigger for its sparse furnishing. There was merely the sofa which she was herself occupying, Edith's easy chair and one other, besides the nest of small tables which was generally, as now, shut up.

'I would not myself call them poky,' she said with an air of detached calm which in no way expressed the true state of her emotions. 'Restricted perhaps.'

Her old governess eyed her from the depths of the large chair that comfortably accommodated her well-rounded form. She was of the type of figure that had been buxom in youth, but was now merely overlarge for her height with a tendency to waddle when she walked. Which was why, as she was apt to say when urged to exercise, she preferred to remain idle.

'I suppose you told him so,' she suggested, after a pause.

'I can't recall what I told him,' Timothia said flatly. 'He informed me, if I remember rightly, that all three of my parlours would fit into one of his.'

Mrs Hawnby grunted. 'I presume he didn't drive himself over here merely to tell you that.'

'No. He came to make me an offer of marriage. I think

the comment about the parlours was designed to persuade
me of the desirability of exchanging my residence with
Wiggin Hall.'

Mrs Hawnby looked her over in silence. Timothia did
not flinch from her gaze, although she knew well how
easily Edith read her. She was conscious of the heat rising
in her face and was relieved when the elder lady folded
her arms and turned her eyes upon the ceiling.

'You could do worse.'

She did not doubt that! 'Very much so.'

'Good property,' continued the other, apparently still
intent upon the ceiling. 'The boy looks well. He is young
enough—seven-and-twenty, if I add it up correctly. Reasonable income. You couldn't know him better, which is
an advantage. Yes, very eligible.'

Timothia had nothing to say. It was a legitimate sum-
mation. Leo could not have put it better himself, had he
wished to tot up his own attractions. Perhaps it would
have been more to the purpose if he had used them as his
arguments. She might have taken him for a coxcomb, but
that was better than taking him for the insensitive brute
he undoubtedly was!

After a moment or two Timothia became aware that
Mrs Hawnby had withdrawn her gaze from the ceiling,
and was once more training those intelligent eyes upon
herself. She met the look with challenge in her own. It
was rewarded.

'You don't want it.'

Timothia's feelings gave way. 'I certainly don't want
the *bargain* he offered me!'

'Bargain?' frowned the other. 'What do you mean,
child?'

'Leo wishes for a wife to run his estate, which is apparently the root of his reason for choosing me. I am to

gain the run of his enormous parlours, I suppose, and the enjoyment—so Leo says—of working at what I enjoy.'

'That sounds to me remarkably like pique, child,' observed Edith sapiently.

'I should think I am entitled to a trifle of pique,' said Timothia roundly. 'It was scarcely the most flattering of offers, Edith, I assure you. And from Leo!'

'Why should he flatter you?' demanded her erstwhile governess. 'Knows you like him. You even respect the fellow.'

'I both like and respect him, but that does not mean that I want to marry him.'

'Knows you get on exceedingly well together. Have you not been close friends ever since I came to you?'

'Oh, before that. I do not remember a time when Leo was not my friend.'

'Apart from the odd squabble,' put in Mrs Hawnby.

'There is nothing in that. Sparring with Leo is by way of intellectual exercise for us both. But it is hardly the stuff of marriage.'

'On the contrary. A marriage without a fight or two is a bloodless marriage.'

'Oh, but Leo does not want a *bloodsome* marriage, my dear Edith,' Timothia said acidly. 'All his thought is for the convenience of it. My convenience as well as his own, you know, for among other things he is very kindly rescuing me from the shelf.'

Mrs Hawnby eyed her with comprehension. 'He has put you in a pet.'

'I am not in a pet,' stated Timothia with dignity. 'Leo spoke no less than the truth. It is a fair assessment of my circumstances to say that I am on the shelf. As you say, why should he flatter me? He knows me so well that he has no need of subterfuge or deceit.'

'Which is more than can be said for most such marriages.'

'Such what marriages?' demanded Timothia with heat.

'Of convenience,' said the old lady, quite unperturbed. 'You admit him to be eligible, you like and respect him, and he offers a solution to your very uncertain future which you would do well to consider deeply.'

'I am considering it,' Timothia pointed out, rising again in a surge of annoyance. 'But the truth is that I am not at all sure that I want such a marriage.'

'Then you are a great fool, my girl,' declared her old mentor roundly. 'You can't stay moping here for ever, driving yourself into a frenzy of boredom.'

'And if I were to marry Leo, and move to Wiggin Hall, I may just as readily be driven to moping and boredom. Since Leo means to indulge his addiction to sport to the utmost, I should very likely not see him from one month's end to another! And since I am only to be in his precious house on sufferance, merely to chaperon his sister and slave to death over his estate, I fail to see how I am to derive any satisfaction from it. I loved working for Dulverton because it was my home. Leo does not intend that Wiggin shall become *my* home—only that I should come and live in *his* home. There is a vast difference, Edith, I assure you.'

She stopped, aware of having thoroughly betrayed herself. Edith had received her tirade with every evidence of indifference, but Timothia was not deceived by that expressionless face. She swung away to the windows.

'You did not, I take it, express yourself with this degree of warmth to Mr Wetheral,' came from behind her.

Timothia let out a muted yowl and turned. 'I did, Edith, and you were perfectly right—he put me in a pet! Only I would not myself describe my state of mind by so little a term. Leo has put me, if you must know, into a *fury*.'

There. She had admitted it. She had been trying vainly to suppress a very torrent of rage!

With the admission, strangely, came relief. She found that her erstwhile mentor was looking at her with a degree of comprehension in her eyes, but no shred of compassion.

'That's better,' said Edith, in a voice both flat and unemotional. 'Get it all out, and then you may think more clearly.'

Timothia's discomfort began to subside. It had ever been thus. Edith had never suffocated her with unwanted displays of affection or compassion, but her shrewd mind had nevertheless commanded respect, even admiration, from her young charge. She had been able to check her with a look, or a few pertinent words. At seventeen, Timothia had dispensed with her services, feeling herself to be no longer in need either of guidance or chaperonage. But an absence of six years had not lessened the power of Edith Hawnby's good sense.

Timothia began to laugh. 'I think I have already got it out.'

'Good. If I were you, I would take a turn in the shrubbery, and try to look at the matter in a fresh light. Remember that men are not adept at expressing themselves in a way that finds favour with women—more particularly when they are making a proposal of marriage. No doubt there is occasion for some dissatisfaction, but you would be wise to consider well before you throw away such a promising opportunity for the sake of a scruple or two.'

She then closed her eyes and fell, to all appearances, into a doze. There clearly being nothing further to be got out of her for the present, Timothia left the room and went outside. Not that she expected to derive much help for her very considerable scruples from a walk in the shrubbery!

This large term served to describe a somewhat forlorn area of formal garden to one side of Fenny House which had been coaxed, at Timothia's instigation, into providing a single walkway leading from a lawn of untidy shape at one end, to a large chestnut tree at the other.

Timothia managed to make a couple of relatively carefree turns up and down the walkway, her attention determinedly on the selection of flowering shrubs, as she deadheaded here and there where shrivelled petals ruined the beauty of the blooms. One of the only signs of femininity she displayed, Leo had often said, was a love of flowers.

Leo again! Was that the trouble? Leo was so inextricably bound up in her life that she could not think of him with fresh eyes—in the light of a husband. Evidently he'd had a similar difficulty in persuading himself to think of her as a wife. She was too unfeminine, it seemed. Too 'indecent'! What was it he was used to say?

'What I like about you, Timma, is that there is rarely any need to accommodate my pace and strength to yours, whatever the pursuit. You are built on the lines of an Amazon!'

A little hollow seemed to open up in her chest, and Timothia paused in her perambulations. Leo had never given the slightest indication that he found anything to admire in the figure or stature of an Amazon. Nor, to be fair, had she any evidence to support a conviction to the contrary. He had never openly admired anyone, to Timothia's knowledge—not in their neighbourhood at least. But there was no saying but that he had been madly in love during his seasons in London, for all she knew, and with a female built on quite other lines than herself. Except that he was still unwed. But might that not betoken a disappointment in the pursuit of some female's hand?

She was conscious of annoyance—that he had not told her. Ludicrous, because of course he would have told her, such close friends as they were. He did not come to her with a bruised heart; of that she might be sure. On the other hand, he did not come with a full heart either.

Should not there be some sign of a warmer feeling between prospective marriage partners? Warmer than mere friendship dictated. What had he said? Their friendship was a basis for a closer relationship. Closer, yes. But warmer? Leo evidently did not think so, for such a sentiment had not formed part of his well-reasoned proposal. Oh, so very well-reasoned it had been! But not one word had been put forward about her personal attributes. Perhaps Leo thought them unimportant.

Well, they were not so to Timothia. She might be lacking in the feminine graces, but she was woman enough to wish to be desired by the man who might take her to wife. And how was she to know whether Leo was to her taste?

In a flash, she recalled those odd symptoms that had attacked her when Leo had seized her hands. Did that mean that she found his masculinity attractive? No! No, it was not possible. Was it? Surely not. That had been merely the shattering effect of her realisation that his offer was in earnest.

Even as this thought came to her, an echo of those earlier disagreeable sensations rose up inside her. With a kind of detached interest, she felt her pulse increase its rhythm a trifle, and a hot tingle at her skin. And it was Leo who had caused this? *Leo*.

Before the inevitable reflections could quite overwhelm her, she was hailed by the light, breathy tones of her friend Susan Hurst.

'There you are, Timma! Did you not hear my carriage drive up? Oh, now, Timma—you are walking without a hat in this heat. If that is not typical of you, dearest. I do wish you will come inside.'

Why in the world Susan persisted in treating her in this elder sister fashion, Timothia was never able to understand. Not only was her friend all of two years younger than herself, but she was also more than half a head shorter and the epitome of youthful femininity. She was reed-slim, her slight figure arrayed in pink muslin, with little puff sleeves and a *décolletage* over a petite bosom adorned with frills and a satin bow, which was echoed in the rows of ribbon decorating the straw hat. Large pansy eyes peeped up at Timothia from beneath this confection, out of a countenance otherwise unremarkable. But her mouse-coloured hair curled riotously, and a flair for fashion made up for a limited intellect. She was a devoted friend, and Timothia valued both her good heart and her loyalty. Susan's ill fortune in the matter of romance made her fiercely defensive, but that did not prevent her from responding with irritation to her gentle reproof.

'Don't you start on me, Susan. I have had enough to bear from Leo already today.'

'Oh, has he been here?'

'To some purpose,' said Timothia, glad of the opportunity to unburden herself. 'Would you believe it, Susan? He has offered for me!'

The pansy eyes widened. 'Already? I had not thought it would have been so quick.'

Timothia eyed her with suspicion. 'You knew?'

Susan clapped a hand to her mouth, consternation dancing in the large eyes. 'Oh, dear! Oh, Timma, I am sorry!'

'You did know. Famous! Only wait until I see Leo!'

Two small hands reached out to grasp her arms. 'Oh,

*pray* don't say anything to him. Oh, dear, how stupid I am! I ought not to have said anything. Valentine warned me to dissemble.'

Timothia took the hands and removed them from her arms, pushing them away. 'It is of no use to say that now, Susan. In any event, I had already discovered that Leo talked the matter over with Valentine. Only I had not thought that you were in the plot, too!'

'It is not a plot, dearest Timma,' said her friend, distressed. 'How could you think I would ever plot against you?'

'Only tell me this,' demanded Timothia sternly. 'Did Leo come to you with his uncertainties?'

'Oh, no, no, no! It was Valentine who told me of it.'

'I might have guessed it! I warned Leo that he would spread it all over the neighbourhood.'

'I am sure he has not done so, dearest,' Susan uttered breathily. 'He told me that Leo had sworn him to secrecy.'

'Yet he broke his word immediately and disclosed the business to you.' She began to move with hasty, if undetermined, steps, pacing towards the chestnut tree.

'Only because he knew that you were bound to tell me,' pleaded Susan, hurrying after her. 'Poor Valentine could not decide whether it would be a good thing for you to marry Leo. He wished for my opinion.'

Timothia halted. 'And just what is your opinion? Or dare I hazard a guess?'

'Timma, pray don't be so out of reason cross! Of course I told Valentine that I thought it a splendid notion, but—'

'Of course you did. What else were you to think? Here am I, stuck in this wretched little house, positively yearning to be rescued. And there is Leo, desperate for someone to run his estate for him and look after Barbara. What better solution?'

Susan blinked at her. 'Is that indeed the case?'

'It is how Leo put it,' Timothia said savagely.

There was no mistaking the disappointment that clouded Susan's brown orbs. 'Oh, no! Oh, *Timma*. And I had been thinking how romantic it was that Leo should fall in love with you after all these years.'

A sharp pang smote Timothia's bosom, taking her unawares. She stared at Susan for a moment, without seeing her. Then a choked laugh escaped her.

'Love? Nothing of the sort. That is the last thing—' She stopped, her breath catching. Why in the world should she be wanting to weep? It was hardly a matter for tears. And she was not going to behave like a watering pot, all for Leo's sake! She drew a steadying breath, and stated coolly, 'You are mistaken, Susan. Leo is not in love with me.'

'Are you sure?' asked her friend anxiously. 'Perhaps he might have been embarrassed to express himself in those terms—to you, Timma.'

Timothia frowned, recalling her cousin's odd behaviour before he had broached his unflattering proposal. 'If he was, the cause had nothing to do with his feelings towards me. On the contrary, he was extremely outspoken on that head.'

'What did he say?' asked Susan anxiously.

Timothia gave her a fluent account, underlined by a commentary of her own—an exercise which allowed her to discharge a good deal of her spleen.

Under the chestnut tree, Timothia had caused to be placed a wooden bench which provided an arbour of sorts, admirably suited to intimate discussions of this kind. To gravitate to this seat seemed natural under the circumstances, and the two females were soon ensconced, and deep in discussion of the day's event.

'After all,' offered Susan, once in possession of the story, 'you are admirably suited to one another. And perhaps a more intimate relationship would make him fall in love with you.'

'I wish you will not keep harping on this laughable romantic fancy, Susan,' said Timothia crossly. 'If Leo has not found it in him to cherish that sort of feeling for me in all these years of friendship, it is scarce likely that he will do so now—or in the future.'

Susan's big eyes were trained upon her in a look she knew well. Her lips, Timothia guessed, were trembling on words that she hardly dared to utter, although she was plainly bursting to say them. It always reminded Timothia irresistibly of a spaniel doubtful of its welcome.

'Oh, do say it, Susan!' she urged, between laughter and exasperation. 'I promise I will not bite you.' She put out a hand to Susan's, squeezing it briefly. 'I am sorry I accused you of plotting against me. It is not your fault that Valentine talked to you. Only Leo put me in such a fume that—'

'Timma, what about you?' interrupted her friend without ceremony.

'I? Why, what do you mean?'

'It is all very well to talk in this airy way, Timma, with Leo said this, or Leo said that. But what of your feelings? You care for him, don't you?'

Timothia stared at her, struck. It had not occurred to her to question her own heart. 'I had not thought.'

'Think of it now,' urged Susan, both hope and anxiety in her voice.

The image of Leo crept into Timothia's mind. It was odd, but with all the memories she could only recall him as he'd looked that morning. Ill at ease, ill-tempered, a trifle hostile even. Only once or twice had the warmth of their close friendship been apparent. He had been almost a stranger, not truly the Leo she knew, with whom she shared a strong bond. Or she had thought she shared it.

A wave of violent sensation swept over her, and tears stung her eyelids. Would she have approached him thus? Would she have gone to Leo with a proposal based on *convenience*? No, indeed she would not! She would have had more regard for his feelings. Had it been the other way about—had she thought of marrying him—she would have spoken of the strength of their mutual affection. She would have lauded the long years of empathy, the give and take of every new thought upon the happenings of time, the growing bond that could only grow dearer in the closer unity of wedlock.

Now it was borne in upon her that these things encompassed her own experience. She could no longer be sure—as comfortably as she had been, without question—that Leo felt the same way. For all that she knew him, as she had thought, she felt him now a stranger. The promptings that had led him to make this offer were not—could never be!—the stimulus that could prompt her to accept.

She became aware of Susan's breathy tones. 'Timma, what is it? What ails you, dearest?'

Timothia's gaze focused, and she discovered that she was still staring into Susan's face, quite unaware. She found Susan's fingers in hers and gently released them. A sort of calm had descended upon her, and she spoke steadily.

'There is nothing the matter, Susan. I have only realised just what my feelings are towards Leo.'

'Oh, then you do love him!'

'I did not say that.' Timothia thought about this, and felt only numbness. 'If I love him, it is in the way I would love my brother. He has been a brother to me. I suppose

that is why it is so very difficult to think of him in any
other way. I dare say he feels the same.'

Susan sighed. 'Yes, that is what Valentine said. He
thought it must be like offering for your sister.'

'Is that what he said to Leo?'

'I do not know. He said it to me. It was what gave him
qualms, he said.'

Valentine had qualms, had he? If he had, they were as
nothing to her own! 'And what did you say?'

Susan blushed. 'Just what I said to you. I had often
thought of Leo's marrying you, though I have never said
so.'

Timothia eyed her, conscious of a sliver of sensation.
Why this unusual reticence? 'Why not?'

'I did not think you would like to hear it,' Susan confessed, hanging her head. 'I knew you had never thought
of Leo in that way. But sometimes I did wonder whether
perhaps you felt about him the same way that I did
about—' She stopped, biting her lip.

'About Valentine,' Timothia finished for her. 'Susan,
whence this shyness? You have been besotted with Valentine, heaven knows why, ever since you came to share
my schoolroom with Mrs Hawnby. Surely you can never
have seen me mooning over Leo in the same way?'

'I did not moon!' protested Susan hotly.

'Pardon me. You did nothing but gaze at him with the
most blatant adoration every time he set foot in Dulverton
Park. Everyone noticed it—except Valentine himself.
Which only goes to prove how insensitive men are. Why
I should have expected anything different from Leo, I do
not know.'

Susan's face fell. 'You mean to refuse him.'

'In no uncertain terms!' Timothia said. Then she
thought of the alternative, and sighed. 'At least, I think I

mean to refuse him. Only Edith said I should be a fool to do so without serious consideration—and the melancholy truth is that she is right.'

Valentine appeared delighted to see her. Trading on their long friendship, Timothia had waived formality to one side, much to the disapproval of Lord Pentre's butler, and accosted him in the gun-room at Bluntisham where he was engaged in fencing practice with his secretary. Valentine was as eager a sportsman as Leo, and Timothia had no mind to wait while he finished his bout and spent an eon of time at his toilet.

'You need not escort me for I know my way,' she had announced. But the butler had insisted on guiding her through the numerous corridors to the old wing—the only part of the original castle still standing—where his master was to be found, in stockinged feet and shirt-sleeves, bounding to and fro across the bare wooden boards.

Interrupted just as he executed a neat thrust in quarte, his lordship appeared not in the least put out. Leaping back out of range of his secretary's foil, he looked quickly round at the butler's discreet cough.

'Good Lord, Timma, is that you?' Removing his mask, and handing his own weapon to his adversary, he advanced with outstretched hand. 'Couldn't be more pleased to see anyone! Was just thinking about you.'

'I can't imagine why you should be thinking about me while you were engaged in swordplay,' Timothia returned, in a tone deceptively friendly.

'Well, not just at that precise moment, of course. But earlier, you know.'

Timothia greeted his secretary, with whom she was acquainted, and asked briefly after some matter concerning the estates. But Valentine did not permit of his responding in any detail, and dismissed him along with the butler, with a careless disregard for the proprieties. He began to draw on his boots, inviting Timothia to be seated at the wooden surround of one of the window embrasures.

Timothia declined, choosing rather to wander down the room, pretending to become engrossed in the portraits of dogs that hung above the gun-racks placed along the wall at intervals. She spoke blandly.

'What made you think of me, Valentine?'

'Was wishing for an opportunity to offer my felicitations,' he said, hopping on one leg as he reached for the second boot which had fallen away from him.

Timothia stopped and turned to watch him. 'Indeed? Are you meaning to felicitate me on my emergence from mourning, or on my betrothal to Leo?'

He looked up from dragging on the boot, his face lit. It was a good-humoured countenance, of the type the world was apt to regard as pleasantly pretty, with a well-sculpted lip and good cheekbones. He was fair, of average height, with a good figure, honed by an active sporting life, which showed to advantage in breeches and shirt-sleeves. Timothia was glad that Susan had not opted to accompany her on this quest, for she would undoubtedly have swooned at sight of him!

In fact, so far from evincing any desire to come to Valentine's home, her friend had flown into a taking.

'Oh, you must not!'

'Oh, but I must,' had argued Timothia. 'I wish to know exactly what Leo discussed with him.'

'But Valentine will be furious with me for saying anything to you. You must not say that I told you.'

'I have no need to say so, since Leo told me himself that he had spoken to Valentine when he made his offer.'

Susan had been relieved. 'Oh, yes, thank goodness!

Would you wish me to tell Valentine that you want him to visit you?'

'That would rather defeat the object of my not telling him you had spoken to me on this head, would it not?' Timothia had pointed out drily. 'Besides, I am in no mood to wait for Valentine to visit me. If I know him, he would be off to some race meeting or other and forget all about it.'

Susan had been obliged to admit the truth of this, and had reluctantly abandoned the idea. But Timothia, fired by her urgent need to thrash out the minutiae of Leo's proposal, had barely had patience to wait for luncheon to be over before ordering Bickley to fig out the gig.

Valentine's reception of the subject was not encouraging.

'Then it is all settled? Excellent!'

Timothia eyed him frostily. 'It is not excellent at all, Valentine. Nor is it settled.'

His grey eyes questioned. 'But has not Leo popped the question? I quite thought he must have done when you asked—'

'He has suggested that we get married, yes. I have not, however, given him my answer.'

'Ah.' Valentine stood up, stamping his foot to get his boot in place. Then he picked his waistcoat off a hook and shrugged it on. 'Lord knows why you females like to keep a fellow on a string! Mean to say, either you wish to marry him or you don't.'

'It is not that simple.'

Turning away from him, Timothia crossed the room to the window and stood gazing out upon the overgrown grass that led towards the stable block. She heard Valentine following her, and, glancing round, watched him button his waistcoat. Then he looked up again and she caught his eye. Alarm came into it.

'Uh-oh! I know that look. Now, Timma, I can't—'

'Exactly what did Leo say to you, Valentine?' she interrupted without ceremony.

'I knew it!' he uttered in a fateful way. 'Can't be done, Timma. You can't expect me to betray Leo.'

Timothia was within an ace of retorting that he had already done so—to Susan. Recalling her promise to her friend, she held her tongue.

'You will be telling me nothing that he has not already said to me himself,' she pointed out instead.

'Then why do you want to hear it?' he demanded reasonably.

She sat on the window seat, and patted the place beside her, giving him her inviting smile. His suspicious manner of sitting amused her, but she pressed her advantage.

'Valentine, we are friends, are we not?'

'Always been friends,' he agreed with wary enthusiasm. 'Not quite like Leo, of course, but still.'

'Just so. Leo is your best friend, and my friend too—as well as my cousin. Only consider, Valentine. If we should make a mistake by marrying, it will ruin all our friendships.'

Valentine frowned in obvious puzzlement. 'But why should you make a mistake? Don't mean to interfere, but seems to me a very good match.'

'I don't deny it,' Timothia said quickly. 'But a good match is not necessarily a successful marriage.'

He nodded sagely. 'True enough.'

'There you are, then.'

Valentine appeared to be thinking the matter over, and Timothia was obliged to curb her impatience. It never answered to bustle Valentine. It only turned him mulish and she would get nothing out of him at all. Her patience was rewarded.

'All very well, Timma, but I still don't see that I can tell you any more than Leo has. Did he mention Babs?'

'Yes, he did.'

'And that you should manage his estate?'

'That too.'

'Well, that's it. Leo seemed to feel you'd like it.' He added, with an air of confidentiality, 'Mark you, I did tell him he could as well employ a secretary. It's what I do. Leo said it's not the same, and I don't say he's wrong. Know you did far more than a secretary at Dulverton. I told him I thought you'd be glad to get out of that silly little house. Much better move to Wiggin Hall.'

Timothia could have screamed. 'Better than what? Marrying someone else? If I merely wanted to live at Wiggin Hall and run Leo's estate, I dare say I could do so without marrying him.'

Valentine shook his head with decision. 'Not without a chaperon, you couldn't. You may be cousins, but it still ain't respectable. And who's to bring out Barbara?'

'The chaperon,' said Timothia cattily.

'But then he'd have to run to the expense of hiring some decent woman instead of a secretary,' protested Valentine. 'Much better marry you and be done with both problems. Besides, Leo must have an heir.'

Rising in some haste, Timothia swung away. 'Pray do not speak to me about Leo's heir. If that is all he wants, let him go to London and pick up some willing little débutante.'

'No use,' said Valentine, rising also and following. 'Been on the town for years, and never once succumbed. It ain't likely he will, especially since he's got this idea into his head about marrying you.'

Timothia turned on him, conscious of a swelling sensation in her chest. She looked Valentine over, wondering whether to ask the question hovering on her tongue. Once again, she saw his expressive eyes register a trifle of panic.

'He has never succumbed?' queried Timothia quickly, before he could think of hedging. 'Do you mean that Leo has never been—in love?'

Valentine coughed. 'I don't say that exactly. Never fallen for any of the girls on the market, that's all.'

Eyeing him with a degree of suspicion, Timothia caught her breath. 'But you think he has been in love?'

Valentine looked uncomfortable. 'Well, not in the way of marriage. Dash it, Timma, a man don't think of that sort of female for a wife.'

'What sort of female?'

A deep flush stained his pretty features. 'Lord, Timma, the things you ask!'

'I suppose you mean a female he would take for his mistress. A doxy, would it be?'

'Timma!'

'Oh, come, Valentine, there is no need to look so shocked,' she said impatiently.

'I am shocked,' he said sternly, shifting a little away.

'Why, when you know I never mince words?'

'Well, you ought to—mince them, I mean.'

He was backing away, but Timothia moved to him and seized hold of his arm. Her voice was urgent. 'Valentine, are you saying that Leo has been in love with one of those women?'

'Happens to everyone,' pleaded Valentine excusingly, squirming with embarrassment. 'Nothing to it. Mean to say, a wife isn't supposed to know anything about a man's ladybirds. Even if she does, she pretends she don't.'

Timothia released him. 'Indeed?'

Valentine became agitated. 'Lord, if Leo ever finds out I told you! Timma, you won't say anything to him?'

She drew a breath, for she must reassure him, much as she might feel inclined to open her mind to Leo. No, unthinkable.

'I shall say nothing. Provided,' she added as he let out a sigh of relief, 'that you tell me what I want to know.'

He sighed in a defeated way. 'That's blackmail, Timma. What do you want to know?'

'When was this? That Leo was enamoured of this ladybird?'

'Lord, I don't know,' he said impatiently. 'I don't remember precisely. A year or so ago, perhaps.'

'And is it over?'

'How should I—? I mean, he wouldn't be asking you to marry him if it wasn't.'

'I thought you said gentlemen didn't think of marriage to these women.'

'They don't,' he said in a harassed tone. 'Only they don't think of marriage to anyone else either—not if they're in the throes.'

This seemed logical. Timothia did not know why the matter was of such importance to her. Except that it was rather galling to find that a woman of that sort was privileged to have Leo's affections, when she was not. What attractions had she, to bring him to his knees? An image of dazzling beauty invaded her mind—dark and sultry, with luxurious eyes and rouged lips that beckoned for a kiss. She had seen such women at public assemblies— from a distance, naturally. One did not approach them. On the other hand, it was no matter for wonder that the gentlemen did!

She took an agitated turn about the room, fetching up

at the window again. Aware of Valentine at her back, she yet could not face him.

'What did she look like?'

'Who?' he asked stupidly.

'You know very well whom I mean,' she snapped, unable to help herself.

Valentine did not answer, and she forced herself to look at him. A frown of unusual severity marked his features.

'Well?'

'Can't expect me to answer a question like that, Timma,' he said heavily.

'I don't see why not. What difference does it make?'

'If it don't make any difference, why do you want to know?' he demanded reasonably.

Timothia felt herself unable to answer truthfully. She tried for an airy note. 'I am interested, that is all. I simply can't envisage what sort of female would be to Leo's taste. He is himself so dark, and I know that my father—who you may recall was fairer than you are, Valentine—'

'Often thought how much you resemble him,' observed her friend, nodding.

'Just so. But Papa, you know, told me that he had been attracted because my mama was so very much a Wetheral—dark and blue-eyed. He loved the combination, he said.'

'Ah, yes,' said Valentine, evidently thrown off guard. 'Leo has it too, don't he?'

'But does he prefer the opposite, or does he go for dark women too?' asked Timothia in as innocent a tone as she could manage.

'Can't say as I've noticed a particular preference,' mused Valentine. 'Though the chit who caught him in her toils was neither. Redhead, she was. Improbably so, I always thought. Tidy little piece, though. Very neat figure.'

Timothia felt sick. She had got what she wanted. Valentine had spilled it all, just as she had known he would, if only she could get him chattering. Now she wished very much that she had let it alone.

A redhead. Leo had fallen in love with a red-headed ladybird. Little—and neat. So much for Amazons! She was obliged to clamp her teeth upon a burgeoning complaint against the stupidity of men and their lovesick fancies. But there was still something more to be probed. And Valentine was best placed to give her an answer.

She looked at him and saw that he had realised how he had been tricked. 'You need not look like that, Valentine,' she said reassuringly. 'It does not affect me, you know.'

'Don't it?' he asked doubtfully.

'Not a whit.' But she held his eye. 'Yet answer me this, if you please. Suppose then that it is over between Leo and this female.'

'Long ago,' put in Valentine hastily.

Timothia ignored this. 'If he should marry me,' she pursued, 'only for the convenience of it, mind—what is to stop him falling in love with some other ladybird at a later date?'

'Why, nothing,' he replied in a voice of surprise, adding thoughtfully, 'Though I shouldn't think myself that Leo could afford to waste the ready. Mean to say, you can't go keeping a mistress if you've a wife and family to support. Though you can't blame a man for wishing to mount one if his marriage bed don't offer him that sort of comfort.'

# Chapter Three

The pen splattered across the paper, and split. With a curse, Leo threw it down on the blotter where its contents soaked into an untidy stain. Then he snatched up the ruined sheet, screwed it into a ball, and flung it across the room.

How was he supposed to work under these conditions? Bad enough that he had a mountain of correspondence to answer, without having his mind constantly seized by the dreadful uncertainty of his immediate future. Why could not Timma answer him? She'd had all of three days to think it over. When Saturday had come and gone with no word from her, he had accepted it, and naturally he had not expected to hear from her on Sunday. But it was now Tuesday! What the deuce ailed her to be keeping him in suspense in this fashion?

He got up impatiently from the large oak desk, and crossed to pick up the wasted paper which had bounced off a glass-fronted bookshelf and come to rest against the foot of one of the small settles that were placed between each of the three large library windows that gave brightness to the spacious room, bouncing off the unadorned white ceiling. Otherwise, the massy cases of books that stacked the place from end to end would have rendered it as dismal as the parlours of Fenny House.

Leo stopped as he turned to return to the desk, caught by the beam of light that showed to disadvantage its disgracefully paper-cluttered surface. How many times had he imagined Timma seated there? It would not, he knew, be in that state if she were. It was odd to think that Timma, who was so careless of her dress, had ever been scrupulously neat in her work. Whereas he, who had rarely a crease out of place—other than when engaged in sport—and who could tolerate no mess either in his bedchamber or the running of the stables, could never keep the desk in anything but the most frightful muddle. Timma, he recalled, thinking of her office in her father's house, had always every paper in its place, and knew exactly where to lay her hand on the correct box for any document she required. She'd had assistance from Crimdon, of course—an excellent agent!—but she had dealt with every letter herself, and kept meticulous accounts.

Sighing, Leo threw the paper into the waste basket with an accurate aim and picked up the pen to see whether it would bear a further repair. Wiping off the ink, he examined the nib. The devil! It was near ruined. He perched on the desk and armed himself with a small paring knife. But as he attempted to mend the pen his attention wandered back to the nagging question that was never far from his mind.

If Timma meant to refuse him, what was he to do? Valentine had suggested a secretary, and he supposed it must come to that. He was not in any way straitened in his circumstances, but secretaries did not come cheap. Nor, for the matter of that, did wives! But there was allowance for that particular expense. He was expected to marry, and the estate must bear it. A secretary was a luxury.

Did she mean to refuse him? It was a fear that had been steadily growing into a conviction over the uncomfortable days that had elapsed since he'd made his offer. He had half expected a summons from Timma on Saturday, after Valentine had sent that note. Lord knew what Valentine had actually said to her! He was beginning to fear that more had been revealed than he would have wished, although Valentine had assured him that he had done nothing more than reiterate what Timma had said had already been discussed between them.

Would it had remained a discussion! Though he knew the degeneration into argument had been the result of his own folly. How he had bungled it! But what else could he have said? The one thing he had determined on, before ever approaching Timma, had been that he must be truthful with her. He owed that much to their friendship. He would not palter with her intelligence, nor offer her false protestations that must insult rather than flatter.

Only it seemed as though his very truthfulness had offended her! He could not understand it. Had he not spoken of their long friendship? Could she not see the advantage of remaining within the area that she knew and loved? She had familiarity with Wiggin Hall, and he knew that she had as much fondness as he for the hilly region in which it was set. It made for stimulating rides, and the view of his home where it nestled in the valley below was superb from the hills. And what could be better than an unexacting partnership where both parties understood each other so well? They were much of an age—four years only between them—and he had ever treated her as an equal. Deuce take it, what more could she wish for?

He had tried to understand when she'd failed to accept

him without hesitation. But if the truth be told, he had never been so put out! He had driven away in something of a rage, and had spent at least four-and-twenty hours persuading himself that he hoped she would refuse him. For he was committed now—whatever she decided. But then nothing!

And a return to his arduous duties had, he must confess it, altered his mind. True, he had given Timma a number of reasons for the decision to marry her. But they were none of them as influential as this! After all, any other female would serve if all he needed was an heir and a chaperon for Babs. But there was no other female of his acquaintance—and none that he knew of with whom he had no acquaintance, come to that—who had Timma's application and experience in the matter of running an estate. It was a rare woman who had anything to do with such matters.

The nib of the pen in his hand came into focus, and he realised that it was satisfactorily mended. Sighing again, he sat back down and took up the letter he had been attempting to answer. A complaint from one tenant of another, who would not keep his grazing sheep to his own land. As if Leo knew how to make him do so! If only he had not given his agent leave of absence to attend a family funeral. Lord, what was it that he had determined to say to this fellow?

He applied himself to the letter again, and struggled through a laborious response. He had barely completed the task when his butler entered to say that a trader had come to see him about an order for fencing in the north wood. Leo threw up his hands in despair.

'I can't see him, Crieff!' he declared. 'I know nothing of fences in the north wood. Tell him he must wait until Beauleigh returns from this funeral.'

'I believe the man only wishes to ascertain the area of the land to be enclosed, sir.'

'But I don't know!' Leo reiterated in a harassed way. 'Beauleigh told me nothing of it, and I cannot arrange it without consulting him.'

'Very well, sir.'

The butler withdrew, and Leo dropped his head in his hands. Fences in the north wood! He might be sure that if this had been Dulverton, he reflected bitterly, Timma would have known everything there was to know about fences in the north wood.

Abruptly, he thrust back his chair and got up. To the devil with it! She had no right to keep him waiting this long. He would have an answer—and today!

Leo eyed the Hawnby dragon with an echo of the unease with which she had always inspired him. He had not thought of the distinct advantage in marrying Timma that would arise from the inevitable removal from the vicinity of her old governess. The woman had an eye that could pierce minds at twenty paces!

Cursing Padstow for showing him into the front parlour—if one could dignify this paltry room by such a name!—he moved to the window and affected to look through the leaded panes.

'Timothia is not in the garden,' came Edith Hawnby's flat tones from behind him.

Leo turned. 'Padstow said she was walking.'

'Not in the garden,' reiterated the old governess. 'Probably gone to the Fenns. Marshy ground seems to favour her mood.'

Denoting a grim smile on Mrs Hawnby's face, Leo felt himself colour up a trifle. Devil take the woman! Was he supposed to take that for a jibe? No doubt she knew everything—including Timma's mind. His interest quickened. She must know! He might probe for some inkling, and so prepare himself for Timma's answer. He moved into the room, rather closer, it seemed, than the old lady appreciated.

'No need to stand over me, young Wetheral! Though I dare say you can't help it in this poky room.'

Leo retreated. Was that a wicked gleam in her eye? Teasing wretch! Very well, since she knew so much, let him take what advantage he might of Timma's temporary absence.

'You appear to be very well informed, ma'am.'

She looked blank. 'At my age, I ought to be.'

'I think you know what I mean,' Leo said tersely. 'Have you any indication of what Timma intends?'

'To walk back home, I imagine,' said the other blandly.

Leo all but ground his teeth. 'Don't trifle with me, ma'am, I beg of you! These days of suspense have given me no small cause for anxiety.'

'Then you are probably wise to have shortened the time of waiting,' came the unemotional response.

'Yes, but has Timma yet made a decision?'

'Concerning?'

'Her future!' said Leo impatiently. '*Our* future.'

'Ah.' Mrs Hawnby rose from her chair. 'That, sir, is outside my province. I am afraid I cannot advise you.' With which, she waddled to the door, and was gone.

Leo was left to glare at the open doorway. Why Timma must needs keep company with a brusque female, with whom no one of her acquaintance could comfortably converse, was a matter passing his comprehension. When they were married—

He caught himself up on the thought. There was as yet no question of *when*. They were still at the point of if.

Had he not elected to come here today to gain an answer, he dared say they would remain at that point, awaiting his cousin's pleasure, for a good deal longer. What was that remark of the dragon Hawnby concerning the Fenns? That they suited Timma's mood? The devil! That was as much as to say that his offer had thrown her into gloom. Not content with hurling this at his head, the woman had not only refused to answer his questions, but had left him flat to kick his heels until Timma might deign to put in an appearance. He dared say he would have got better fortune by asking Padstow.

But the thought of Mrs Hawnby's iniquities could not occupy his mind for long. He found himself instead going into the vexed question of what he was to do if Timma refused him. It struck him all at once that it was little more than two weeks since he had first hit upon this solution to his difficulties. Yet already it was so set in his mind to be the best solution that he could think of no other. He could not even remember what it was that had prompted the idea—something Dulverton had said concerning Timma's way with management, had it been? Or had he said it?

He had met Dulverton out riding, and turned to accompany him back to the Park since it lay in his way. It had been done in a purely companionable spirit for he had little acquaintance with the man. Not unnaturally, the conversation had turned upon Timma, for whom Dulverton had expressed the greatest admiration—along with some regret that he had not her skill with management. Leo had suggested that he seek Timma's advice, adding that he had been thinking of doing so himself.

From there to the germ of his idea seemed to have been but a short step. And once it had taken root in his mind it had grown rapidly, springing so readily into bloom that he had been almost as taken aback as had been the subject of his plan when he'd put it to her. Yet he had taken some days before he'd determined to do so. Several days— along with a lengthy discussion with Valentine. And then he had felt himself obliged to wait another few for her mourning to be at an end, during which time he had become so fond of the notion that it had seemed to him to be almost a settled thing, save only for Timma's certain agreement.

Deuce take it, he had been unreasonable! Why should he have expected Timma to jump to the offer when he had himself been obliged to spend a good deal of time thinking it over? He should not have come here to press her for an answer. It was only fair to allow her to reach her own conclusion in her own time. After all, if she had not sent to refuse him, it must mean that she was still considering the matter.

Yes, he should certainly go. Now, before she returned. The less he harried her, the more likely was it that the outcome of her cogitations must be favourable.

Crossing quickly to the door, Leo passed down the narrow passage and picked up his hat and gloves from the little table in the meagre hall. The weather being so fine, he had not troubled to wear his caped driving-coat over the blue cloth coat and buckskins. He scanned his image in the barely adequate wall mirror as he paused to don the wide-brimmed beaver. With his gloves clasped together in one hand, he let himself quietly out of the house. And came face to face with his cousin.

'The devil!' he burst out.

'Oh, heavens!' she uttered simultaneously.

There was a brief pause. Timothia tried to speak, and failed, finding that her tongue seemed to have become entangled with her vocal cords. Her heart was thudding—

with shock! What did Leo mean by arriving unannounced? She had not sent for him. She was not ready!

'I beg your pardon,' Leo managed, trying for a calm he was far from feeling. 'I did not mean to startle you. I was just leaving.'

'So I see,' Timothia said, finding her voice. She glanced towards the road. 'Did you drive? I did not see your phaeton.'

'Tarbert is walking the horses.'

'Why have you come?' No, that was stupid! 'I mean, you're early. I am not—I don't— Oh, the devil!'

'That is excessively unbecoming language!' Leo rapped out, hardly conscious of using the exact same expression only moments before. He regretted the impulse at once, for Timma's eyes flashed.

'If it is, you have only yourself to blame, for you taught it to me!'

Which was undeniable. Inevitably, perhaps, Timma had picked up his habitual expressions over the years. It had never before occurred to him to object. He grimaced.

'I didn't mean to say that. It slipped out.'

'I dare say you could not help yourself,' said Timothia shrewishly, 'having already accustomed yourself to the idea of having the mastery over me.'

'No such thing!' He kneaded his gloves with unquiet hands. 'I wish you will not leap to absurd conclusions.'

Aware of the idiocy of her own remark, Timothia strove for a measure of calm. 'You took me by surprise.'

Leo sighed down his ill temper. 'I know. I have already begged your pardon. I should not have come, only I have been beset by anxiety. But I had just realised how unfair this was to you, and that is why I was leaving.'

Timothia was silent for a moment, her ruffled temper damping down. At a vague level of consciousness, she took in that the shock of the meeting had flung them both into betraying the confusion into which the whole business had thrown them.

'Why are we doing this?' she said impulsively. 'We have been so much to each other, Leo. I have relied upon your friendship more than any other relationship—excepting only Papa. Even he has not been privy to some of the secrets I have shared with you. Why—oh, why must we spoil it?'

He could not but be touched by this appeal. A rueful smile lit the blue eyes and he reached unconsciously for her hand, grasping it strongly. 'I never imagined that it would spoil it, Timma. Had I thought so, I should not have broached the subject.' He brought her fingers to his lips and kissed them briefly. 'I promise you, I truly believed—I still believe it!—that our closeness ought to be a sound basis. I cannot imagine setting up the level of trust we have with any other woman.'

The feel of his hand had warmed Timothia, but the touch of his lips caused a flushing sensation in her breast—quite out of keeping with the words that followed. She could not endure it! Withdrawing her hand, she turned away, walking directly onto the lawn, and automatically lifting the amber-coloured petticoats of her kersey gown clear of the grass. She was aware that Leo followed. Aware also of the expression of hurt in his eyes as she had removed her fingers from his hold.

'Have we grown so far apart so quickly?' came his voice, insidiously soft, and with an echo that hinted at the pain she had caused him.

Pausing on the grass, Timothia turned to look at him. 'Do you wish for the truth, Leo?'

He frowned, aware of a sliver of apprehension that accompanied the hurt of Timma's withdrawal. Leaning back in a pose of unconsciously defensive arrogance, he placed a hand on his hip, and eyed her. Her countenance was solemn under the inevitable disarrangement of her pale yellow locks, where a straw hat had fallen awry behind, resting on a short brown cloak.

Leo almost sighed. Did he want the truth? 'Have we ever lied to one another?'

'I am sure we must have done,' Timothia returned, smiling a little. 'Not knowingly, perhaps.'

'Then why boggle at plain speaking now?'

He saw the green eyes darken, and his apprehension deepened. He did not think he did want to know this truth. But it was too late to draw back.

'We grew apart, Leo, at the first moment that you conceived the notion to make use of our friendship for the purpose of convenience.'

'But I never meant—'

He was overridden, the flame of Timothia's fury fanning too fast to be contained.

'What you meant was innocent enough. That is not the point. What you did was to throw my affection in my face! It was of so little account that it could be turned to any purpose that suited you.'

'That is quite untrue!' he rejoined heatedly. 'Deuce take it, Timma, how can you say such a thing? It is your very affection that led me to think—'

'The trouble is, Leo, that you didn't think!'

The ribbons of the hat hanging behind her seemed to choke her. She ripped at the tie with unsteady hands, and whipped the straw bonnet away, unaware of the clenching of her fingers about the curled brim.

Leo was staring at her, torn between perplexity and the inevitable rise of temper. 'I do not understand you. I know

I put it badly, but what is there in the matter of what I said to merit this reaction?'

Timothia gazed at him in her turn, and slowly shook her head, wonder in her tone. 'We are poles apart.'

'How can you say so?' he uttered, mystified. 'Explain it to me, for I am quite at sea.'

'I cannot,' she said, shrugging helplessly.

A heady sensation of loss gripped Leo. She was slipping away from him. He grasped her shoulder urgently.

'Timma, don't let this happen! If you will not marry me, then, for the Lord's sake, don't let us lose our friendship! Will you throw away these fifteen years?'

Timothia grimaced. 'Is it that long?'

'It must be that long.' He shook her a little. 'You can't mean to let this divide us. Don't you see? I want to be close to you. Closer! If I have led you to believe otherwise, I did not mean it. Above all, I do not want to lose our friendship.'

She did not speak, but it seemed to him that she searched his face, as if she sought for something more than he had said. Leo felt as if he would say anything— only as long as she would not renounce him. He was a trifle startled by his own need. Did her friendship mean so much?

Timothia found herself bewildered. The manner of his plea, if not the words, wrought havoc within her. She could not listen to him unmoved, yet she was at a loss to account for the pulsing beat of her heart. There was that in his voice that had tugged at an answering chord—but it had little to do with what he had said. A thought sprang unbidden into her mind, and she spoke on its impulse.

'There might be a way to keep it so. Leo, what if we did marry for convenience?' He made as if to speak, but Timothia quickly put her fingers up to his mouth to silence him. 'Wait! Let me speak.' He sank back, removing his hand from her shoulder, and she drew a breath to start anew. 'There is no denying the benefits on either side; that I grant. But there is too much complication in the fact of marriage. The demands cannot be met. Why should we not marry—and remain upon terms of friendship alone?'

It was so unexpected that Leo could not quite take it in. Did she mean what he thought she meant? He frowned. 'Are you suggesting a platonic relationship?'

Timothia nodded, smiling. 'That is it exactly. We may have all the advantages, and none of the difficulties.'

'Not quite all the advantages,' he pointed out drily. 'Are you sure you know what you are talking about?'

A laugh was surprised out of her. 'Do you take me for an ignorant miss? I am proposing that we marry without becoming bedfellows. What else did you suppose I could mean?'

Leo was blank with astonishment. 'Have you run mad?'

Timothia frowned. 'Why should you think so?'

'Have I been talking to the air?' he demanded forcefully. 'How could such an arrangement possibly serve me?'

'Serve you! I thought the advantages were supposed to be mutual.'

'So they are. But there is little point in my marrying at all, if my wife is not to provide me with an heir!'

Her eye kindled. 'Oh, so we are back to that, are we?'

'Of course we are back to that!' he snapped. 'It is almost the only reason why a gentleman of property even considers marriage. If I wished only for the other aspects of the case, I would have no need to wed you, you simpleton!'

'So now I am a simpleton!' uttered Timothia dangerously, unconsciously rolling her ill-used straw hat between agitated fingers. 'Did you not specify that your prime motive in asking me to marry you was to get me to run your estate?'

'Yes, but—'

'And did you not also say that begetting an heir was only one of your reasons?'

'Well, of course I did. You don't suppose I should have dreamed of putting the emphasis on it? But anyone with the smallest pretension to common sense—which I believed you to be!—must see that it is something that cannot, under any circumstances, be put aside?'

'Well, if you wish me to be your wife,' Timothia announced furiously, 'it will have to be put aside!'

Leo stepped back a pace, heat in the blue eyes. 'If that is an ultimatum, let me tell you that nothing could be more insulting!'

'In that case, I am very glad I said it,' Timothia retorted. 'It will pay you back for the insults I received at your hands when you had the effrontery to make this ludicrous proposal!'

Leo nearly hit her. 'Effrontery? You dare to call it that?'

'I would call it worse than that, if I could only call something worse to mind!' Timothia threw at him.

Balked for the moment, Leo could only scowl at her, stiff with anger. She returned his thunderous stare with one of equal ferocity, her bosom heaving. But the pause was enough to damp down his fire a trifle. His eyes roved unconsciously over her features, and the thought flitted through his mind that she looked magnificent when she was aroused. Green eyes afire, and about the amber skin a sheen that threw the flaxen locks into strong relief. They were a very mane tossing about her face, for the fight had disarranged her plait. Oh, Timma, so much passion! And she wanted to withhold it!

'No, Miss Dulverton,' he said evenly. 'I will not take you upon those terms. My offer stands, but it is all or nothing.'

Timothia answered from the heart. 'Then let it be nothing, for I cannot give you my all.'

For the second time, she watched him turn on his heel and walk away. But her emotions on that first occasion were as nothing to what she was feeling now. For under the consuming heat of her rage lay a vast well of molten lead, dragging her down.

Striding up and down the ramparts of the south wall at Bluntisham Castle, Leo spoke his mind at some length, with Valentine obliged to keep pace beside him, if only in order to hear what he said. The winds at this height had a tendency to carry the words away. Which was perhaps as well, as Valentine once remarked, for Leo had torn his cousin's character to shreds.

'Good thing there's only me to hear you,' said his friend severely. 'I hope you didn't tell Timma to her face that she was a temperamental shrew with a brain the size of a walnut.'

'If I had her before me now,' Leo threatened savagely, stopping short, 'there is no telling what I might not say— let alone do. I could cheerfully strangle her!'

'No, you couldn't,' Valentine argued, perching thankfully upon the parapet and drawing in large breaths to get his wind. 'You know very well you wouldn't hurt a hair of her head. Dash it, Leo, you're a gentleman!'

'You need not remind me,' Leo snapped. 'If I were not, I should never have put myself into this impossible situation.'

He found that much of his spleen had now been discharged, and the desire to rail against Timma was lessening. But he still could not understand her!

'What should take her to make that suggestion?' he demanded of his friend. 'She is no fool. She knows perfectly well that I could not possibly marry her on those terms.' He frowned as a thought struck him. 'Unless she meant always to refuse me, and used that as a means of causing me to withdraw?'

He became aware of his friend's face. Why in the world should Valentine look so conscious? Then he remembered. That interview Timma had sought with him! What had been said?

'Valentine—' he began on a dangerous note.

His friend flung up a deprecating hand. 'Know what you're going to ask me, old fellow.'

Leo watched him draw breath and blow it out again, puffing out his cheeks. He waited, grimly expectant. Valentine met his eye, and grimaced.

'The fact is, Leo, it may well have been something I said. Not that I meant it. I couldn't help myself. Mean to say, you know what Timma's like. Dashed well blackmailed me!'

'Go on,' said Leo, impatient of these preliminaries. It was no surprise that Timma should have wormed something out of Valentine. But what?

'Thing is, she got it out of me that you'd been head over heels for Lucy,' confessed Valentine ruefully.

'Lucy?'

'Little redhead. You must remember, Leo. Dash it, she was your—'

'Yes, yes, all right,' Leo said hastily. 'Of course I remember. But what—?'

'Well, Timma wanted to know if you'd ever been that

way over a female, and I insisted that you hadn't—not in the way of marriage. And that led Timma to saying that she couldn't think what sort of female might take your fancy, and next thing I knew she had dragged Lucy out of me.'

'Oh, my God, you clodpole!'

'I know, but I did my best, Leo,' pleaded Valentine. 'Tried to mend it. Told her you'd not be likely to take another mistress after marriage—'

*'What?'*

'Well, you probably couldn't afford to, could you?'

Leo gasped for breath. 'You—told—Timma—?'

'Couldn't help myself, old fellow. She asked me flat out if I thought you'd fall for some other ladybird after she married you. What was I supposed to say?'

For several moments, Leo was obliged to fight for control. If his murderous instincts had before been directed at Timma, they were now fully concentrated upon his misguided rattlepate of a friend!

'By God, Valentine,' he said at last, 'if you were not my best friend, I'd tip you over that parapet!'

Valentine rose hastily from his perch and moved out of range along the ramparts. 'Now, Leo, don't be hasty! Not that I blame you, mind, for I can't but feel that Timma may have been influenced by—'

'May have been? *May* have been?' Leo resumed his restless pacing, muttering baleful threats. Small wonder he had been treated to Timma's insulting proposition! She must suppose he meant to use her only for the purpose of bearing his children, and take his pleasures elsewhere. As though he would dream of treating any woman so shabbily, let alone Timma! The devil! Was a wife a brood mare? Lord, what must she think?

'She must think all that is a mere matter of duty!' he

uttered aloud as realisation hit him. He found himself face to face with Valentine again, having crossed back and forth along the ramparts without knowing what he did.

'Does she imagine that I don't find her desirable?' he asked his friend. The question was posed in a rhetorical spirit, but Valentine chose to take it up.

'Do you?'

Leo frowned. 'Do I what?'

'Find her desirable?'

The question stopped Leo's very thoughts. Blank, he gazed at his friend, utterly unable to answer him.

'Shouldn't have thought so myself,' pursued Valentine in a musing way. 'Mean to say, she ain't the type of female you have ever looked at. Besides, it stands to reason. You can't keep close acquaintance with a female right through your childhood, and then expect to find her bowling you over. Know her too well, that's the trouble. If you ask me, the thing would have manifested long ago, if at all. Far more likely to happen when you was both adolescent and starting in that line.'

Leo heard the words with every evidence of understanding. Valentine made perfect sense. He had never experienced the smallest vestige of desire in Timma's presence—and there had been every opportunity for intimacy. No curb had been put upon their friendship. They had spent endless hours alone together in those vulnerable years. Except that he had been well ahead. Four years was a long time in childhood. When he was fifteen or sixteen, experiencing all the pangs of early maturity, Timma had been—what, eleven? Twelve? No loverlike ardour could ever have occurred between them.

Then, by the time Timma was grown up, he had been on the town for a number of years. He'd sown his wild oats like all young gentlemen—and yes, there had been

Lucy. He had been badly hit there! Yet all the time Timma had been in the background at home. And still there had not been the slightest sign of—

His thoughts suffered a check. A vision leapt into his mind: Timma, all fiery eyes and heaving bosom, flaxen locks awry. His blood quickened. A stabbing in the groin. Devil take it! Could this be happening? A second image nudged out the first: that 'indecent' spectacle when he had come to make his offer. He saw her again in his mind's eye. The casual pose, the creamy yellow mane slipping from its place, the glimpse of bosom, and the golden sheen of her skin. Oh, how seductive had she looked then! He had not seen it at the time—or had he? For had he not been quick to condemn her for it? Was it *this* that had prompted him to do so? His breath caught in his throat, and he turned away to grasp at the edge of the parapet.

'What's to do, old fellow?' came Valentine's concerned tones.

Leo straightened, drawing a steadying breath. He turned to confront his friend. 'You are mistaken, Valentine. The thing has manifested all right. Late in the day, perhaps. But, by God, it's there!'

A beaming smile swept across his friend's face. 'By all that's wonderful! Who would have believed it? Not Timma, I'll lay my life!'

'What do you mean, not Timma?' said Leo quickly, frowning. 'That she would not think it of me? Or that she—' A horrifying thought gripped him. He seized his friend by the coat. 'Valentine, what exactly did she say? Do you suppose she was jealous, or—?'

'Good Lord, no!' stated Valentine firmly. 'Said it didn't affect her—the business about your ladybird, I mean. Besides, it don't make sense. If she favoured you, she wouldn't refuse to participate in that side of the marriage.'

It hit Leo like a douche of cold water. Valentine was right. 'She does not find me to her taste.'

'What has that to say to anything? Lord, I know you ain't a coxcomb, but you must rate your personal attractions higher than that!' uttered Valentine in disgust. 'You can make her like you, can't you? Have you made love to her?'

'Made love to Timma? Of course I have not! I would not dream of—'

'Well, if you wish to win her, hang it all, you must dream of it,' said Valentine severely. 'Tell you what, Leo. I'll go and see Timma and pave the way, so to speak.'

'You will do no such thing!' said Leo, alarmed. 'You have done quite enough already.'

'Yes, but that's exactly why I feel I ought. All I have to do is tell Timma that you favour her and—'

'And she will instantly favour me in return? No, I thank you, Valentine. It is quite clear to me now why Timma has been recalcitrant all along.' He made for the small tower at the end of the rampart where a narrow winding stair led down into the castle. 'Evidently she did not wish to say outright that she could not like me in that way. Did I tell you how she was convinced that marriage would spoil our friendship?'

'Yes, you told me,' said Valentine, hurrying after him, 'but I can't see what that has to do with it.'

'It has everything to do with it,' responded Leo, clattering down the stairs at a rate that made Valentine dizzy. 'You did not see her face when I first made the suggestion to her. I did. She was shocked, Valentine—and now I see why. She could not envision herself tied to me in wedlock. Of course she could not. I am only Leo! Her cousin, yes. Her friend, yes. But husband? The thought disgusted her.

I see it all now. She could not say so, naturally. She would not wish to hurt my feelings, but—'

'Leo, you've taken—leave of your senses!' protested Valentine breathlessly from behind him. 'For the Lord's sake, don't be such a chucklehead! If you didn't—give Timma to understand that you find her desirable, how—' He broke off, crying despairingly, 'I do wish you will stop for a moment!'

Leo paused by one of the slit windows let into the tower walls. Turning, he searched his friend's face in the gloom. 'What are you trying to say, Valentine?'

'For all you know, Timma might change her mind if she knew of it,' Valentine suggested. 'That's a female all over—contrary. Ask my sister Chloe. Time and again it's happened. A female don't feel anything for a fellow until she hears that he finds her ripe enough to warm his bed. Then—whoosh! Suddenly she's all over the man.'

'Indeed?' said Leo sceptically.

'Assure you. If I've heard Chloe say it of some friend or other of hers once, I've heard it a dozen times. You ask her.'

'I have no intention of discussing such a matter with Mrs Devenick, I thank you—even if she is your sister. Besides,' he added, turning to start down the stairs again, 'Timma isn't like other females. To my knowledge, she has never even looked at a man in that way.'

'Then you won't even try?'

Leo halted again, turning wrathfully on his friend in the darkness of the narrow stairway. 'Do you know me so little as to suppose that I would force my attentions upon an unwilling female? If I were to marry Timma, that is precisely what I would be obliged to do. No, I thank you, Valentine. Timma does not wish to marry me, and if she is not attracted to me—which cannot be in doubt!—then I certainly do not wish to marry her! The matter is closed.'

'It is of no use to say any more, Susan. My mind is made up.'

'Yes, but I am going to say more,' announced her friend with unaccustomed determination.

'Oh, for pity's sake!'

With a distinct sensation of being persecuted, Timothia rose from the bench under the chestnut tree where the tête-à-tête was taking place. To her annoyance, Susan got up and followed her as she made for the shrubbery.

'Timma, you have not considered!'

Timothia halted, turning. 'I have had all night to consider, and there is nothing further to think about.'

But Susan grasped her arm and caught her glance with that spaniel look in her eyes. 'For my sake, Timma! I could not reconcile it with my conscience to allow you, without argument, to fling away a bond that means everything to you.'

A sharp pain thrust into Timothia's breast, but she fought it down. 'It *meant* a great deal, Susan. It is past.'

'I don't believe you,' said her friend, greatly daring. 'Leo has been all in all to you. He is so still.'

Timothia pulled away. 'Leo is not the man I thought him! And it is ludicrous to say that. You are quite as important to me as he is—was!'

'But I am a female. It is not the same.'

'Just so. One cannot have that friendship with a male. They have not the same mentality. Their priorities are different.' She added acidly, 'As for Leo's priorities, they are all of them at odds with my own.'

She found that her friend was eyeing her with a look of scepticism in the large brown eyes. 'They were never so before. It is only this foolish misunderstanding that makes you say so.'

'Misunderstanding!' Timothia shifted away, ripping at petals on the brink of wilting with vicious indiscrimination as she moved down the line of shrubs. 'My cousin presents me with a mockery of an offer that scorns my feelings and ruins our friendship—and you call it a misunderstanding?'

'But he never meant to scorn your feelings,' protested Susan. 'You know that he cares for you, Timma. You said yourself that he was desperate not to lose your friendship.'

'Then he should not have done his best to alienate me,' said Timothia ruthlessly. 'I wish you will not take his part, Susan. He has behaved in a perfectly heartless fashion, and I can only thank providence that my eyes have been opened to his true character.'

'Oh, this is quite dreadful, Timma! You know you do not mean that. Why, you like Leo beyond anything.'

'Correction. I loathe Leo beyond anything!'

Having said which, Timothia discovered that tears were trickling down her cheeks, and dashed them away with an impatient hand. Not fast enough for Susan, however.

'I knew it! You are utterly cast down. Oh, Timma, dearest, why will you persist in this obstinacy?'

'I am n-not cast down,' said Timothia, sniffing. But the welling at her eyes persisted, and she was obliged to search with frantic hands in her blue muslin petticoats for a handkerchief. By the time she had managed to stem the flow, she found that Susan had somehow succeeded in manoeuvring her back to the bench. She allowed her friend to take her hand, but meeting the dejected air of the brown eyes had the effect of hardening her again.

'Do stop looking at me like that, Susan!' she begged crossly. 'I am merely tired, for I slept badly.'

'I don't wonder!'

'Yes, well, I have no intention of allowing myself to indulge in this sort of weakness.'

'If you will only stop being silly, and agree to marry Leo, you would not be in this upset,' Susan said forthrightly.

Timothia eyed her with hostility. 'Are you so little my friend? Even could I bring myself to overlook his conduct, do you suppose I am stupid enough to tie myself up in subservience to such an autocrat as Leo has turned out to be?'

'He is not an autocrat, Timma. You have always held him to be the kindest of men—despite your squabbles.'

'Kindness has nothing to do with it. He has merely offered for me, and already he believes he may order me about as he chooses. At present he is only my cousin, and I may defy him with impunity. Do you think I will barter that freedom for the hideous situation of a wife?'

'But, Timma,' ventured Susan doubtfully, 'it is only fair that a gentleman, who has all the duty and burden of providing and protecting a wife, should require obedience. It is in the marriage vow.'

Timothia rose in haste. 'Nothing would induce me to vow to obey Leo! I would die first!' She added sourly, 'And if I wait upon Leo's provision I should very likely starve! He is incapable of running his estate, and will undoubtedly end in bankruptcy.'

Susan looked so shocked that Timothia was betrayed into a giggle. She sat down again, finding that she felt several degrees more comfortable, having given full rein to her seething emotions. A sort of lethargy was creeping over her, and although she was aware that Susan was speaking she did not really hear the words. She could hardly even remember what she had been saying herself.

She knew that a vast disruption had occurred in the even tenor of her life, and saw with a barely felt unease that the ripples were only beginning to appear.

Before she could follow the thread of her own thoughts, an interruption occurred. Some change in the presence beside her brought her senses alert, and Susan's voice penetrated the blanket of calm.

'Valentine! Oh, he must have come on an errand for Leo. I am sure he will prove to be Leo's emissary.'

Timothia watched her friend leap up from the bench, and, holding up her muslin petticoats of a becoming shade of pink, run quickly towards the figure of Valentine Lord Pentre, who had evidently espied them from the path to the front door, and was swiftly crossing the meagre lawn.

'Valentine!' Susan called out. 'Are you come from Leo?'

'Not exactly,' he replied, and Timothia saw his grey eyes trained upon her face.

An inward sigh shook her. No more, she begged silently. But she summoned a smile for him as he came up and held out her hand. He shook it, but was obliged to give his attention to Susan, who was tugging at his arm.

'Valentine, surely you can do something? It is all too dreadful! Pray, pray, try to talk some sense into Timma, for she will not listen to me.'

'Ain't likely she'll pay any heed to me either, Sue,' he said ruefully. His eyes came back to Timothia. 'Truth is, Timma, I've come to set things straight. I know it's my fault that you took against Leo yesterday.'

'Oh, surely not!' struck in Susan.

'Yes, it is, though. Couldn't sleep for thinking of it. Thought I'd do best to come and try to patch it up.'

Susan's eyes shone—with tears, as Timothia knew. It

would not take much for Susan to see Valentine's conduct as heroic!

'That was well done of you, Valentine,' uttered Susan breathily. 'I might have known you would come to the rescue.'

Valentine looked uncomfortable. 'Hardly that, Sue. Made a muff of it, that's all. Tongue runs away with me, that's the trouble.'

Timothia intervened before Susan could dispute this obvious truth. 'You need not take all the blame. I provoked you intentionally into saying what you did, so it is quite my own fault.'

'Yes, but the thing is, Timma, that Leo—well, when I think of some of the things he said about you—'

'I see,' said Timothia drily. 'So he has once more seen fit to discuss me with you, has he?'

'Dash it all, Timma, what do you expect?' demanded Valentine with some heat. 'The poor fellow was so put-about, he had to talk to someone. Better me than anyone else. And what of you and Sue? Don't tell me you haven't been discussing the whole business between the pair of you, because I should never believe it.'

'It was not my wish to discuss it with Susan, I assure you,' Timothia retorted. 'Only she would insist upon harping on the subject.'

Susan bridled. 'I should think I might! Why, Valentine, would you believe it? She would have me keep mum and leave her to her fate. As if I could!'

'No, indeed,' agreed Valentine earnestly. 'As well suppose that I could let Leo go wrecking his life. Timma, you must listen to me! The poor fellow was wretchedly cut up. I could hardly bear it when he left me—looked so devilish distressed about the whole affair.'

Timothia tried not to allow these words to affect her,

but in vain. It was with difficulty that she kept her countenance. But she had no intention of showing how powerfully Valentine's communication was operating upon her, nor indeed of discussing the matter further with either of her friends. She drew a breath and stood up.

'I must thank you, Valentine, for these tidings. You too, Susan. I know that you have both of you only my interests at heart. Leo's too, I must suppose. You are good friends to me. But pray, leave me alone now. I—I need to think. Valentine, do you, if you please, make sure that Susan gets home safely.'

She pressed both their hands, gave a tremulous smile in an attempt to respond to the concern in each friend's face, and then fled.

Reaching the safety of her bedchamber, she found that the desire to weep had subsided. But her knees were shaking, and she sank down upon the big four-poster, gazing unseeingly through the leaded casement, her thoughts in turmoil.

## Chapter Four

Leo distressed? She ought to be glad! Had he not caused her enough confusion of mind to wish to be revenged? She could scarce believe now that she had almost persuaded herself into acceptance of his proposition only yesterday. The more fool he to have lost patience. He deserved to feel distress of mind!

She had gone to the Fenns that day to think. There was a solitude and silence about the old marshlands, despite the reclaiming drainage that had enabled the numerous lots to be sectioned off for crops. Mr Dulverton had introduced his daughter to the Fenns for the purpose of instruction, but instead an elusive imaginative fancy in Timothia had been captured by the grey air of mystery that hung about the low-lying land which gave off a musty stench. It was the very place for brooding.

Timothia had brooded to some purpose. Against all her instincts, the words of Mrs Hawnby had worked upon her with near disastrous results. For what had there been against the match, if she was honest with herself, bar a laughable conceit that her cousin approach her with some sort of loverlike ardour? Instead, Leo had been honest, true to their friendship. And she, taken by surprise, had allowed herself to fall victim to vanity!

What was it to her if Leo had been in love with some doxy? Valentine was right—it was none of her concern. And if Leo should, by some chance, be lured into the bed of another such creature after they were tied up in wedlock, the likelihood was that she would know nothing about it. Would she even care? It was not the part of a wife of convenience to concern herself whether or not her husband enjoyed sharing her bed! In all probability, her cousin would do his duty in getting her with child and then leave nature to take its course. She need not be fearful of the continued embarrassment of providing him with his conjugal rights. Let him by all means find solace elsewhere! Indeed, Timothia might well with impunity deny him any further access to her once she had provided him with the necessary heir. After all, a marriage of convenience ought to be just that.

By the time she had returned to Fenny House she had been within an ace of sending to tell Leo that she would accept him. Had he refrained from giving in to his impatience, she would probably have done so. She could only be glad that Leo had abandoned caution, for she had been thus exposed to a most disagreeable side of his character. If he was distressed, she decided defiantly, he had only himself to blame!

Had he not taken up that despicable attitude in regard to his heir, she would not have delivered her ultimatum. She had not meant to marry him without providing him with one. The suggestion of a platonic relationship had been impulsive—the natural outcome of her cogitations. Only Leo had not given her time to amend the suggestion, but had got upon his high ropes and behaved in the most disgustingly selfish fashion. Had he not been so defensive of his own needs, she would have explained that she had only meant to withdraw herself from his bed once an heir had been created. What could have been fairer than that?

But, no. Leo must needs demonstrate that his offer had been just what she thought it at the outset. Framed purely for self- interest. And she had nearly given in to it!

She was obliged at this point to have recourse to her handkerchief. Oh, she was glad that Leo was distressed! He could not be more so than she. The only difference was that where he was upset only at the loss of her companionship—which she could not doubt—her sorrow found its root in the discovery that her cousin had feet of clay. He had been all along unworthy of that degree of friendship with which he had been entrusted. She could hardly regret the passing of such a friendship! And it was past. There could be no return to intimacy after this.

Yet there was no diminution of Timothia's melancholy as the days passed. True to her character, she kept it hidden. She flattered herself that neither Susan nor Valentine, who had visited her both separately and together, ostensibly with the purpose of urging her to relent towards Leo, could guess the true state of her emotions. Indeed, quite otherwise.

'I never thought you could be so cruel, Timma,' had said her despairing friend, shedding tears.

Valentine had been no less outspoken. 'Dashed if I ever thought to see the day when you could be such an enemy to Leo!'

She had answered both with the same curt dismissal. 'It is of no use to speak to me on the subject. It was not I who began it.'

Whether either of them spoke to Leo, Timothia was not in a position to know. She must suppose that Valentine had done so. But when next she heard from Susan, by a scribbled note sent round from the Rectory at Old Hurst on the Monday—with apologies for not delivering the news immediately yesterday, the Reverend Mr Hurst insisting on his household keeping the Lord's day correctly, so that no servant was permitted to take the letter—it was to understand that Valentine had gone off to a shooting party at Peterborough. Susan thought Leo had very likely gone along with him.

Timothia could readily believe it. The news did little to ease her discomforts. She felt irrationally annoyed that Leo should have so readily accepted the breach. Was he so capable of enjoying a party of pleasure? How little their long friendship had meant to him! One would suppose that he might make some effort to retrieve it. But had he? No, not in the very slightest. Had he bothered to try to see her in these last days? Had he written—if only to express his regret at the outcome of his bizarre proposal? No, he had not.

Not that she had really expected him to do so. Despite Edith's ludicrous comments.

They had been sitting at breakfast in the parlour which served for all meals. It was a truly 'poky' apartment, except that Timothia, soon after her arrival, had dealt ruthlessly with its contents. She had thrown out the aged table with which the place was already furnished, and which took up far too much space for comfort. Instead, she had begged of Dudley the neat round worktable that had long stood unused in her mother's old sitting-room. Even with six chairs around it, this afforded sufficient accommodation in the room for a long sideboard. And, once a serving-hatch had been cut into the panelling through to the pantry behind so that Polly need not struggle through the narrow corridors loaded down with dishes, the place afforded a cosy arrangement for meals.

Timothia had snatched up the letters from the silver salver presented to her by Padstow, and flicked swiftly through them until she came upon Susan's letter.

'Seems to me,' had observed Edith evenly from the other side of the table, 'that you've developed a habit of doing that of late.'

'Of doing what?' had enquired Timothia without looking up from breaking the seal on the note.

'Grabbing your correspondence up as if your life depended upon it, and then tossing it aside in disgust.'

Timothia had glanced up, frowning. 'What do you mean?'

Edith had chosen not to answer this, asking instead, 'What's that letter?'

'It is from Susan.'

'Ah. Didn't think it was what you were waiting for.'

To Timothia's consternation, a flush stained her cheeks. 'I am not waiting for anything! That is a ludicrous suggestion.'

'Is it?' said Edith flatly. 'I suppose it is just as ludicrous to suggest that you spend a great deal of time watching the driveway.'

'I do no such thing!'

'Don't you?' For a moment or two, Edith continued to regard her with that all-seeing eye. Then her gaze returned to her plate. 'Then I must have been mistaken.'

'You are mistaken!' stated Timothia stoutly, and was annoyed when Edith addressed herself to her food and neither replied nor looked up again. She read Susan's letter in a spirit of resentment, which was in no way dissipated by its contents.

She knew what Edith had been at. She meant to suggest that Timothia was waiting for some sign or appearance from Leo. Well, perhaps she had been. It was not unnatural. If only her days were not so empty, she would not have leisure to think about her cousin. Heaven knew she did not wish to think of him!

At length, in a fit of rebellion against the relentless intrusion into her mind of her cousin's ill-advised conduct, she found an excuse to give her something to do.

Her lawyer having visited on Tuesday to pay her the allowance from her trust fund, she directed Padstow to note down any household necessities they might be needing. It was a meagre list, consisting of such items as wax candles and various oils which were not available from the local farms or village traders which adequately furnished most of their day-to-day needs. But Timothia added to it a few necessities for the stables after consultation with Bickley, and decided that this justified the excursion to the nearest town. Next morning, she instructed Bickley to harness one of the two carriage horses to the gig.

There was a deal of relief to her lowered spirits in driving the few miles to St Ives. The day was overcast but warm, and the breeze generated by a good pace did much to blow the cobwebs from her mind. She conducted her small purchases with a lighter heart, and spent some few idle moments browsing in the haberdasher's. She supposed that with her emergence from mourning she ought to be thinking of some refurbishment to her gowns. Fresh ribbons, perhaps, for the green silk? A pink seersucker caught her eye, and she wondered if she could run to the expense of a new gown. Not that she would purchase anything without first consulting Susan. No one was more knowledgeable about fashion than her friend.

She had worn her habit for driving, and recalled how Susan had deprecated her choice of mustard, though Timothia herself still thought it suited her. Nevertheless, she turned out of the shop, deciding that Susan was bound to advise her against wearing pink with her hair and complexion. Truth to tell, she was not in a mood to purchase frivolities.

Glancing at her list, she discovered that she had forgotten one of the horse ointments, and moved to cross the road towards the saddler's. In her abstraction of mind, she almost collided with a gentleman in a caped driving-coat, and stepped back only to discover that it was Leo.

'Timma!' he exclaimed, recognising her.

Shock held Timothia silent. It also shot her pulse rate up, so that her chest became overwhelmed with the thudding of her heartbeat. She wanted to run away! But that would be stupid and cowardly. What in the world could she say to him? She did not know that her green eyes signalled the frantic unrest within her, her mind taken up with the hideous embarrassment of this meeting—and the gaunt shadows that seemed to have settled in her cousin's features.

Leo, no less disturbed by her sudden presence, experienced a resurgence of the morbid regret with which he had been scourging himself as he recognised the inner turmoil to which Timma was undoubtedly subject. He said the first thing that entered his head.

'You have been making some purchases?'

He could have cursed himself for his inanity. But Timothia was relieved by the innocuous subject, and grasped it thankfully.

'A few necessities,' she managed, half thrusting forward her basket as if to show him the packages therein, and then pulling it back again. 'What about you?'

'I am here on a matter of business.'

'Ah.' Timothia nodded vaguely.

Silence fell again between them. The sensation of embarrassment mounted.

It was too absurd, Leo thought. Anyone would suppose them to be strangers. He tried to gather his scattered wits. But before he could think of anything further to say Timothia forestalled him.

'I thought you were gone to Peterborough.' Why had she said that? Now he would ask why.

But the question did not occur to Leo. 'I was not in a mood for it.' His complexion darkened. What the deuce had possessed him to say such a thing? She would take it for criticism. Now she would poker up again, if he knew Timma. He ought to have given her some kind of opening.

Sure enough, Timothia drew herself in a little, looking away. 'I only mentioned it because Susan told me that Valentine was gone to a shooting party thereabouts.'

'Yes, I know. I declined the invitation.' Warily, now, he warned himself. Tread warily. 'I am—I am rather busy at present.'

Timothia breathed a little more easily. 'You have the advantage of me, then.'

It was on the tip of Leo's tongue to respond that she need not have been idle had she accepted his offer, but he curbed the words. He was trying to think of something else to say that might not hark back to the division between them, when they were both hailed by a fluting voice.

'My dear Timothia!' it sang out. 'And Mr Wetheral. How very fortunate to see you both!'

Timothia jumped, and turned. The lady who had accosted them was one she knew only too well. A female of considerably greater age than her girlish aspect warranted. Not only was she dressed in the height of fashion, but her high-waisted gown of flowered muslin was of a style more suited to a débutante. Over it she wore only a light shawl pelisse, which did little to conceal the upper flesh of a wilting bosom. A straw hat covered over with knotted ribbon completed this toilette, together with an open parasol to shade her from the non-existent sun.

'How do you do, Lady Hurst?' Leo was saying politely, and Timothia caught the warning look he threw at her.

He must be no less aware than she of the danger in which they stood. For this was the same loathsome female who he had sarcastically suggested might bring her out. Of all people Timothia might have chosen to run into in this terrible state of consciousness, Lady Hurst was the last. She could not be more unwelcome. She had a nose like a bloodhound! If there was the slightest hint to be noticed of this appalling breach between herself and Leo, Susan's obnoxious aunt was bound to sniff it out.

Timothia knew not how to dissemble in her present state of discomfort, but she did her best. Smiling, she put out a hand. 'I trust I see you well, ma'am?'

'Very well indeed, my dear Timothia,' uttered the lady, taking her hand, and casting sharp glances from one to the other. 'A fortunate chance that I should run into you both.'

'Is it?' asked Leo, throwing a frowning question at Timma that clearly asked what the woman would be at.

Timothia raised her brows. 'Fortunate, ma'am?'

The lady simpered. 'Why, surely? I would hope I might be the first to offer my—' She stopped, artistically throwing up a hand to her mouth, as though she had said something out of the way. 'Don't say I am beforehand?' She gave a silly giggle that did not sit well upon her years. 'How foolish of me! Do forgive me, my dears. I am too eager. But at my age one positively longs for any little whiff of romance!'

It was the last thing Timothia had expected. Her consciousness was acute. So far from discovering the breach, it seemed that Lady Hurst was bent on receiving confirmation about their betrothal. Heavens, what could be said? She threw an anguished glance at Leo, and saw that he was stiff—with anger or resentment. Or both?

'You are mistaken, Lady Hurst,' he said icily. 'I cannot imagine where you came by such a notion.'

Quick to follow this lead, Timothia drew herself up with haughty disdain. 'It is too absurd, ma'am. As if there could be the slightest question—I mean, we are too much *friends*.'

To her consternation, Lady Hurst did not look in the least discomposed. Instead, her eyes widened, and a knowing smile curved her mouth. 'Oh, have you quarrelled?'

'No such thing!' snapped Leo.

'Of course not!' uttered Timothia strongly at exactly the same moment.

'Dear me,' said the lady, and simpered again. 'A lovers' tiff already? Now that is romantic! I had better leave you to have it out, had I not?'

With which, she let out a shrill laugh and went on her way. In growing horror, Timothia watched her go. What in the world were they to do? Now the news would be all about the countryside! She turned back to Leo, and found him tight-lipped, disgust all over his face.

'I suggest,' he said stiffly, 'that this requires some private discussion. Shall we meet at the old monastery?'

'Yes,' said Timothia hastily. 'Oh, yes! This is appalling! In ten minutes?'

'Let us say fifteen. I left my phaeton outside the chandler's, and it is all of five minutes' walk.'

Without further words, Timothia hurried away towards

the spot where she had left Bickley with the gig, quite
forgetting the missing purchase from the saddler's. She
drove rapidly to the ruin of the disused monastery, which
was a little outside the town, and pulled up just as Leo's
phaeton came into sight, at a rattling pace. He must have
made the short journey in considerably less than the seven
minutes it had taken Timothia.

'Just what are you about, Miss Timma, may I ask?'
demanded Bickley, with the freedom of long service. 'Secret meetings, is it?'

'Don't be stupid, Bickley,' she said as calmly as she
could. 'It is merely that I have business with Mr Wetheral.'

'Don't tell me, Miss Timma! Me as have known you
from the cradle, too. No one don't doubt as you're going
to marry Mr Leo one day, but what should take you to
meet him in this havey-cavey fashion I'm sure I don't
know.'

Incensed, Timothia would have speedily undeceived
him of his ludicrous delusion, had not Leo driven up. Any
such speech was now out of the question, so Timothia
contented herself with a threatening glare, which was received with a comprehensive snort of derision.

Fortunately, Leo was too preoccupied to notice. And in
any event would have paid no heed, Timothia reflected,
since he was used to the manner in which Bickley addressed her. Indeed, he had frequently commented upon
the freedom which she allowed to both groom and butler,
to which Timothia invariably responded that Bickley and
Padstow were more like uncles to her than servants. She
was far too beholden to both to treat them with anything
other than the easiest familiarity.

Leo was in fact so concerned about the outcome of their
encounter with Lady Hurst that he cared not a fig for

anything else. He swung himself down from the phaeton, and grasped Timothia's arm without ceremony, forgetting the terms upon which they now were.

'Come on!'

'Let me go!' she said in a low tone, wrenching her arm away.

'Hurry, then!' he snapped, and walked swiftly down the cracked path and through the monastery entrance into the overgrown cloisters.

Little remained of this part of the building but some standing pillars and a broken parallel wall that had once enclosed the paved walkway along which the monks had prayed. Leo took a few steps down one side, and then paused, waiting for Timothia to catch up.

'Why you should insist upon driving like a maniac, I can't think!' she said as she came up.

'Never mind my driving!' he said curtly, stripping off his gloves. 'We have more important matters to discuss.'

'If anyone had seen you, they must immediately suppose that something is amiss.'

'Let them think it,' he rejoined carelessly. 'It will be no less than the truth.'

'Yes, but the whole point of this meeting is to think how we are to keep people from talking,' she objected.

Leo uttered a short bark of laughter. 'Some hope! If that woman has it, we are quite undone.'

'Yes, thanks to Valentine's idiotic tongue!' flared Timothia.

'How do you know it was Valentine?' demanded Leo, bristling in defence of his friend. 'It may just as likely have been Susan who talked of the matter.'

'To Lady Hurst? Unlikely, I think.'

'Not to Lady Hurst,' conceded Leo briefly. 'But what of Claud? Do you tell me she would refrain from speaking of this matter to her brother? And Claud is rector at Hursting Stone.'

Timothia had not thought of it, but she was obliged to admit that Susan might well have talked it over with Claud. From Claud Hurst to the ear of his aunt and patroness was but a step. He had been a favourite with Lady Hurst since childhood, and had never recognised how unkindly she had treated his sister—who was not to blame for this! Hostilities having been resumed, Timothia had no hesitation in hitting back strongly.

'And I suppose that Valentine would not open his lips to Chloe Devenick? Perhaps he does not know that his sister is as thick as inkleweavers with Lady Hurst.'

'Of course he knows it,' returned Leo. 'Don't think I absolve Valentine, for I don't. In fact,' he added, recalling Valentine's words about his sister's remarks on the frailties of females, 'I have every reason to suspect that he may well have spoken to Chloe. I am merely pointing out that one avenue is as likely as the other.'

Timothia could not deny the truth of this. The more so because of the slight rift that had been created between herself and Susan. And if Valentine had gone off to Peterborough without Leo it was probable that there was constraint between them as well.

'How much harm has been done by this stupid proposal of yours!' she exclaimed impulsively. 'We are all at outs, and now see what has come of it!'

Leo flung away. 'You need not speak as if that is what I intended! Nothing could have been further from my thoughts than—'

He broke off, slapping frustratedly with the leather gloves in his hand at one of the remaining pillars of the cloister. Why must Timma taunt him thus? Could she not see how much he was regretting ever having ventured on this course? He had been within a hair's breadth of breaking his resolve and running to beg her forgiveness any time this past week! Only the discovery he had made rendered it impossible that they should ever pick up their erstwhile ease of friendship. He could not hope to keep company with Timma again without re-experiencing a kindling of desire. And that, given her feelings, would be unendurable.

This was getting them nowhere. He turned back to Timma, and found her watching him, a frown in her eyes. Was there also distress? Something gave in his chest. As if unable to help himself, he went to her, stretching out his free hand.

'Timma, I cannot bear this!'

Automatically she took the hand, and as the strength of his fingers clasped hers she felt their warmth even through her glove. A tattoo started up in her pulses. For a moment neither spoke, and Timothia was struck once again by the gaunt look about his cheeks.

'You look dreadful,' she uttered without thought.

'I feel it,' he answered, low-toned.

A shadow of her smile trembled on her lips. It was, to Leo, almost intolerably touching. Without thought, he lifted her gloved hand and dropped a kiss on the fingers. Then his eyes found hers again, and the smile had gone, giving place to a wary unease. To his dismay, Timma withdrew her hand from his clasp.

Timothia was all too suspicious of the gesture—which had done nothing to ease her physical discomfort. Quite the contrary. What was Leo at now? Almost unconsciously, she put both hands behind her back and clasped them together, as if she would withhold them from the possibility of his seizing her fingers again. She was not going to be beguiled into forgetting what lay between them. Their friendship was over. It was impossible that it could ever be renewed—not, at least, on the same footing. Though, for the sake of appearances, some sort of truce must be achieved.

'What are we going to do?' she asked, as neutrally as she could.

Hurt threw Leo on the defensive. 'Do you mean about the rumours, or our own situation?'

'There is no situation!' Timothia retorted.

Leo dropped back a step. He only now perceived that there might have been in his mind a half-formed intention of renewing his offer. If it had been there, Timma's attitude slew it at birth. Oddly, he felt less troubled now by Lady Hurst's impertinent hints. He hardly knew why it should be so. Set against the blighting of his hopes, it seemed a little thing.

'I dare say it will blow over in time,' he suggested dully.

'Blow over?' uttered Timothia, amazed at his apparent unconcern. 'How can you say so? Lady Hurst and Chloe between them will spread it all over the countryside. We shall have everyone watching us, looking to see how we conduct ourselves towards each other. Or, worse, asking guardedly when they may expect to hear an interesting announcement.'

Leo shrugged. 'It would have been just the same had you accepted me.'

'Not at all. We would have endured a barrage of surprise and congratulation for as long as it took the novelty of the notion to wear off.'

'Then you have only yourself to blame for refusing me,' Leo pointed out irritably.

Timothia regarded him with narrowed eyes. Her voice

was silky. 'If you wished only to quarrel, Leo, I wonder at your having requested this meeting.'

Leo stiffened. 'I have no wish to quarrel, Timma. I never have. All the unpleasantness in this matter is of your making.'

'My making!'

'Had you received me with a vestige of proper feeling, instead of flying up into the boughs, all might have been settled with no rancour on either side.'

'To your satisfaction, yes,' said Timothia acidly.

'To both our satisfactions,' he insisted.

Her temper rose, but she repressed it. 'Don't let us discuss it any further since we will clearly never agree.'

'As you wish,' he said, and made as if to leave.

'Wait, Leo!'

He hesitated, looking a question.

Timothia drew a determined breath. 'Since we must needs meet, and in public, let us at least do so with some semblance of civility.'

Leo bowed, unsmiling. 'It would ill accord with my honour to do anything else.'

Timothia could have hit him. 'That is just the sort of remark that is likely to undo us.'

'Is it indeed?'

'You know very well you only said it to provoke me!'

He bowed again. 'Be sure that in public, ma'am, I will refrain from passing any comment that you may take even remotely amiss.'

With which, he doffed his hat, and left her, pulling on his gloves as he went. He had not thought himself so apt to be provocative! He had not meant it so. He had wanted, if the truth be told, only to get away. Timma had cut him to the quick. She clearly did not know it. Did not recognise how her physical rejection had both galled and hurt him. She had been—yes, cruel! He had not thought it of her.

Indeed, he decided as he swung himself up into the phaeton and took the reins from his groom, Timma's whole attitude from start to finish of this affair had been both insulting and inexplicable. She was not the woman he had thought her. To find himself mistaken in her character after all these years must be a grief to him. He had believed that there was scarce a thought or opinion that they did not share.

He recalled abruptly what Timma had said. 'We are poles apart.' The remark had been hurtful to him. At the time, he had been unable to understand it. Now it seemed as true to him as it evidently did to Timma. He ought to be thankful, deuce take it! It was clear that they did not share enough common ground for the close partnership of marriage. To the devil with it! He was well rid of her.

From the crumbling doorway to the monastery, Timothia watched Leo drive away. At a pace that threatened to unseat both himself and his groom! Well, it would serve him out. What did she care if he took a toss?

As she moved towards the gig, the grumbling tones of her groom took her attention. 'I don't know what you said to him, Miss Timma, but he's fair rattled. Never knowed Mr Leo to spring his horses in that fashion afore. Now don't you go aping his game, Miss Timma, for all you're in as bad a temper!'

'I am not in a temper at all,' replied Timothia with dignity, accepting his help to climb into the gig. 'And if I were I should certainly not take it out on my horse.'

'No, because you'd have me to reckon with,' said Bickley frankly, handing over the reins and hopping nimbly up onto the seat beside her. 'And if Mr Leo had any sense he'd use his whip where it might do some good!'

'If that means what I think it means, Bickley,' Timothia stated warningly, 'you had best take care—unless you wish to find yourself back at Dulverton Park working for my cousin!'

Bickley grunted. 'Where I'd be a deal better off! But where would you be, Miss Timma? Tell me that.'

'I can perfectly well employ another groom,' she retorted, but without much conviction. As Bickley was well aware, it was an empty threat. She had as well rid herself of her closest family. Recalling the groom's earlier lapse, she added, 'And I'll thank you, Bickley, not to indulge this nonsensical idea of my marrying Mr Wetheral.'

'Try telling that to Padstow, that's all I say,' returned the groom, unheeding. 'Me and him have been discussing how we'd fit into your new arrangements when you wed.'

'Well, you may stop discussing it, because I am not going to be wed. The suggestion has already been put out of court, and the matter is settled.'

'Is it, now?' remarked the groom, in a tone that all too readily betrayed his disbelief. 'Ah, well, it's young yet you are, Miss Timma. And if you don't fancy Mr Leo he ain't the only gentleman hereabouts.'

Incensed, Timothia took refuge in silence. If she was not to marry Leo, it was inconceivable that she would marry anyone else! What, exchange her freedom for shackles to some other man? Some man unknown, moreover, who would no doubt expect both obedience and that she adapt her tastes to his. At least Leo would not have interfered with her pleasures. He knew her too well to try to change her. He must know her, indeed, better than anyone alive!

Her cousin, for all his present distasteful showing, had

been so much a part of her life that she could recall nothing of her childhood without the intrusive addition of his presence. In fact she could recall very little of those periods when he was necessarily absent: away at school, or visiting relatives or friends with either parent. It was invariably to those memories of happier times spent together that she returned when thinking of the past. Like that occasion when they had pored together over his books so that Timothia could help him understand mathematical principles which eluded his grasp.

She had been ten or thereabouts, Leo in his teenage years. He had cursed Isaac Newton and his *Principia*. But Timothia had sat with him for several hours, demonstrating over and over again the basic formulae until Leo finally understood. In return, Leo had taught her how to clean and load a gun. Not that she had felt she was likely to have much need of such knowledge, but since Leo had offered the exchange in a manner that suggested he was conferring upon her an honour seldom applied to females Timothia, not wishing to offend him, had accepted with the proper degree of gratitude.

There had been a similar episode with Leo's inability to spell correctly. That time, Leo's magnanimity had extended to showing her how to shoot the gun—which was more to her taste. It was ironic that this training had now come into its own. For at Fenny House her proximity to the Fenns made her vulnerable to marauding poachers. Timothia felt safer for the possession of her pistol, which she kept cleaned and loaded in her bedchamber. So she had something for which to thank Leo.

She sighed, thinking what a pity it was that there should be such a painful end to their long association. If meeting with him was only to incur a repetition of the sort of experience she had endured today, she could only dread the future. For how was she to avoid meeting him? He would not visit her again, she dared say. Yet she could hardly incarcerate herself at Fenny House. She had done so for a year already! Besides, she was heartily sick of sitting about with no vestige of occupation worth the doing.

The problem loomed larger still when she arrived home. For, if the rumour of her possible betrothal to Leo had not yet penetrated far afield, the news of her emergence from mourning had certainly gone the rounds. It was some few weeks since the local gentry had returned to their country residences for the summer months, and it was plain that the indefatigable hostesses, revived from the natural exhaustion incurred by the London season, were once again itching for pleasure. A number of invitations awaited her from various matrons of her acquaintance in the neighbourhood—and they were all of them as thick as thieves with Lady Hurst.

Timothia's heart sank. Heavens, but it was not yet over!

Leo had driven all the way home in an unforgiving black cloud. But no sooner had he got within his own doors than he was hit by a tide of despair. What had he done? Timma had been right. They were all at outs! Even now he felt a furious resentment against Valentine. The clodpole had thrown him to the wolves! For would it not be he who came worst out of this? If Lady Hurst was to be trusted, it was Leo Wetheral who must look as foolish as bedamned. For he was the rejected suitor. Did he dare doubt that this aspect of the matter had been released? No, he dared not.

A curse upon Valentine's loose tongue! How often had he and Timma had occasion to deprecate this failing on the part of their mutual friend. No, friends—for Susan had been as foolish as Valentine. What of that time he had felt obliged to save Timma from a thrashing? It had been Valentine and Susan who had blurted out—upon enquiry, to be sure, but could they not have held their tongues?—that it was Timma who had instigated the childish prank that had resulted in them setting fire to a woodman's cottage.

Lord, they had almost caused a forest conflagration! It had undoubtedly been Timma's idea to play at cavemen. But Leo and Valentine, older—but regrettably at fourteen no wiser, he reflected ruefully—had joined in. None of them had supposed that rubbing two sticks together would truly start a fire. Leo had been more shocked than anyone when the sticks began to smoke, and the dry grass had caught rapid fire from flying sparks.

His uncle Dulverton had been justly furious when the four of them had been brought before him by the forest keeper. But when he had ordered Timma to her room to await his coming, and her face had turned hideously white, instinct had caused Leo to intervene. He remembered moving quickly to Timma and seizing her hand, holding it so tightly that she winced. He had never afterwards been able to recall what he had said, but he had somehow persuaded his uncle that he and Valentine, as the eldest, ought to take the blame. Timma's sentence had been commuted to confinement to her chamber on meagre rations, and Leo had returned home to the inevitable painful interview with his own father—in this very library.

The memory of his punishment had long faded, among the shadows of many others. He and Valentine had ever been far too keen sportsmen to resist staying out of trouble.

Hardly aware of his own movement, lost in thought, Leo rose from the desk and crossed to the window embrasure, looking out upon the rolling lawns that fronted the mansion. The hills beyond were misted, but his eyes sought automatically for the place where ran the well-worn path between that hilly surround which led him by a short cut to the road to Dulverton Park. How often he had ridden it! He had done so—not without some discomfort!—that next day, only because he'd wanted to be sure of Timma's safety.

He had entered the grounds by stealth, climbing secretly up to Timma's window by her own ivy-clad escape route. She had hailed him with joy, and some misgiving about what he must have suffered in her stead. He had assured her—untruthfully!—that his sufferings had been as nothing to her own. Timma, the minx, had agreed with him!

Leo found himself laughing at the memory. He could hear her complaints in his mind.

'I am as hungry as a hunter! I have had nothing but gruel and water this morning, and last night Papa sent me only dry bread,' she had related indignantly, adding that she had not dared risk a foray in search of food for fear of the certain evil consequences of capture.

To her delighted gratitude, Leo had produced the contraband with which he'd had the forethought to stuff his pockets: apples, sweetmeats and a hunk of cheese. He had been rewarded with a hug from Timma's skinny arms, and they had spent an agreeable half-hour—while Timma munched greedily, and with Leo suspended precariously upon the thin branch that served for her illegal entries—in abusing the wagging tongues of their mutual friends.

That had been the worst, but not the only time that one or other of those two had landed them in difficulties. They had been an adventurous foursome, young Susan tagging along after Valentine. Though it was often enough that

Leo and Timma, yearning for freedom from the encumbrance of the other two, had secretly set off alone. His childhood memories seemed more full of Timma than of Valentine!

Yet now the intimacy they had shared, and which he had thought to deepen, was at an end. He had nothing to do but to reconcile himself to a future without her. What was the difficulty? They were no longer children. What difference did it make to him now? After all, if she had opted for being brought out, she would no doubt have married someone else. She ought to have done so! His uncle should have insisted upon it. It was extremely foolish not to have secured her future. It would then never have occurred to Leo to marry her himself!

Leo continued in this unsettled frame of mind for a couple of days. An unacknowledged reluctance to face his acquaintance had caused him to withhold himself from any callers, like a hermit. But a visit from Valentine, when he returned from Peterborough on Friday, encouraged him to suppose that talk was not as widespread as he had feared. His friend had nothing to relate bar the lack of good sport that had attended his forays.

'Nothing but a wood pigeon or two. I tell you, some of us took to potting rabbits!'

When the merits of what gun to use for rabbits had been thoroughly thrashed out, Valentine took his leave without once referring to the rift. Either he was being uncommonly tactful, or he had forgotten all about it. Which was the more likely, Leo thought cynically. In either case, it emboldened him to believe that no serious harm had come from Lady Hurst's discovery, and he decided it was safe to present himself at a dinner party at Somersham on the following evening.

There was nothing in the demeanour of his hostess to

dissipate this confidence, and he entered without qualms the sea of blue brocade and gilt that constituted Mrs Baguley's drawing-room. There were some fifteen couples assembling, showing the disparity of elegance inevitable at a country do between the attire of the fashionable London set and the more dowdy die-hard stay-at-homes. Leo belonged, he felt, neither to the one nor the other. He preferred a degree of comfort and sobriety in the quiet discretion of a tabby coat with matching breeches in his favourite blue, and a lighter waistcoat of silk. But the cut and quality of his garments proclaimed, he knew, the hand of the London tailor who had made them.

The chatter and laughter was intense. Leo was hailed almost immediately by his near neighbour, Brown of Wood Hurst, who drew him into conversation with Hammond and Pidley, both neighbours to this house. Mr Pidley, being a member of the House of Commons, had been seized upon for some matter of complaint among the local landowners concerning drainage.

'It won't do, you know, Wetheral,' Brown was saying. 'The government ought to do something. Trying to persuade Pidley here to take up our cause.'

Leo groaned inwardly. This was bound to be something about which he knew little, if anything. He loathed this style of conversation, for it meant he must bend his brain to matters which bored him into a stupor. Furthermore, it was unlikely that he would be able to make head or tail of anything that was said! He was rescued by the voice of Dudley Dulverton.

'No use trying to interest Wetheral, my dear Brown. Not in his line—drainage. What you ought to do is talk to his cousin.' He laughed in his self-conscious way. 'What am I saying? She's my cousin too, of course. I mean Miss Dulverton, you know.'

Timma's paternal cousin was a man of early middle age, with a jovial manner that sat uneasily, Leo felt, on his always somewhat harassed features. His wife, who hung upon his arm, had an even more fretful look about her, which might be attributed to the difficulties of bringing up her numerous offspring. Was she again increasing? wondered Leo, with a suspicious eye on the slight bulge below the high-waisted gown of figured muslin.

'Oh, yes,' Ella Dulverton agreed, blinking rapidly. 'Dear Timma must know everything about drainage. I am sure she would be delighted to help you, for she very much enjoys wrestling with that sort of thing.'

'By Jove, yes!' sang out Mr Brown. 'Miss Dulverton is the very person!'

'Oh, good God!' exclaimed Pidley, alarmed. 'You are not going to set Timothia Dulverton on to me? I warn you, I shall instantly take my leave!'

'You have nothing to fear, my dear Pidley,' said Hammond, with a jovial slap on the other man's back. 'The Dulverton chit is still in mourning.'

'No, she ain't,' contradicted Brown, grinning. 'She's here.'

Timma was here? The devil! Leo had not bargained for that. He supposed he should have thought of it. Devil take it, what was he to do? Avoid her? To his dismay, he heard Brown pursuing the subject—to his undoing.

'Tell you what, Pidley,' he was saying on a note of laughter. 'Hide behind Wetheral. By all accounts, she won't come near you.'

These words had the effect of rendering both Mr and Mrs Dulverton tongue-tied and red with embarrassment. Leo discovered a battery of eyes upon him in the little circle. It took all his resolution to laugh it off.

'Brown is teasing you, Pidley. I can afford you no protection. My cousin and I have ever been the best of friends.'

With which, he turned away and sought for Valentine among the throng. Behind him, he heard a murmur start up, succeeding the silence that had greeted his words, and knew that Lady Hurst had been busy. How the deuce was he expected to get through this evening? A short colloquy in the corridor, whither he dragged his best friend, did little to cheer him.

'But you said nothing about this yesterday.'

'Didn't want to upset you, old fellow,' protested Valentine. 'I can keep my tongue between my teeth, you know.'

'If that were only true!' remarked Leo bitterly. 'Only tell me this: did you mention the business to Chloe?'

'Of course not. Talked it over with Sue. Mean to say, she was as upset as I was. I'll tell you one thing. We were at one in blaming Timma for her treatment of you.'

This disclosure had the odd effect of fanning Leo's anger. 'You had no right to blame Timma! It was I who began the business, not she.'

Valentine stared at him. 'Changed your tune a trifle, old fellow, haven't you?'

'Nothing of the sort.'

'Thought you were hot against her yourself.'

'Yes, but it was never my wish that she should be pilloried in the public eye. Whatever I may feel, she has a right to any choice she makes.' He eyed his friend with some suspicion. 'I hope you have not spoken to anyone else on this head.'

'What do you take me for?' demanded his friend indignantly. 'Mean to say, I may have told Chloe the bare bones, but I wouldn't discuss it with her!'

Leo gazed at him in dumb resignation. What was the

use? It was as hopeless to try to make Valentine see sense as it was for himself to battle with the intricacies of drainage!

'What are you looking at me like that for?' asked Valentine, frowning. Then his eyes popped. 'Dash it, I did talk to Chloe!' Consternation showed in his face. 'Beg your pardon, old fellow. Quite inadvertent. Never meant to do so. Wretched female must have gabbed to half the county!'

'And Lady Hurst to the other half,' said Leo dully.

Valentine cursed. 'Should have thought of that. Chloe is thick with that old hag.'

'So also is Claud Hurst. I don't think you are wholly responsible, Valentine.'

This altered his friend's attitude instantly. 'Now don't you go putting this on poor little Sue! If she said anything, it was only because she was in out-and-out despair. Never cared for anybody but Timma, that girl. Worships her, you ought to know that. Sue would rather be nibbled to death by ducks than do Timma a mite of harm!'

Leo was moved to stare blankly at his friend once more. Was he completely blind? Well, it was not for him to open the fellow's eyes. Susan would not thank him for it. And Timma—

But, after all, he preferred not to think what Timma might say. He wondered, as he returned to the drawing-room with Valentine, whether it would be possible to avoid a meeting. Was it even advisable? Perhaps he ought to seek Timma out for the sole purpose of showing the world that they were mistaken. Only he could no longer be sure what exactly was being said. On the whole, he thought it better that they stayed aloof. Meetings between them were so problematic that they would be bound to give themselves away, so providing further food for gossip. He resolved to keep out of her way.

He succeeded quite admirably in this for the next half-hour or so. Then the guests were called in to dinner, and he was requested to take in his neighbour's lady, Mrs Brown, on his arm. He escorted her to her chair, and then moved to find his own place where one of the footmen led him, only to discover, to his intense discomfiture, that he was seated next to Timma.

## Chapter Five

With a sense of outrage, Timothia watched Leo sit down in the place directly to her right. Had she not had enough to bear this night? With a table large enough to accommodate thirty persons, how in the world had she the ill luck to draw him for her neighbour? Glancing down to the bottom of the table to where Mrs Baguley was just seating herself, she caught that lady's eye, and knew that it must have been deliberate.

Indignation rose up. Was she to be made a mockery of? Enough of her female acquaintance had twitted her slyly for her to be fully alive to the damage done by Lady Hurst. She had thought to face it out by coming tonight, but she was fast regretting the decision. She dared swear that there was not a person in the room who was uninformed about the dissension between herself and her cousin—and the occasion of it. Irrationally, she felt her fury veer back to Leo. It was all his fault!

Upon the thought, she felt his glance, and deliberately turned her shoulder, seeking the companion of her other side. She found Mr Brown of Wood Hurst on her left.

'Miss Dulverton, by all that's fortunate! The very person with whom I was wishful to have a word.'

'How do you do, Mr Brown?' she responded, smiling mechanically.

'So you've emerged from seclusion at last. Not before time, I can tell you.'

'You are very kind, sir, but what was it you wanted to talk to me about?'

'Drainage,' announced the single-minded Mr Brown. 'My dear girl, you will not believe the disgraceful…'

Timothia heard his complaint with only half an ear. She was in fact fully conversant with the situation which was stirring him up, despite having been out of the world for a year. Her old agent Crimdon had told her all about it, when visiting on the excuse of discussing her needs at Fenny House. Furthermore, she had received occasional visits from those few members of the local gentry who did not disport themselves in London for the best part of the year.

At any other time, Timothia would have entered with enthusiasm upon a discussion of the disgraces attending drainage. Tonight, with her thoughts so taken up by the intricacies of her own vexed situation, it held almost no attraction for her. Indeed, she was hard put to it to keep her attention sufficiently on what Mr Brown was saying to maintain her part in the conversation.

For this, Leo's conduct was undoubtedly to blame, for he devoted himself for a considerable time to the female on his other side. This happened to be the daughter of another neighbouring family of his, who had—if Timothia's straining ears did not deceive her—just come out this very season. A quick glance served to confirm that it was indeed little Jenny Preseley, the doctor's daughter. Timothia was astonished. She had not thought Dr Preseley to have had the means to send his daughter to London for her début. She had grown up very pretty, it would seem, with a quantity of red-gold curls threaded through with silver ribbon.

Red-gold? *Red?* A stirring of something very uncomfortable entered Timothia's breast. Jenny Preseley had ever had a mop of red hair. Red hair and freckles. She remembered it now. The girl could be little more than seventeen! Was she still freckled? Timothia moved to pick up her wine glass, contriving at the same moment to cast another surreptitious glance at the girl. As she did so, she most unfortunately caught Leo's eye.

A slight flush mounted to her cheeks, and she quickly turned her attention back to Mr Brown, assuming as interested an expression as she could contrive. He was still immersed in earnest exposition of his drainage complaint, and Timothia tried to listen.

'I thought,' murmured Leo's voice close to her ear, 'that we were to be civil to one another in public.'

Timothia stiffened. Affecting to have difficulty in slicing at the meat on her plate, she leant a little towards the table, whispering under cover of the general conversation.

'I doubt it matters any longer. Content yourself with being civil to the infant Jenny!'

She then wished that she had held her tongue, for Leo closed in again on the pretext of reaching for the salt.

'Do I understand you to be jealous, Timma?'

Timothia drew in her breath rather sharply. Without intent, she turned her head and met his eyes fully, her own blazing. 'Don't be stupid!'

The blue of Leo's orbs hardened. 'Take care! You are drawing attention to yourself.'

It was a timely reminder. For a split second, it seemed to Timothia that the whole table was silent, listening. Then the hubbub of voices returned, and she let her breath go. Glancing about, she noted that there were indeed several pairs of eyes trained upon her, in particular from the opposite side of the table, where others besides Susan and Valentine—placed separately, but still within sight of each other and their mutual friends—were interested spectators. Mr Brown had stopped talking, and Jenny Preseley was eyeing her with a mixture of awe and deference. With deliberation, Timothia smiled at her, and received a shy acknowledgement.

Then, without another word to Leo, she turned back to Mr Brown. 'You were saying, sir?'

He resumed his discourse, and Timothia tried desperately to listen to him in an effort to blot out the thoughts in her head. Jealous indeed! Not that the girl was not as pretty as a picture. It would not in the least surprise her if Leo should succumb. Men were such easy prey to innocence and virtue. He was ten years her senior, but what of that? She looked to be malleable, and if she could not administer his estates for him at least she would not set herself up in opposition to his will. Leo might be as autocratic as he chose, and Jenny would never say him nay. She wished him joy of the wench! They might not share a thought in common, but that was a small matter—if Leo should happen to fall in love with her.

The meal began to seem interminable. Try as she would, Timothia could not but overhear snatches of the conversation taking place to her right. There was a good deal of laughter from her cousin, accompanied by shy-voiced protestations from his companion. It would appear that Leo was very well entertained by little Jenny Preseley!

To Timothia's relief, Mrs Baguley at length gave the sign for the ladies to rise and leave the gentlemen to their port. Timothia no sooner found herself in the drawing-room than she sought out Susan, whom she found seated upon a gilt-edged Chippendale sofa of white-painted wood upholstered in blue flowered brocade. A setting that enhanced rather than detracted from her friend's appearance in a charmingly simple gown of lemon-coloured French lawn, with a lace trim.

'Tell me at once how it comes about that Jenny Preseley is here?' Timothia demanded without preamble as she took a place beside her friend.

'Did you not know?' came Susan's breathy response. 'Mrs Baguley took her up. Jenny has been staying with her in London since February.'

'So that is how it was.' Then Timothia realised from her friend's give-away pansy eyes that she was trying to hide something. 'What is it? Susan, tell me!'

Susan grimaced a little. 'My aunt Hurst says that Mrs Baguley placed Jenny in that position at the table on purpose.'

Timothia felt her breath catch. 'I suppose I need not be a genius to guess the reason.'

Her friend nodded gloomily. 'She thinks Leo may take to her, if all is over between you.' She clasped Timothia's hand and lowered her voice. 'Dearest, you must not be angry, but it seems that all the world has been forever inclined to predict a match between you and Leo. I thought it had only been myself who dreamed of it. But, no. My aunt told Claud that everyone believed it a settled thing, especially when you failed to take up anyone's offer to come out.'

'Did they indeed? No doubt that accounts for their present interest.'

'Yes, because of course no one ever dreamed that you would quarrel.'

'But how charming of Mrs Baguley to ensure Leo's

future by placing myself and Jenny on either side of him—as if he need only choose between us!'

Susan squeezed the hand she held. 'I am so sorry, dearest. I know just how you must be feeling, for I had been led to imagine that Mrs Baguley intended Jenny for Valentine.'

Timothia was conscious of a rush of sympathy for her friend. 'I suppose your hateful aunt Hurst said so?'

Susan nodded numbly, and Timothia followed her glance across the room to where Jenny Preseley, in a white muslin gown, was standing near an open French window that let onto a small balcony. The days were yet long and it was still light, but the candles had been lit and the haze of evening cast a glow over the young girl, setting off the red in her hair. She was petite, with a neat figure, and it did not seem to Timothia that the faint speckling of brown across her milky complexion did anything but enhance her looks.

'She is very pretty,' Susan said, on a forlorn note.

'Very pretty, and very young,' agreed Timothia.

'Only just seventeen, I think.'

'Ten years younger than either Valentine or Leo. I cannot answer for them, but in all honesty, Susan, do you not think that she is more likely to fall for a younger man?'

Susan turned large and doubtful eyes upon her. 'But who? Claud is spoken for, you know. And Adam is away soldiering against the French.'

'Susan, there are other young gentlemen in the world besides your brother and my young cousin.'

Susan shook her head. 'Very few others in this circle. And Valentine is a great catch. I am sure she is to his taste.'

Timothia refrained from pointing out that Jenny

Preseley was far more likely to prove to Leo's taste—if Valentine's testimony was to be trusted. A little redhead, with a neat figure. But if Leo was coxcomb enough to suppose her to be jealous she would speedily undeceive him!

'Well,' she said instead, 'if a flirtation with Jenny takes the gossips' attention away from me, either of them are welcome to it.' She met head-on the reproach in Susan's brown eyes. 'You need not look at me like that. I have no doubt at all that you had a hand in spreading the word.'

The spaniel eyes changed instantly. 'I didn't. Oh, Timma, I didn't. I only told Claud, and—'

'That I had already deduced. I suppose it did not occur to you to remember that Claud is very much in with your aunt.'

Susan gaped at her. 'Oh! I never thought. Oh, Timma, I am so sorry.'

Timothia relented. 'Never mind it. I dare say everyone would have seen it for themselves in any event, if it is true that they supposed Leo and I were intended for one another.'

The gentlemen entered the room soon after this passage. Despising herself, Timothia watched for Leo, waiting to see whether he would seek out Jenny Preseley. In the event she did not see him enter, for Valentine came up.

'Timma, I have to beg your pardon. Now, you must not blame Sue!'

'But, Valentine, I—' began Susan.

'No, Sue,' he interrupted. 'I will not allow you to be at fault. I talked to Chloe, and from there to Lady Hurst was inevitable.'

'But I know for a fact, Valentine,' insisted Susan, 'that Claud spoke to our aunt on the subject. It is just as much my fault, I assure you.'

Timothia intervened before Valentine could argue the point. 'I wish you will both be quiet! What does it matter whose fault it was? If it makes you both happy, by all means share the blame between you. But, for pity's sake, have done!'

A short silence greeted this outburst. Timothia looked from one shocked countenance to the other, and sighed. She rose from her chair.

'Forgive me. I am a trifle overwrought. I think I will go home.'

Valentine made to speak, but Timothia saw Susan quickly shake her head. She was thankful that her friend understood her so well. With a brief word of farewell, she left them, and threaded her way through the animated guests to find her hostess. She had just caught sight of Mrs Baguley settling at a table where the tea-tray had been deposited, when she felt her arm taken in a firm grip.

'One word, Timma.'

Timothia's pulse quickened. She looked round at Leo's frowning features. 'What is it?'

'Not here.'

Resistless, she allowed him to draw her out of the crowd gathering about the tea-table, and in a moment she found herself standing with Leo on the very balcony before which Jenny had been talking earlier. Looking back into the room, Timothia saw that most people were turned the other way.

'If anyone sees us here, it will only add fuel to the flames,' she said, and was dismayed to find that her voice was shaking.

Leo had detected it. His frown deepened, and he wanted very much to take her hand. But such an approach had met with so hurtful a rebuff that he could not do it. The evening had upset him. He had been angry with her, yes, for her conduct at the dinner table. And had taken his revenge by devoting himself to the little Preseley chit. But with the departure of the ladies it was Timma who had filled his thoughts.

He had never in the past given a thought to her appearance, but tonight he had been struck almost immediately by the alluring way in which the low-bosomed green silk gown set off her figure. That it was otherwise plain, and a trifle out of fashion—the waistline being marginally lower set than he observed to be current with those newly returned from the metropolis—served only to deepen his dissatisfaction, for he guessed she could not afford to replenish her wardrobe this year. As his wife, she might have decked herself out as fashionably as she chose!

He could hardly blame her for behaving as she had done at dinner. The situation in which they found themselves tonight was enough to make any woman defensive.

'I have to beg your pardon, Timma,' he said quietly. 'The circumstances are impossible.'

Timothia sighed, and a little of her discomfort left her. She looked at him. 'Are we to expect this sort of thing every time we set foot outside our doors? How long do you think we will be obliged to endure it?'

He shrugged. 'Until, I must suppose, we end it one way or another.'

A frisson shook her unexpectedly. She was barely aware of her own lowered tone. 'I thought we had ended it.'

It seemed to her that Leo moved a little closer. Or it might have been a trick of the light that was beginning to fail. His voice was a breeze, murmuring on the air.

'Have we?'

His eye caught hers, and the look that she encountered sent a spread of warmth scuttling through her veins. She knew not how to interpret his expression, only that it disturbed her. She felt as if her very soul was being searched by the light in the depths of his eyes.

Confused, Timothia broke contact, pulling away. She grasped the iron railing with one hand, and with the other sought to quiet the perturbation below her breast.

'Are you in pain?'

She looked back at him, shook her head briefly. 'N-nothing of that sort. I—I must go home.'

Leo's hand covered hers on the railing. Timothia's glance flew from his face to the hand and back again. She gripped the rail harder, to prevent the tremble that began in her fingers.

'May I escort you?' he said.

Panic took her, though she could not have said why. Snatching her hand from under his, she took a hasty step backwards. 'No!'

His features tightened. 'Very well.'

'It—it would look too particular,' she said quickly, driven by some unnamed quality she detected in his tone. 'We have been talked about enough.'

But Leo was no longer looking at her. His frowning gaze was sweeping the room, as if he sought for someone. Then he turned back to her, and a new note was in his voice.

'The devil! I had not realised until now. Where is your dragon? Do you tell me you have come alone? What in the world do you mean by coming out without a chaperon?'

Timothia stiffened, the confusing symptoms thrust aside in a surge of wrath. 'You have not won the right to question my actions, Leo!'

'I need no other right than being your cousin,' he retorted.

'Let me tell you that I recognise no such right,' she threw at him. 'And if you imagine that Edith will be dragged to such affairs as these you very much mistake the matter.'

'A pretty sort of companion!'

'She suits me very well, I thank you. Furthermore,' she added with venom, 'in answer to your earlier query, Leo Wetheral—yes, by heaven, we have ended it!'

Turning her back on him, she moved into the room and thrust as quickly as she could through the persons blocking her passage, ignoring the popping eyes and questioning glances that came her way. Her hostess greeted her with dropped jaw.

'Timothia! What is amiss?'

'Nothing, ma'am, nothing at all,' Timothia responded with barely repressed irritation. 'I must go, for it is getting late and the light is failing.'

'But will you not—?'

Timothia cut her short. 'I must thank you for a most enjoyable evening. Goodnight!'

She passed through the door without looking back, and fairly ran down the stairs. At a word from her, a footman was despatched to summon Bickley with the gig, while with unsteady hands Timothia took her cloak from the butler and gathered it about herself, hugging into its folds as if she meant to hide away within that comforting disguise.

Leaving the house, she climbed into the gig. The hood was up, and Timothia sank back into its merciful shadows and bit hard on her lip against a threatening storm that was whipping up inside her.

'Now what's got into you, Miss Timma?' asked the groom in his avuncular way.

'Drive, Bickley!' she uttered harshly. 'Take me away from here. At once!'

The horse bounded forward, setting off down the drive at a lick. At the turn into the road, Bickley slowed the carriage a little, and kept a steady pace through Somersham.

'I'll pick him up again when we're through the town, Miss Timma.'

'Do as you will, but pray don't talk to me!'

'I've a better regard for me skin nor that, Miss Timma! Mum as a corpse.'

A faint smile curved Timothia's lips in the darkness. But it was a momentary respite. She felt wrung out—as if she had run a gamut of emotion this night. She was left bewildered. How was it that her responses to Leo had become so unpredictable, so explosive? It was as if, whenever he came within her vicinity, she no longer had control. Some dark force took over, tossing her this way and that.

Yet her relations with Leo had always been so *comfortable*. They had sparred, yes. But never had she struck at him with so poisonous a tongue! She could not imagine what had thrown her into this uncharacteristic distemper. Oh, that wretched offer! What, was she determined to punish him over and over again? But for what? What had he done, in all honesty?

At once the unknown force took flight. What had he done? He had cut up her peace! He had destroyed their friendship and made a laughing-stock of them both in the eyes of the world. Worse yet, he had made her stupid! She was ashamed of her own conduct, of her own thoughts, and that she had never been. How could she be so silly over poor little Jenny Preseley?

She sighed. The night was fine, and stars dotted the

heavens. A romantic evening—if one had leisure or inclination for such things! They were not for her.

The thought brought a tightness to her chest, and she was relieved to see that they were approaching Fenton. Yet the thought of Fenny House and its poky little rooms was stifling. She wanted air.

'Don't stop at the house, Bickley,' she said, making a sudden decision. 'Drive to the Fenns.'

The groom did not hide his astonishment. 'The Fenns, Miss Timma? At this time of night?'

'Yes, the Fenns. I want to go there.'

'It's mad you are, Miss Timma, and no mistake,' observed Bickley in a grumbling tone. 'Why should you be wishful to go down there? Horrible, smelly place. And it's only a track. We don't want to go losing a wheel in the ruts.'

'We have the lantern, Bickley,' argued Timma. 'Besides, it has not been raining these many days, so I dare say the road will not be so very bad.'

'And I dare say we'll be lucky to come out of it without no broken bones! You must have been in the sun, I should think, Miss Timma.'

But Timothia was adamant. 'Well, if you don't like to go, Bickley, I shall set you down and drive myself.'

'That you won't, Miss Timma!' stated the groom, outraged. 'I know me dooty. I'll go if you needs must, but like it I won't, and that's me last word!'

Timothia had to laugh. 'I'll believe that when I see it.'

But despite his qualms and grumbles Bickley drove on past the entrance to Fenny House and on through the village, turning off the road onto a narrow farm track that was indeed full of ruts and bumps. The gig took it slowly, and Bickley was obliged to shift from side to side to avoid the potholes which increased the further down the track they went.

At length the visible marks made by the wheels of carts gave out, and Bickley pulled up. 'Seems to be the end of the track, Miss Timma.'

'It does not matter,' Timothia said, preparing to alight. 'We must be less than a hundred yards from the edge of the Fenns.'

'Wait a minute, Miss Timma!' said Bickley suddenly. 'Do you hear that? Sounds like someone else had the same idea!'

Timothia paused, listening to sounds from behind. Another set of hoofbeats! More than one horse? And carriage wheels! The sounds must earlier have been covered by the inordinate noise of their own progress. 'Heavens, who in the world could that be at this hour?'

'Belike another lunatic!' said the groom sourly. 'Now, don't you go jumping down until we know it's safe, Miss Timma.'

He was too late. Timothia was already climbing to the ground just as the vehicle behind them was pulling up. Moving behind the gig, Timothia ignored the agitated protests of her groom, for a pool of light was thrown by lanterns on either side of a coach. A pair of horses were shifting, and blowing steam into the cool night air.

The coach door opened as Timothia moved into the light, and her cousin Leo jumped down. Surprise held her momentarily silent. He took a glance round, found her face, and came quickly forward, his long greatcoat swishing about his ankles.

'What in the world are you doing here?' she demanded as he reached her.

'The exact question I was going to ask you!' he returned. 'I followed you to be sure you got home safely,

and have been wondering for the last ten minutes whether
you have taken leave of your senses.'

'Is it you indeed, Mr Leo?' came the voice of Bickley
from somewhere in Timothia's rear. 'Thank the Lord! Do
you talk some sense into her, sir, for I can't!'

Timothia swung round. 'Hold the horse, Bickley, and
your tongue, too!'

'That's just what I ain't going to do, Miss Timma. I'm
hoping as how Mr Leo will prevail upon you to return
home.'

'Well, he will not!' declared Timothia, and without further words walked off in the direction of the Fenns.

'The devil!' uttered Leo.

He moved back to his coach where the groom had already jumped down, and barked an order. 'Unhook one
of the lanterns!'

What the deuce was the idiotic wench up to? he asked
himself for at least the twentieth time as he waited impatiently for the lantern to be detached from the side of
his coach. In a moment, armed with the light, he was
easily able to catch up with his cousin, whose progress in
the near pitch-darkness had been necessarily slow.

Making no attempt to stop her, Leo took his place
alongside her, holding up the lantern. 'What do you think
you are doing, Timma?'

Timothia halted. 'Leo, you have two choices. Either
you may stop spoiling sport and go away—'

'Save your breath!'

'—or, if you insist on accompanying me—'

'Which I do. Who knows whether you may meet a
poacher or some other felon? You know how dangerous
are these parts.'

'—pray…'

'Walk!'

'Yes, walk,' she insisted.

'At close on midnight? And in such a place as this?'

'What is wrong with it?'

'Everything,' he said crushingly. 'In the first place—'

Uttering a bare grunt of defiance, Timothia turned from him and started off again, moving purposefully. Breaking off his complaints, Leo perforce accompanied her, keeping the lantern poised so as to light the way as far ahead as possible.

'I was thinking the other day,' he said conversationally after a moment or two, 'of that thrashing I took for you once. Now I see that I was mistaken. A salutary whipping or two might have served to instil some common sense into you.'

Timothia refused to allow herself to be goaded into retort. Ignoring him as best she could, she marched doggedly on until a faint glimmering on the dark outline of the landscape ahead began to permeate the darkness. Yes, there it was! Impulsively, she stopped, seizing Leo's arm.

'There! Do you see it?'

'What, the will-o'-the-wisp?' he asked prosaically. 'It is given off by the marshy gases.'

A slight sensation of disappointment clouded Timothia's mind as she moved on. He ought to have remembered. Of course she knew the cause of the apparent phosphorescence that seemed to flit across the top of the still uncultivated parts of the Fenns. But once Leo had spoken of it very differently. There had been romance in his soul. Or so she had then thought.

They were getting closer to the edge of the old marsh, and the wispy lights became more distinct, dancing above the ground. Almost as if he read her thoughts, Leo put the lantern behind him as they stopped, shading its light so that the green flickers brightened.

For a short time, they watched together in silence. Then he saw Timothia's head turn towards him, her face a silhouette.

'You have a short memory, Leo.'

There was a wistful quality in her voice. Almost without intent, Leo brought the lantern up so that he could read her features. Timma did not move, but her eyes seemed to glitter in the glow. Her warm skin gleamed, and Leo experienced the oddest sensation of melting within himself.

'What is it you mean?' he asked softly.

Her lilting smile curved her lips. 'Don't you remember? Papa took me to look at the Fenns one night, to show me the will- o'-the-wisp. I was seven. The next time I saw you—next day, or later; I don't remember precisely—I told you all about it. You said they were fairies. I dare say you said it only to tease me, but I believed you. I have never forgotten it. Will-o'-the-wisps have been fairies to me ever since.'

'Oh, Timma!' A light laugh escaped him as warmth radiated through his chest. 'I never thought to discover in you a hopeless romantic. It had certainly escaped my memory. I dare say you are right, and I did say it to tease you.'

She was looking again at the flickers that glowed and died as they seemed to shift position. Leo's gaze remained upon the outline of her hair, its shade almost silver in the lantern's light. She had gathered the heavy folds of it into a looped braid perched at the back of her neck, adorned with a filigree comb. Leo was seized with an insane desire to snatch away the confining ribbons that held in place the mass of hair, that he might watch it tumble down, and feel it ripple through his fingers. He had not seen Timma's hair loose since—oh, since she'd crossed the boundary into womanhood at seventeen!

Something of his heated thoughts penetrated Timothia's consciousness. She looked back as if impelled, meeting his eyes in the gloom. The strangest sensation beset her, as of an altered reality wherein the spoken word had no relation with the apparent thought behind it. What she said she knew not. What Leo answered was as alien in its portent.

'There are some corners of my childhood that remain untouched.'

'Your love of fairy stories? I was used to think it odd in a girl like you. I had thought you must have grown out of them.'

'I grew out of the stories, but I have never shaken off your idea about will-o'-the-wisp.'

Her smile was magic, transporting him into the past. For a few instants in time, she was the Timma of his remembrance, the bond between them untrammelled and free. His fingers came up, lightly caressed her cheek.

'And are they fairies still?'

'They look no different to me. If ever you have children, Leo, you must tell your daughters just the same.'

The words echoed in Timothia's head. She saw in Leo's eyes the exact instant when they registered with him. The sense of unreality vanished. Her spirits plummeted, and she drew away just as the line of Leo's jaw stiffened.

Constraint returned. All that lay between them seemed to rise up in an invisible wall, the harsh words that had been bandied to and fro crashing in like shot from a cannon, scattering the friendly ease that had returned so briefly. On a sudden, the cold of night made itself felt, seeming to penetrate to Timothia's very bones. What in the world was she doing here? She became conscious of squelching mud at her feet, which were encased in slippers wholly inadequate for such a terrain. What had possessed her?

Brusquely, Leo hefted the lantern and turned his back upon the phosphorescent gleam. 'It is time we were going. I shall follow to see you safe home.'

Timothia swept about, and started back towards the carriages, hugging her cloak about her as if to conceal the inward shivers that seemed to rack her. Not one word further was exchanged. Leo parted from her in silence, and she climbed in solitary dignity into the gig as he vanished into the interior of his coach. Bickley had turned the gig about to face towards Fenton again, as had her cousin's coachman, who waved them to go ahead.

Timothia did not even notice the rattling of her own conveyance, for the only sound that penetrated to her ears was the double clip-clopping of the horses behind mingled with the heavier rattle of coach-wheels. Long after it had died into the distance, Timothia fancied she heard it still, bearing her cousin away.

Faithful was skittish. His chestnut mane tossed with the jerking upward motion of his head as he threatened to rear. Timothia tightened the rein, murmuring soothing words, and then slackened it once more as the stallion quietened again. But he fidgeted still, sidling and flicking his ears.

'What in the world is the matter with you?' demanded his mistress impatiently. 'Is it a gallop you want?'

If the horse could speak, she might swear that he would have greeted the suggestion with acclaim. A ripple of muscle answered her, and a whiffling movement of the proud mouth.

'Very well, then.'

She could not be more willing to oblige him! They had trotted a good three miles over rough country, cantering only now and then when the lie of the land permitted. Timothia's blue devils were so insupportable that she had vowed to throw them off—or die in the attempt! Accordingly, she had set off for her morning ride in a fresh direction from the norm, travelling south. Crossing through the corner of Crow's Nest Wood, she had skirted Wood Hurst and ridden on towards the Sparv, wishing that she might lose herself in the hills.

Anything were better than to continue in this intolerable state of depression! She had experienced nothing like it since the early period of her mourning, when the ceremonials were over and she'd had time to take in the full aftermath of Papa's death. Loneliness dug like a spur into her heart.

It was not even as if she had lacked company in the hazy distance of these many days. Susan had been to visit her, and she had herself dined cosily at the Rectory at Old Hurst. Susan's reverend father had spoken kindly of the old days, and she had enjoyed a brief little chat with Mrs Hurst, who seemed to feel that Timothia might have power to persuade her daughter to forget Valentine and look elsewhere. Had that been all of a week ago? She'd had other visitors since, but they blurred as readily as had time. Oh, yes. Mr Brown had called to enlist her further support for his demands upon Pidley's influence with the government about the matter of drainage. Timothia had found that drainage, at one time a fruitful topic of conversation, for once failed to interest her. Then she had attended a soirée at Hursting Stone—with some reluctance. And she thought the small gathering at the house of Chloe Devenick had been only two days ago. At neither of these establishments had her cousin Leo put in an appearance, although she was assured by both hostesses—who seemed to make a point of telling her!—that he had been invited.

Not that she would have wished to see him. Quite the contrary. But there was an inevitable let-down when one had braced oneself to face a person in public, with determination that no-body—least of all the individual concerned!—should perceive anything amiss, only to find that the effort had not after all been required. It put an unnecessary strain upon one's social veneer. And took up far too much attention which could better have been used for something more worthwhile.

Despite all these entertainments, Timothia had been unable to halt a creeping sense of isolation. It had seemed to permeate her very soul, bringing her spirits so low as to become utterly oppressive. Now here they were in July, and she was as dismal as ever. She had so lost count of time that she could not even remember what day of the week it was! She could no longer continue in this way. Something had to be done.

Discounting such attractive remedies as throwing herself off the top of Valentine's castle towers, or blowing her own brains out with the pistol that Leo had most thoughtfully taught her how to shoot, Timothia had opted instead to ride as hard as she could to the devil. Literally. Only she was by far too careful a guardian of her cattle to allow her own inclination to run her horse into danger.

She had held Faithful in while she picked her way through unknown country. But once she spied the hills of the Sparv ahead she knew she must take advantage of the last of the open country if she was to shake off her own fidgets—which she knew she had communicated to the stallion.

She took a precautionary moment to adjust herself in

the saddle, slid her foot more firmly into the stirrup, and then gave Faithful his head. He flew, racing across the meadows, ears laid back, limbs pumping muscle as his full strength soared into play. Timothia kept her seat with relative ease, for she was an accomplished horsewoman, and the exhilarating sensation of speed blew freshness into the dark corners of her mind.

The hills loomed larger as the ground flashed by, and as of instinct Timothia headed her mount into the growing gap ahead appearing now between two vast mounds that had seemed as one, only dipping at the centre. She did not slacken Faithful's pace, but only guided him a little to the familiar route.

Familiar? But she had not ridden here before. Her eyes searched the outlines of the hilly range ahead. They struck her as alien at first, then all at once everything fell into place. She knew this country! That view was as etched in her mind as it must be in Leo's. Heavens, what had she done? In her desire to avoid Wood Hurst she had strayed unseeingly across country—and now she was come within full sight of Wiggin. This was Leo's land! That very gap in front of her was the route he had taught her as a short cut that led from his estate to her own at Dulverton. They had ridden it both severally and together innumerable times.

What had she done? What deep-seated thrust of memory had drawn her here? Fool! Unthinking simpleton!

Under her, the rhythm broke. Inattentive, she had lost her union with the horse. In an instant, she realised that her rein was too slack, and tried to draw it in. Too late! The stallion veered sharply. Timothia was unprepared. Her foot slipped from the stirrup, and she was flying free.

Landing hard, Timothia was aware of a juddering crash, and then a momentary blackness. It was over in seconds, and she opened her eyes to a whirling sky—and violent pain at the extremity of one leg.

# Chapter Six

For several moments, the agony of injury was everything. But presently Timothia's senses triumphed a little and she dragged herself up, leaning on one elbow. Dazed, she wondered what had happened. She had taken a fall, but her clouded mind could not recollect the occasion of it. That it was bad she knew, for she had let go of the rein. Had her horse bolted?

Peering about as best she could for the inconvenience of her position, she saw with relief that Faithful was grazing some distance away. Thankful for his phlegmatic temperament, she gathered herself together, for she must get up. If she could only get Faithful to come to her, she might catch the rein and so pull herself to her feet. How she would mount again, she could not imagine, for she had undoubtedly hurt herself rather badly. But she would deal with that problem as it arose.

Taking a breath, she called to the horse, but her voice was too weak to carry. She would have to sit up! She pulled in her left knee for extra support, making ready. But as soon as she made a motion to shift the right leg a dizzying sensation of pain flared up instantly.

Timothia closed her eyes, biting her lip on a groan. As

the pain dulled a little, she peered at the leg, trying to see what damage had been done. In a moment, the ache became localised at her ankle. Heaven send she had only sprained it!

Dragging at the mustard petticoats of her habit, she freed the ankle, but could see nothing for the leather boot that covered it. A feeling of helplessness began to invade her. What was she to do? Perhaps she should just lie here, succumbing to lassitude. Someone was bound to come by sooner or later.

Setting her teeth, she berated herself severely. What kind of a stupid female was she? To have come off her mount was bad enough. But she was made of sterner stuff than this, was she not? If she could only get a trifle of help, she was sure she could get up. Only when she put her weight on the leg would she be able to judge the severity of the problem.

But to her consternation, as she tried to glance about for some means of succour, she was overcome by wave after wave of dizziness. She could barely see. A problem that worsened as despairing tears forced their way through her tight-shut eyelids. Then, as her eyes opened again, she saw through blurred vision two running figures coming in her direction.

Relief swept over her, and she gave in momentarily to the weakness threatening to consume her, sobbing thankfully as she sank back onto the ground.

Moments later, two men were upon her. Rough-clad working men in homespun smocks over corduroy breeches, one of middle years, the other a thick-set youth, leaning over her with sweaty faces contorted in concern.

'Miss? Are you hurt, missy?'

'Don't be daft, boy!' said the elder. 'If she weren't, she'd 'a got herself up by now.' To Timothia he touched his forelock. 'We were working our land, ma'am, and saw you fall. Is it bad?'

'It is my ankle, I think.' Timothia pulled up onto her elbow again and reached out a hand. 'Help me, pray!'

Wiping his own hand first on his breeches, the man gingerly assisted her to a sitting posture. Then his jaw dropped. 'Why, it's Miss Timma, ain't it?'

She peered frowningly at him. It was a round-featured countenance, burned brown from working out of doors, and vaguely familiar. 'You know me?'

He nodded. 'It's Clent, ma'am. I'm one of Mr Leo's tenants.' He pointed. 'We have the farm up yonder.' Nodding at the younger man, he added, 'This here's my son, ma'am. Bit of a noddy, but he's right at heart.'

Timothia was in no fit state to respond appropriately to this disclosure. 'Can you help me up?'

'Was you meaning to ride again, missy?' asked the younger Clent. 'Shall I fetch the horse?'

He received a clout round the head from his father. 'Nodcock! How d'ye think the missy is going to ride in that state?'

The young man did not appear to resent the blow. 'Well, shall I fetch the horse?' he repeated.

'No, no, for you will never catch him,' Timothia said, distressed to find her voice a trifle faint. 'He—he would not come to you, and if you chase him he will only run off. He won't stray. He may even follow me wherever I go.'

'Ah, you've put your finger on the nub, ma'am,' put in Clent doubtfully. 'For where you're to go has me in a fair puzzle.'

Timothia was as much puzzled. It was becoming difficult to maintain concentration, for she was beginning to feel sick and rather faint. 'I think—I think I had better...'

Her voice faded, and she put a hand to her head, aware in some corner of her mind of the increased concern in the features of her would-be rescuers.

'Seems to me as I'd best send Ned here for Mr Leo,' observed Clent in anxious tones.

That did penetrate. Send for Leo? Oh, no! She could not have Leo find her in this condition—and here on his lands!

'No, no…pray do not bother Mr Wetheral. I think—' Breaking off, she asked hesitantly, 'What—what day is it?'

Both the farmer and his son gazed at her, the younger in blank amazement, the elder in growing concern.

'Lor', miss!' exclaimed the lad. 'Don't you know?'

'You must've taken a knock on the head, ma'am,' opined the other.

'No, no, I am sure I have not.'

'Thursday,' stated the younger Clent matter-of-factly.

'Is it?'

He nodded, repeating it slowly. 'Thursday, miss.'

More than ever did Timothia desire that Leo should not find her here. He would think her a very simpleton! 'Pray, could we not—might you not between you help me get to your farm?'

'The farm! I'd not take that risk, ma'am,' said the farmer firmly. 'You might have taken a concussion. And especially seeing it's you, Miss Timma, I'd be afeard of Mr Leo's wrath.' With which, he turned to his son and grabbed him by the shoulder. 'Now you listen to me, boy! Go directly to the farm, unhitch the cob from the plough, and ride as fast as the devil to Wiggin Hall.'

Timothia heard it with consternation, but was curiously relieved at the younger Clent's eager response.

'I can do that. And am I to tell Mr Leo as how the missy is here?'

'Nodcock! You'll tell Mr Crieff, as is the butler. Say as Miss Timma fell off the horse and is hurt, and we're in a puzzle how to bring her off safe. Understand?'

'Fell off the horse and is hurt,' repeated the boy obediently. 'I can do that. I'll be as quick as winking.'

With which, he sped off across the turf in a manner likely to prove his boast. Timothia watched him go, beset by gratitude not unmixed with apprehension. If only Leo was at home! Yet if he was, and he found her here…

Her distressed mind failed to grapple with the problem, and the pain at her ankle was increasing so that she was willing to compound for anything so long as someone brought relief. With a sigh, she sank back on the ground and closed her eyes.

She must have lost consciousness for a while because the next thing she was aware of was a cool sensation at her brow, her hands being chafed, and a woman's voice, scolding.

'To think I've a simpleton for a son, and a husband with not much better wit! Why didn't you think to remove this boot first thing? Now it'll have to be cut, for this ankle is swollen up proper.'

'Oh, no,' moaned Timothia faintly, taking in the sense of this.

Another round face came into view above her. That of a female, and adorned with a large mob-cap, an apron visible over an ample bosom. Evidently this was the farmer's wife.

'So you're awake again, ma'am. Now just you lie still until Mr Leo gets here.'

'What if he ain't home?' demanded her spouse.

'Then we'll just have to fetch Miss Timma to the farm.

I dare say as our good neighbour and his lads will fashion a hurdle for her at need.' A podgy hand wiped Timothia's face with something comfortingly wet. 'This'll keep you cool, ma'am. It's a hot day for a mishap like this.'

But Timothia had been seized by the notion of being taken to the farm. If she could get there, someone might go for Edith to come and rescue her. But when she tried to put this to Clent's wife that efficient dame would have none of it.

'We ain't doing nothing, ma'am, not until Mr Leo gets here, or until we hear from my boy as he ain't been able to find Mr Leo at home.'

'If he ain't gone tearing off in the wrong direction,' said his fond father gloomily.

'You keep your tongue, Clent! Now don't you fret, ma'am. I can't deny as my Ned ain't got a deal of wit, but he won't let you down, never fear.' As if to justify her confidence, there came a distant sound of hoofbeats. 'Ah, now, there he comes.' But a moment later, 'Oh, no, it ain't! It's Mr Leo—and riding fit to bust hisself!'

Timothia was moved to struggle up. She could hear it herself now. From between the two hills that had so startled her wayward memory came a horseman, thundering across the ground. Recognising Leo's black, Timothia felt a rush of warmth at her heart, and a swell of fresh tears made the vision dance in her sight. That Leo should come for her—and hell for leather too!

'Let's hope as he don't come off, and all!' uttered the pessimistic Clent, and received a cuff from his wife for his pains, who adjured him once more to hold his tongue.

In very short order, the horse was thudding to a stop, and before Timothia knew what had happened Leo had flung himself off his mount, thrust the reins into the hands of Clent, and was kneeling beside her with one supporting arm about her back.

'What has happened to you? My God, my God, Timma, what have you done?'

Grasping feebly at his lapel, Timothia could only choke out a confused explanation, looking up into Leo's blessedly familiar features. 'So stupid! A—a moment of—of inattention. My ankle, Leo! I don't know why I came here—it was a mistake—I am all too conscious of it. You must not pay any heed! Pray don't put yourself out—'

He cut her off curtly. 'That will do! If you can only talk nonsense, it will be better for you not to talk at all.'

Timothia let out a weak laugh. 'I might have kn-known you would not be in the l-least sympathetic.'

Leo grinned down at her. 'So you might.'

She felt him hug her closer, and sank into the welcome strength of his embrace, dissolving into tears. His voice softened.

'Come, don't cry!' he said gently. 'We must get you to Wiggin, and—'

Timothia raised her head. 'Not Wiggin! I cannot possibly go to your house.'

'You can't possibly stay here,' he countered. 'Now, stop making nonsensical objections and leave this to me.' He drew back a little, glancing down at her leg. 'How to get you there, though, without causing you a great deal of pain?'

Timothia was too overwrought to think, but the question was in fact rhetorical. For Leo, thrusting down on the surging anxiety in his breast, entered into debate with the Clents as to the most practical solution. A coach was out of the question for there was no fit track for it and the jolting must put Timma through unnecessary agony. By the time a hurdle had been fashioned and brought, he

could have carried her back to Wiggin. No, the only thing
for it was to take her up before him on his horse.

The scheme was not to be accomplished without difficulty. Just as Leo was working out how to manage it,
young Clent most fortunately came riding up on the
farmer's cob.

'Ah, excellent!' said Leo. 'A stout arm immediately to
hand. Ned may lift Miss Dulverton up to me. I will mount
first. Do you, Clent, go to the other side of Barbarian here,
to be ready in case of difficulty.'

Mrs Clent was detailed to hold the horse's rein, and
Leo turned back to Timma. 'I am going to stand you up,
Timma. Don't try to help. Only put your arm about my
neck.'

By this time, it was as much as Timothia could do to
obey, although a number of expostulations passed through
her brain. How could Leo hold her? And how were they
both to fit into his saddle? Then she felt herself lifted,
Leo's strong arms under her shoulders.

'Don't put your foot to the ground!' he warned.

Timothia was panting with effort, even so small an effort as holding her knee bent. For on rising the blood
drained speedily from her head and she sagged against
Leo.

'Faint…' she murmured.

His arms cradled her to his chest. 'Hold up! I forbid
you to faint! At least, not yet.'

This bracing treatment had the effect of encouraging
Timothia to pull herself out of the dizzy spell. She stead-
ied herself on her sound leg, and pushed away a little,
grabbing Leo's upper arms for support.

'Well done! Gently, now. Ned, take hold of her!'

But the young Clent, for all his brawn, turned brick-
red, hesitating. 'Hold the missy, sir?'

'Come on, man!' urged Leo. 'Hold her round the waist so that you may lift her up to me.'

'Ned Clent,' said his mother shrilly, 'just you do like Mr Leo says, or I'll fetch you such a basting as you'll be sorry for!'

Thus adjured, the youth seized his charge with alacrity, and as Timothia felt his large hands clasp strongly at her waist she could not forbear the ghost of a smile. She could not doubt but that the rotund little form of the farmer's wife would carry out the threat, comical though the image might be.

But next moment all desire to laugh had dissipated. The exquisite torture that followed left her breathless. For she saw Leo mount up, and then lean down to her.

'Reach up to me, Timma, and clasp your hands behind my neck. Hold tight, now!'

Complying as best she could, Timothia then felt herself lifted from two directions, and her injured foot caught inevitably at the horse's flank. She cried out, and heard Leo curse. When next she was able to take anything in, she found herself seated across Leo's saddle-bow, his arms encircling her. He caught at the reins.

'That's it. She will do now. All right, Timma?'

Her ankle ached unbearably, and she could not help but grasp at Leo's coat, sinking her head onto his shoulder. But she uttered as strongly as she could, 'I will do, thank you.'

She heard Leo express words of thanks to the Clents, and she recalled how much in their debt she was. She tried to add her voice to Leo's.

'My thanks, too—you have done so much!'

She could not be sure that she had been heard, for the horse was already moving. She tried to look back, anxious that her rescuers should not think her ungrateful, but Leo intervened.

'There will be time enough to express your thanks, when you have recovered. Try to relax, Timma. I will walk Barbarian. It will take longer, but I think you will find it more comfortable. And I can hold you the more easily, for I daren't attempt to settle your knee about the pommel—the jolting would be a deal worse.'

Timothia was only too relieved to leave such decisions in his capable hands. She nodded wearily, for even this slow progress, in the position she had been made to adopt, caused her foot to rock with every motion of the horse's back, sharpening with each jar the agony at her ankle. It was fortunate that Barbarian was such a big stallion. She could not think that Faithful would so readily have carried the weight of two. Faithful!

'My horse,' she uttered fretfully, bringing her head up. 'Leo, I had forgot him. Did you see him? He had not bolted—was grazing somewhere near.'

'What, did you not notice?' Leo said, on a note of surprise. 'No, I suppose you would not in the condition you are in. He came over to investigate while we were mounting you. He is following at a little distance.'

'You will see him safe?' she asked anxiously. 'You know he does not like—he will not go to anyone he does not know.'

'Tarbert can manage him. Don't let it trouble you.' He shifted his arm to give her more support. 'This is agony for you, is it not? I am sorry, Timma. It will be over soon.'

Timothia shook her head, biting her lip on the tell-tale gasps that she guessed must have given her away. 'It makes no matter,' she managed, speaking in short bursts. 'I am only glad—to be no longer lying out—in that field.

Besides, it is…quite my own fault. I cannot think how… how I came to be so stupid.'

'It happens to us all,' Leo reminded her reassuringly. 'Thank the lord you chose to come off on my lands!'

This comment served only to recall to Timothia's hazy mind the foolish realisation that had caused her to lose concentration. She fell silent, conscious of a degree of embarrassment swelling the sum of her discomforts. It was a question whether the intermittent waves of faint-ness, accompanied by a growing nausea, were a worse affliction than the spasms at her ankle. The one must nec-essarily be aggravating the other, she supposed. By de-grees, she sank into a half-dreaming, half-waking state, where thoughts no longer followed one another in logical sequence, and the only effort she was aware of making was to keep herself from crying aloud. This was a simple refusal to give Leo added concern about her well-being, because there was nothing he could do to ease her.

But Leo was all too aware of that frustration. If he could have flown Timma back to his house in a minute, he would have done it. He had all to do as it was to keep her secure, and hold his restive mount at a walk. He knew each time the uneven ground caused a jolt at Timma's injury, for he could feel her so close against him that he could not miss her indrawn breaths against the pain, try as she might to conceal them. Would he might have spared her!

Yet he must thank providence that he had been still idling near the stables when young Clent came hurtling into the yard on his father's cob. Another few minutes, and he might have already been away with Valentine. That did not bear thinking of! Timma thrown, and he not by to come to her aid? He would never have forgiven himself. It had taken some few precious moments to get the boy's story from him, overcome as he was with the importance of his message.

'Pa said as I was to tell it to Mr Crieff, Mr Leo, sir,' he had stated doggedly, apparently unable to grasp that telling it to Leo himself was of even more urgent necessity.

But as he had begun the news with a mention of Timma's name Leo had been in no case to wait for common sense to penetrate his slow wits.

'Never mind Crieff! Tell me at once what has occurred, Ned!' he had ordered tersely, holding the cob's bridle fast. 'Where is Miss Timma?'

'Fell off the horse and is hurt, Mr Leo, sir,' the sturdy youth had answered, repeating the litany he had rehearsed.

Leo had felt as if someone had punched him in the ribs. He had known his own voice came out hoarsely from lack of air.

'Where?' He had repeated it impatiently as the young Clent had stared at him stupidly, obviously thrown by his reaction. '*Where*, boy? Is she at the farm?'

Ned had shaken his head dumbly, wide-eyed. 'Not at the farm, Mr Leo, sir.'

'Where, then? Speak, man!'

The youth had pointed at the hills. 'Over yonder, in the fields as is lying fallow these five year.'

Leo had thrown a hasty order to his groom to saddle Barbarian instantly, and then turned back to Ned. 'How badly is she hurt? Do you know, Ned?'

He had nodded. 'I know that, Mr Leo, sir. Hurt bad, she is. Couldn't get up, nor Pa wouldn't get her up. She couldn't ride, Mr Leo, sir. Nor she didn't know it were Thursday!'

'Where the devil is that horse, Tarbert?' Leo had yelled,

driven by still deeper anxiety. Then he'd said sharply to the boy, 'But she is conscious? She is talking?'

Ned had nodded again. Then his eyes had lit. 'I remember, Mr Leo, sir! The missy said as how it were her ankle.'

A measure of relief had entered Leo's soul. But, knowing Ned for a simple fellow, he had been unable to satisfy himself that the boy's report had been accurate. Leaving a brief message for Valentine, he had leaped into the saddle and ridden like the wind. Every second's delay had driven his anxiety deeper, for he had been unable to forbear imagining a series of horridly unpleasant consequences that Timma might have suffered in taking a toss. To find her relatively little harmed had given him immeasurable relief, bad as the injury was.

He wished now that he had thought to send someone for Dr Preseley at once. Still, it was no use thinking of that. He would have to cut Timma's boot off himself. Mrs Clent had explained that her husband had been too flustered to think of removing it. A pity, because now it would cause Timma an agony to be rid of the thing— besides ruining a perfectly good pair of boots. But that was a small thing. First and most important was to get Timma to his house.

It came into sight a few moments later, and he at once brought this to Timma's attention, encouraging her.

'See there, Timma! We are almost home.'

With an effort, Timothia brought her head up, forcing her hazy vision to focus. Home? The combined effects of pain and nausea made it difficult to see. In a dim corner of consciousness she half expected to find herself looking at Dulverton Park. For a moment or two the sight of the great secluded mansion nestling in the lee of the surrounding hills seemed an alien thing. Its grey square shape, squatting among the belts of trees around it where it lay below her eye-line, was nothing like home. Then the image adjusted in her mind's eye, and she recalled that it had once been home—to her mother. Upon her marriage, Mama had come from here to Dulverton. And over the years Timothia had grown almost as familiar with the place—as familiar as Leo had become with the Park. Was it coincidence that she should return here thus, where Leo had offered her a home?

'I will head for the front,' he said, interrupting her train of thought. 'It will be easier to bring you through the main doors.'

In a moment Timothia did not care, only as long as she could be released from this hideous journey. The inconsequent thoughts were swept away, for their progress to the house was necessarily downhill, and the increased jolting shot spasms of agonising pain up her leg. She wished desperately for an end, and longed to be in a horizontal position that she might sink into the stupor that threatened every second to overcome her.

She saw little of the approach to Wiggin Hall, bar the occasional flash of the sun on one of the sixteen windows set between a dozen fluted pillars. Leo had taken a course across the rolling lawns, ignoring the drive that wound around them, and Timothia recognised with relief the approach of journey's end as Barbarian's hooves scrunched on the gravel of the drive, and a battery of shouts and running footsteps smote her ears.

'He is here, sir!'

'With Miss Timma and all.'

'That's her Faithful, that is, coming behind.'

'Crieff, send someone instantly for Dr Preseley!' called out Leo's voice over her head. 'Is Mrs Salcombe at hand? Ah, there she is. I will need you, ma'am. Tarbert, look to Miss Dulverton's horse!'

'I have him, sir.'

It seemed to Timothia, in the glimmers permeating through her half-shut eyes, that a veritable crowd accompanied Barbarian's progress to the front steps.

'Good Lord, Leo, have you really Timma there?' cried a voice Timothia recognised as the horse at long last came to a halt. 'What in thunder has gone amiss?'

Leo hailed it with relief. 'Valentine, is that you? Thank the Lord! Take her from me, would you? But mind you keep her foot off the ground.'

'Here, fellow, hold the horse!' ordered Valentine, grabbing a nearby servant.

'Timma, we are arrived,' Leo said gently. 'Come, your agonies are almost over. Valentine is waiting to catch you.'

Timothia thrust her lids fully open, saw the anxious eyes in Valentine's pretty features, and gasped out only, 'It is my ankle,' then all but fell as she was lowered from the horse, into his waiting arms.

She could hear Leo's voice issuing orders right and left, and knew that she was being carried immediately behind him.

'The downstairs parlour, Valentine. I must first get that boot off. Crieff, get me a knife. Make sure it is good and sharp! Mrs Salcombe, do you run ahead and prepare. And someone fetch me brandy. At once!'

Footsteps clattered ahead as Leo led the way up the short stone stairway to the high portico, and through the open double doors into the airy hall. A medley of voices penetrated Timothia's consciousness.

'This way, Valentine.'

'Take care, sir! The doorjambs!'

'I have her safe, don't worry.'

'Lay her down, sir. The head here, sir, where I have piled the cushions.'

'No, no, the other way, Mrs Salcombe. It is the right ankle that is injured and I cannot get at it from that side. Give me those cushions!'

Profuse apologies followed from the housekeeper, and a flurry of movement at the sofa, presumably to change the arrangements to suit Leo's purpose.

'There, Valentine, all is ready.'

'Here we go, Timma. Gently, now.'

Timothia felt a softness at her back, and her head came blessedly to rest upon a bank of cushions.

'Not her legs! Wait a moment. We must support the ankle… There, that will do it.'

Her legs were laid down, and as the injured foot came to rest its protest drew a groan from her lips.

'Have you the cognac there? Give me the glass!'

Timothia felt her head raised. Something cool was put to her lips, and Leo's voice came from near at hand.

'Timma, drink this!'

Timothia forced her eyes open again. Leo's features, looking stern and determined, met her dazed vision. 'What—what is it?'

'Brandy. Open your mouth, and drink. It will help you bear the pain when I remove your boot.'

She tried to shake her head, a protest more against the promised additional pain than a refusal to drink. But Leo was insistent, and she did as she was bid, feeling the fiery liquid burn down her throat. She spluttered a little, but felt the better for the warming sensation that swept through her chest.

'Take this, Valentine.'

Timothia found Leo's face again, and Valentine somewhere behind, hovering with a glass in his hand. Both were exhibiting anxiety, but Leo met her eyes and smiled. He drew her hand to his lips and kissed it.

'You'll do now, dear one.'

Timothia's heart contracted, and tears stung her eyelids. But Leo was turning away to speak to Valentine, and he did not see. He stood up, and Timothia closed her eyes again, fighting for control. There was a murmur of voices, and she thought she heard mention of the doctor.

'Should not you wait for him, if he has been sent for?'

'Who knows whether he will be immediately available? It has waited long enough. I am sure Preseley will say I should go ahead.'

Preseley? Oh, but what of his daughter? Little red-headed Jenny, who must be disappointed in her hopes now that Timothia had been brought home to Wiggin Hall. Home? What was she thinking? This was Leo's home, not hers. But what had he said? *Dear one.* His voice cut into her inchoate thoughts.

'Timma, I'm afraid this is going to hurt.'

It was an understatement. There was a cutting sound, and such a resurgence of pain that Timothia only now realised that it had before dulled a trifle. Like a scorching fire, it endured for several seconds, until Timothia came within an ace of begging for a halt. Then her foot was moved, and a wave of violent agony hit her. Her head swam, she was aware of a scream somewhere in her mind, and then she knew no more.

A pulsing throb penetrated into Timothia's unquiet dreams, and she shuddered into wakefulness. The throb continued, and at length she identified its source. Her ankle! Oh, yes, she remembered now. She had fallen from Faithful's back. Leo had brought her to Wiggin. She was on the sofa in the parlour downstairs.

Her lashes flickered on surroundings she did not recognise. What was this? A tester above her head? Daylight streaming from the windows, two of which were open to the sun-filled air. Between them, a chest of drawers, and a large armoire across the room. She was in a bedchamber! Lifting the sheet in sudden question, she discovered that she had been stripped of her habit and every garment under it, barring only her shift.

Timothia started up, and saw that her bared foot and ankle were protruding from the blankets, resting upon a pillow. To her fascination, despite the continuous throbbing ache, she discovered the huge puffy goitre that protruded from her ankle.

'It is twice the normal size!' she uttered in a dazed voice, noting that quite half her foot had grown.

'I'm afraid that was my fault,' came Leo's voice.

She started, looking frantically about. He was standing by a small table on her other side. He grinned at her shocked expression.

'You need not look like that. All the proprieties have been observed. Mrs Salcombe is here. Look!'

Timothia followed his pointing finger, and discovered that the elderly housekeeper was seated in a chair on the other side, just out of the periphery of her immediate vision.

'What a turn you gave us, Miss Timma,' said the woman, clasping pudgy hands against her tubby waist over the bombazine gown. 'Thank goodness Mr Leo was able to fetch you back safe!'

She was well known to Timothia, who knew her to be well disposed towards her, as were most of Leo's staff. Her kinship, as well as her special friendship with the scion of the house, had ensured a warm welcome when-

ever she came to visit. Which, in the past, had been of-
tener than she could count.

'You are very good, Mrs Salcombe,' she said with a
smile, sinking back onto the pillows. 'I trust that it was
you who put me to bed?'

'Gracious me, ma'am, I should think it was! You was
still in the swoon you fell into when Mr Leo took off the
boot—which I can't say that I was sorry for.'

'Nor I,' put in Leo ruefully, perching on the other side
of the bed. 'It was the very devil to get the thing off. I
had to hack it about quite dreadfully, and I am very sure
that the injury has become even more inflamed because
of it.'

He sounded distressed, and without even thinking what
she was doing Timothia put out her hand to him. His
fingers closed about her own, and warmth enveloped her.

'You have done altogether too much for me, Leo, and
I am very grateful. Thank you.'

'Nonsense!' he said curtly, and withdrew his hand. Did
she suppose he could have done less? He saw that her
eyes had clouded, and was instantly conscious of regret.
He should not have spoken like that. She must still be in
a state of shock, poor Timma, though she sounded a good
deal more coherent.

It had been Valentine who had pointed out to him that
she had fainted away. He had been glad of it, for she had
screamed with the pain, and he had known how much he
must have hurt her. Whatever else might be at fault,
Timma was the pluckiest female of his acquaintance—
proven in the way she had borne the ride home with
scarce a murmur. Had she not lost consciousness, he
would have found it hard indeed to continue.

But, the boot once off, both he and Valentine had
agreed that he had done the right thing, for the ankle had

swelled visibly before their eyes. Leo had hastily lifted his cousin in his arms and borne her upstairs to this bed-chamber, detailing Mrs Salcombe to undress her as quickly as possible while she was still unconscious, so that she would not suffer any further discomfort. Valentine had gone off hastily on the next errand which they had agreed between them would be the best solution to Timma's present situation, and he had himself waited outside the door until the housekeeper and a maid had completed their task.

He had been watching Timma from the bedside, torn by mixed sensations. Distress at the pale cast of her features, the flaxen locks spread about the pillows. And another feeling, less welcome, and even more disturbing. To his relief, she had woken a few moments later, pulling him out of it. He had not had time to think of the implications of her present situation on the current disturbed relations between them, but that she should thank him in the manner of a guest had brought them forcibly to his mind. She had withdrawn her gaze from his, and Leo found himself subject to a feeling of constraint. He was relieved when she turned a frowning gaze upon him, breaking the silence.

'My horse, Leo. What happened to him?'

'Tarbert has him safe,' he replied, seizing the subject. 'He is quite unharmed. We will send to Bickley presently to fetch him home, never fear.' He grinned. 'Meanwhile, Faithful is welcome to eat his head off in my stables.'

Timothia laughed weakly. 'I have no doubt he will, insensitive brute! He could think of nothing better to do even while I was lying out there half fainting. I called him, hoping to pull myself up by the rein. But would he come?'

'You mean he refused to leave off nibbling at the grass? The selfishness of horses never ceases to amaze me!'

Although Timothia smiled, she said nothing more for several moments, for the reminder of her accident brought a resurgence of consciousness to add to her discomforts. She bethought her of her rescuers.

'I must send to thank the Clents.'

'No need. I have already despatched some small token to Mrs Clent through young Ned. He rode over with your gloves, hat and whip, which I was too preoccupied to think of.'

'That was kind, Leo. Thank you.'

'I wish you will stop thanking me,' he uttered tetchily. 'Anyone would suppose we had been strangers!'

Timothia bit her lip against an upsurge of distress. But Leo was already remorseful. His hand covered hers where it lay on the coverlet. 'I didn't mean it. Pay no heed to me!' He gave a self-conscious laugh. 'I am still in shock, I believe. To see you lying here, so white and still!'

He was gripping her fingers, and Timothia winced. Leo saw it, looked down, and realised what he was doing. Releasing her, he shifted a little away.

'Was I in a swoon for long?' she asked.

'Mercifully, yes,' he replied. 'It took me a good ten minutes to remove the boot. Then I carried you up here, and left you to Mrs Salcombe and a maid.'

'It's been about a half-hour, Miss Timma, no longer,' the housekeeper assured her. 'Here, do you have a sip of this before the doctor arrives.'

Timothia eyed the cup she was proffering with some suspicion. 'Is it more brandy?'

'Brandy? Gracious, ma'am, no, indeed!'

'It is a herbal infusion,' Leo said quickly. 'I only gave

you brandy for the shock. This is camomile, so Mrs Salcombe says, and intended to help you to relax.'

'You had better have some brandy yourself,' said Timothia, with an attempt at humour as the housekeeper presented the cup to her lips. She sipped a little of the liquid,
but very soon brought a wavering hand up to push it away.
'No more, I thank you.' Suddenly weary, she closed her
eyes.

She was looking drawn, and Leo was aware again of
that unsettling sensation of distress. 'Are you still in much
pain?'

'It is throbbing a trifle,' she admitted, thrusting her eyelids up again.

Inevitably, Leo thought, after what he had been obliged
to do to that boot. Aloud, he said coolly, 'I dare say it
will do so for some while yet. But Preseley will be here
at any moment. I hope that he may be able to make you
a degree more comfortable.'

Timothia did not look forward to the doctor's coming
with any comfort at all, for he was bound to maul the
ankle about in order to find out just what injury she had
sustained. But she was at least the more at ease for lying
down, and, it had to be admitted, for having had her
clothes removed—not to say the offending boot. Her head
was no longer subject to the dizzy faintness she had been
experiencing, and the nausea had subsided. She was able
to think more clearly, and was inclined to believe that the
brief respite of unconsciousness had done her good, despite the throb at her ankle.

A knock at the door made Leo rise quickly from the
bed. 'I dare say this is Preseley now.'

So indeed it proved, for Timothia recognised him the
moment he entered the bedchamber. Dr Preseley was a
dapper little man in his early forties, of attractive appear-

ance and a kindly bedside manner. He was neatly dressed as befitted his calling, in a dark suit and a modestly knotted cravat. He did not affect the physical wig, as did so many of his colleagues in the same profession, but wore his own hair tied in the nape of his neck. It was, Timothia noticed for the first time in her life, the colour of faded autumn leaves. Preseley had served as physician to both the Dulverton and Wetheral families throughout most of her own and her cousin's growing years, following in his own father's footsteps. There had been a Preseley on hand to minister to the ailments of the local gentry for two generations. Unfortunately, this Preseley had no son to continue the tradition.

Timothia was at once struck by the resemblance she was now able to perceive in his grown-up daughter, to whom he had obviously bequeathed his stature as well as the colour of his hair and the set of his features. It was the more noticeable because, to her instant consternation, Jenny Preseley herself followed her father into the room.

'My poor dear Miss Dulverton,' began the doctor, advancing towards the bed. 'I am so sorry to see you in such a case. Your ankle has suffered, as I understand it?'

As she responded in the affirmative, Timothia's eyes went directly to Jenny, as Preseley immediately bent over the injured member and ran his fingers gently about the swelling in the practised manner of a professional.

'Dear Miss Dulverton,' uttered his daughter, coming to the side of the bed that Leo had vacated, 'I do hope you don't mind my coming with Papa.'

'I thought you were staying with Mrs Baguley,' Timothia blurted out, surprise—not altogether welcome!—making her forget her manners. Realising how uncivil it must appear, she added quickly, 'No, of course I don't mind it.'

'I am so glad,' said Jenny, with a shy smile. 'I was only staying with Mrs Baguley in London. Since my return I have been at home, except for accompanying her to parties.'

'Otherwise, she is accompanying me on my labours of mercy,' laughed her father, looking up. 'She is quite useful to me, you know, for I am often in need of assistance.'

'I have been attending my father since I was a child,' put in Jenny.

Yes, thought Timothia, remembering. That was how she had recalled the girl, with her mop of red hair. It was more like burnished bronze now, enriched with gold, the red catching alight here and there as it filtered through the curling locks that fell prettily from under a chip straw hat. She was clad in the white muslin that stamped all the débutantes in these times, but of a cut that bore testimony to Mrs Baguley's fashion sense. Timothia was obliged to admit that she looked enchanting. She felt a sigh from deep within her, and was glad when her attention was drawn from contemplation of the girl by her father's next words.

'Now, Miss Dulverton,' he said apologetically, 'I am going to hurt you a trifle.'

Timothia braced herself, but said lightly, 'You cannot do worse than my cousin has already done.'

'Oh, but I am sure he did not mean it, dear Miss Dulverton,' came the pleading tones of Jenny.

'Nor did Miss Dulverton, my dear,' pointed out her father, laughing. 'If you had known these two as long as I have, child, you would not take seriously anything they say about one another.'

Timothia wondered what Leo might have to say to that, and discovered, on looking about, that he had left the room. Only Mrs Salcombe remained, stalwart in her chair by the bed—presumably in her role as chaperon. She was relieved, for at least Leo had not been here to witness her discomposure at the appearance of Jenny Preseley.

The examination which Dr Preseley proceeded to carry out tried her fortitude pretty high, and removed any spark of interest she might have retained in the fact of Jenny's unwanted presence. He must, he explained, feel for the wound.

'I am suspicious of the extreme amount of the swelling, and I did not care for the description given to me by Mr Wetheral of your sufferings upon the event.'

He asked a series of questions at the same time, which Timothia answered only with difficulty, biting down on the protests at his ministrations that were ready to issue instead from her lips. But at last he appeared to be satisfied, and he laid the limb down again upon its cushion. Timothia sighed with relief, and relaxed into the pillows, trying to overcome the resurgence of dizziness brought on by the increased pain.

Dr Preseley came to the bedside. 'Well, now, Miss Dulverton, I fear that you must resign yourself to a period of inactivity. I cannot be sure, you see, that you have not cracked a bone or two.'

Timothia's chest went hollow. 'Do not say I have broken it! But that will take weeks to mend!'

'Not necessarily,' said the doctor soothingly. 'I suspect one or more fractures, for there are numerous little bones in the ankle, you must know. If it had been a serious break, there would likely be a deformity in the position of the foot. That, I am glad to say, is not the case.'

A ragged breath left Timothia's lips. 'I am relieved to hear you say so.'

'But we are not out of the woods, my dear. What I wish you to do is to lie here quietly, and I am going to cradle this foot and ankle to keep it still. I will not attempt either to bandage or to splint you until tomorrow, when we will see what has happened to the swelling.'

Timothia gazed at him, quite horrified. 'You don't mean that I must remain in bed? But for how long? And how in the world am I to do all that is needful…?' She petered out, unwilling to put into words the horrors she envisaged at being bedridden, even for a short time.

'There are always ways and means,' said Preseley, smiling a little. 'I will advise the good Mrs Salcombe here, who will no doubt arrange everything to your satisfaction.'

Ways and means? Timothia was not in the least satisfied. Apart from the personal routines of the day, how could she remain in Leo's house unchaperoned? Indeed, how could she remain here at all—under the circumstances?

'But may I not be taken home?' she pleaded. Although she could not, in truth, look forward with any degree of comfort to the prospect of another journey in her present state. Perhaps one night at Wiggin Hall would not prove harmful.

'There is no question of your going home today,' replied the doctor regretfully.

'Well, tomorrow, then?'

He shook his head with decision. 'I think, Miss Dulverton, that you must make up your mind to it that you will not leave this house for some little while.'

## Chapter Seven

Dazed by the doctor's words, Timothia could only gaze at him, the substance of them reiterating in her head. She could not go home. She must remain in Leo's house. She must stay here, in this bed, in this chamber, in Leo's house. It was a plot, that was clear. A dastardly plot of providence! At any other time, had there never been this dissension between them, she would have fallen off her horse in some other place. But, no. That did not suit the fates' notion of merriment. Far more of a jest to enmesh her in the embarrassment of lying beholden to the one man with whom she had been utterly at outs!

'Meanwhile,' Dr Preseley was continuing, 'I believe we can make you a degree more comfortable.' He turned to the housekeeper. 'Cold compresses, Mrs Salcombe, if you please. A very light wet towel will serve the purpose. Try if you can to procure some ice.'

Ice? Timothia struggled to comprehend him, the shock of his insistence on her remaining here still operating so strongly that nothing seemed to make sense. What in the world had she to do with ice? But as he went on speaking it slowly entered her mind that he was promising some real relief.

'A little crushed ice inside the compress will speed the process. We want to reduce that swelling for you, Miss Dulverton, with the added advantage that it will numb the pain. There is nothing like ice, I find, but very cold water frequently changed is almost as good.'

'Do you mean to say that I may be freed from pain?' she asked, between disbelief and hope, for the after-effects of his examination were still making themselves felt.

'I could wish I might say as much,' he answered, with a rueful look. 'I fear it will be some time before you are free from the ill effects of this accident. But we will certainly lessen their severity.'

He then called for a bolster, and Mrs Salcombe went off to despatch several maids to locate one. While he waited for its arrival, the doctor kept up a steady flow of gentle chatter, reminiscing about Timothia's father in a way that she suspected was designed to lull her into relaxation. The bolster having arrived, he removed the cushion upon which Timothia's leg was resting and showed Mrs Salcombe how to place the long pillow about the foot and leg in such a way that it both supported the ankle and prevented too much movement.

He then withdrew, with the promise to return in the morning to see how Timothia went on after having compresses applied, leaving in the interim his daughter to keep her company. He would send his gig for her later.

'For Mrs Salcombe must set about procuring a compress, and indeed I dare say she has other duties to attend to. Jenny may nurse you, Miss Dulverton, and at the same time serve in the guise of chaperon until your own may be sent for. I understand that Lord Pentre has been despatched to bring her here.'

It was the first Timothia had heard of it. Would Edith come? Of course she would. Indolent she might be, but she was not the woman to shirk her duty. Timothia knew she would never abandon her. Meantime, she found herself with little Jenny Preseley taking up her station in the chair that Mrs Salcombe had lately occupied.

It was not an arrangement that recommended itself, but there was little she could do about it. The fates were busy today, she decided grimly. Was it not enough for them to tie her here? Must they also play an even crueller joke? What else could it be, that would throw Jenny Preseley at her head to come between herself and Leo?

Come between? Fool! What was there to come between? Had she not ended all association with Leo after their last encounter? Only now that episode seemed to belong to some other time. Some other relationship even. She had not quarrelled with the man who had dashed to her rescue today. That were impossible! This had been the old Leo, her dear friend who would not dream of leaving her to her fate. And he had been so very gentle—under the harsh manner he had used only to brace her up. She bore him no ill-will for that. Had their positions been reversed, she would have doled out much the same medicine. It was never of the slightest use to over-sympathise with an invalid. Leo had known that she would respond to a strong hand. He had dealt so capably with the crisis, and with so much understanding of her needs, that she was altogether in charity with him. Except that she did not want to remain indefinitely in his house!

A soft footfall drew her attention. Jenny was crossing quietly to the far window. She had forgotten that the girl was here! She watched her draw the drapes a little and then turn to see whether she had successfully shut out a shaft of sunlight that Timothia had not noticed creeping up towards her pillow.

'Thank you, Jenny,' she said impulsively, touched by

the thoughtful gesture. 'I am sorry to have neglected you. I was lost in thought.'

'Pray do not regard me, Miss Dulverton. I wish only to be useful to you.'

'Don't be stupid!' uttered Timothia impatiently, wincing as she incautiously shifted her foot.

Seeing it, Jenny cried out, 'Take care!' moving quickly to the bed.

Disconcerted, Timothia blurted out, 'Oh, come! You are not a nursemaid, for all your father's words. And I wish you will not address me as Miss Dulverton.'

Jenny wrinkled her nose in an expression of doubt that was both silly and endearing. 'But I cannot call you Timothia. It seems so disrespectful.'

'You may call me Timma. All my friends do so.' Timothia grimaced. 'As for respect, I am not so very much your senior.'

'Oh, but you are so much more knowledgeable and mature!' exclaimed Jenny, moving from the end of the bed to the side. 'I have always thought so. It seems to me inappropriate to be invited to be upon terms of friendship with someone like you.'

Terms of friendship? She supposed she had so invited her. The chit was right to call it inappropriate. If Leo was to develop a *tendre* for her, they were more likely to be sworn enemies! As it was, Timothia knew she was doing her best to dislike the wench. But she could hardly say so.

'You are making me feel like a maiden aunt,' she said instead. 'Why in the world you should regard me in this bizarre light, I am at a loss to imagine.'

The girl broke into her shy smile, and perched on the edge of the bed. 'I beg your pardon. I never meant it to sound like that.'

She had removed the chip hat, and the loose curls trailing on her shoulders made her appear absurdly young. Timothia found herself hoping very much that Leo might not see her like this. A sharpening of feeling at her ankle told her that her muscles were tensing up. A fitting punishment, she told herself, for her uncharitable thoughts. What did it matter to her? If she did not want Leo, then she had no right to resent his liking another female. But this eminently sensible point of view had no effect whatsoever. She continued to resent Jenny Preseley—very much indeed. It made it very difficult to converse with her.

'The thing is,' continued Jenny, leaning a little towards Timothia in a confiding way, 'that you always seemed to me so important a personage. And I heard of you only such things as made me feel myself to be quite foolish and ignorant by comparison. Only fancy your running Dulverton Park! I could scarce believe it to be possible. Only Papa insisted that it was so, and I have heard the same from a number of others. I admire you so much!'

This was a new experience. It was far more usual for Timothia to find herself looked at askance by members of her own sex, as if by her activities she did them some disservice. Even Susan, though she never expressed disapproval, had done her utmost to interest her friend in more feminine pursuits.

'That is refreshing, to say the least.' She found herself smiling. 'To me it seems so normal a thing that I have ever found it hard to understand why people insist upon finding that occupation so odd in me.'

'Well, but that is only because you are a female,' said Jenny naïvely. She then astonished Timothia by blushing profusely, and looking away, while her fingers fidgeted unknowingly with the coverlet upon the bed.

Timothia could not have affected to ignore it for anything in the world. So very extraordinary a reaction to the girl's own statement of the obvious demanded investigation.

'What in the world is the matter, Jenny?'

Jenny bit her lip, looked quickly back at her, and then down to her lap, whither she drew her hands where they writhed about each other nervously.

'If—if I tell you—' with another quick glance which gave away her anxiety '—you will not laugh at me, will you?'

Intrigued and, despite herself, touched by the plea in the chit's voice, Timothia quickly reassured her.

'You may be very sure that I shall not.'

'Well, I—well, you see, I—' She seemed to gather herself, stilling her hands with some deliberation. Then she drew a breath, and looked full into Timothia's face. 'There is a reason why I admired you. You see, I never really wanted to go to parties in London. I don't want to be a débutante. I want to be a doctor!'

Timothia gazed at her dumbly. It was the last thing she might have expected—and from this little slip of a thing. Her resentment faded. What an ambition, poor girl! A worthy one, heaven knew. But, oh, how was she to achieve it?

Jenny's eyes were brimful of something between hope and fear. She was evidently at a loss to know whether she had done well or badly in betraying herself. Timothia spoke without further thought.

'Have you told your father?'

Relief swept over the youthful features. 'Oh, no. Not that I think he would disapprove or laugh at me. But he would be bound to tell me that it could never be.'

'Perhaps he would be pleased,' Timothia suggested.

'After all, he has often spoken of his disappointed wish for a son to carry on the family tradition.'

Jenny shook her head. 'No, because he must know that I could never replace that wish. I—I have made up my mind to it that there is little hope of my being allowed to do it.' She sighed. 'I had thought perhaps I might marry a doctor instead. At least that would permit me to assist, if I might not learn the science in my own right.'

Timothia was finding it increasingly difficult to dislike Jenny Preseley. She seemed to have approached the barriers confronting her with a degree of common sense that could not but appeal. She should be applauded.

'You did not meet any doctors in London, then?'

At that, Jenny's shy smile emerged again. 'I did not expect to. But on the other hand I could not see how I was to meet any doctors in this district either. Then something Mrs Baguley said—I forget exactly what it was—made me think of another scheme.'

'Which was?' Timothia asked, more than ever intrigued.

'It seemed to me,' said Jenny seriously, 'that a man of property might not object to it if his wife were to busy herself about the concerns of the people on his estate. It need not matter to him if she were to take to doctoring, in a small way. I have learned quite a lot from Papa already, you know, and I am forever reading his books. I do not think he would withhold his advice, were I to find a case that I could not manage.'

Timothia suffered a reversal of feeling. A man of property! Someone like Leo Wetheral, for instance. No, there was no doubt at all that her cousin would have no objection whatsoever to his wife interesting herself in his estate! Not, admittedly, quite in the way he had foreseen. But who was to say that Jenny Preseley, with a mind capable of learning to administer to the sick, could not equally learn how to administer an estate?

'Do you think, Miss Dulverton, that it is very selfish of me to think of marriage for such a purpose?'

What a question! No, Timothia did not think it at all selfish—provided that the man chosen to pave her way was someone other than Leo. But who, other than Leo, had a taste for little red-headed waif-like females who, one could not deceive oneself, had a great deal to offer? Gentlemen found much to admire in innocence, bashfulness and modesty. She had a charming way with her, added to the natural attraction of youth. And she was undeniably pretty, with an abundance of brain to boot. What more could any man wish for?

'Selfish? Nothing of the sort!' she said untruthfully. 'I wish you every success.'

Jenny beamed with pleasure, and Timothia was obliged to bite down on a number of unkind additions to her wish. The entrance of Mrs Salcombe, bearing the makings of the required cold compress, put an end to the conversation, to Timothia's relief. It had so taken up her attention that she had been able largely to blot out the dull ache at her ankle. The prospect of fresh ministrations filled her with apprehension. Had she not borne enough?

Within a very few minutes, she was able to judge for herself the quality of Jenny's doctoring. It did little for her peace of mind to discover that the girl had made no idle boast when she'd spoken of having learned from her father. She took the materials from the housekeeper, and with a profuse amount of thanks besought her to leave the whole to her and go on about her no doubt pressing duties. Since Jenny was detailed to remain until Mrs Hawnby should arrive, Mrs Salcombe waited only to see, for later reference, how the compress should be made up and applied before leaving Timothia in the capable hands of the doctor's daughter.

And they were eminently capable. She had a deft touch, handling the limb with firmness, but with care that the least amount of discomfort should be felt. The relief was almost instantaneous, so that Timothia was much inclined to forgive her the incipient designs upon Leo's hand and heart. A state of magnanimity that lasted until a knock upon the bedchamber door brought Leo himself into the room.

He did not seem surprised to see Jenny. But neither did he look—as far as Timothia could interpret his expression—particularly elated. She could not help a slight rise of triumph when he came directly to her bedside.

'How is it now?' Glancing across at the ankle, he added, 'I see that Preseley has done something for you.'

'Yes, but it is Jenny who has been applying the remedy,' said Timothia before she could stop herself.

'Oh, but only on Papa's instruction,' put in Jenny quickly, throwing an unmistakable plea at Timothia.

Evidently she was afraid that her late confession might be betrayed. She would not wish her quarry to know of her design beforehand. Naturally not. But if she imagined for one moment that Timothia would betray a confidence—even to Leo!—then she understood very little of her character. Not that she could ever have resisted that appeal, even had she any intention of divulging the girl's secret.

But Leo appeared utterly uninterested in the matter, and Timothia was conscious of a feeling of pleasure at his continued interest in herself.

'Is it helping you? Has the pain subsided at all?'

'To tell you the truth, it is so effective that at this moment I hardly feel it,' Timothia admitted.

Relief flooded his features, and he reached down his hand to her. Forgetting Jenny, Timothia put hers into it, and was gratified when he sat down on the bed and clasped it between both his own.

'You cannot imagine how much that means to me! I feared that I had significantly worsened the condition.'

Timothia's lilting smile dawned. 'Oh, Leo, how can you be so stupid? If it were not for you, I might still at this moment be lying on a cot in a farmhouse—or a hurdle even—waiting for Edith to come and fetch me. It was the only thing I could think of at the time.'

He grinned. 'Well, thank heaven Clent had more sense!' Then he frowned. 'But you are looking decidedly pale still, Timma. You must be worn out.'

'I am a little tired.'

'I think you should try to sleep.' He released her hand and got up. 'We will leave you.'

For a moment, Timothia did not take it in. But then she saw Leo cross to where Jenny had remained standing, at the end of the bed where she could more easily reach the ankle.

'Come, Miss Preseley. I think we will do better to leave Miss Dulverton to rest.'

A jolt shuddered into Timothia's breast. He was reaching out his hand to her! And she was smiling. That shy smile of innocence that hid a wealth of determination.

'But Papa detailed me to look after Miss Dulverton until her chaperon should arrive, Mr Wetheral.'

'Lord, that dragon will be hours yet! My friend Valentine has gone to fetch her, but I imagine she will take some time to gather together what may be needed. I told your father I would arrange for your return home in due course.'

'But Papa was going to send the gig for me.'

'Yes, but that would not have been until after he goes to visit at Brown's some time after four.'

'Oh, I had forgot. Yes, they have a case of fever there, and Papa must call every day. Oh, it is not contagious, Mr Wetheral. You have no cause to fear for Miss Dulverton.'

'I am relieved.'

He cast a reassuring glance across at Timothia, who received it in silence. Her heart was beating so loud that she could not imagine why the two of them did not hear it.

'Still,' Leo went on, 'I cannot have Miss Dulverton disturbed with idle chatter. She has had a severe shock, and suffered a good deal of pain. I must insist that she be left alone—at least for some little while.'

If Timothia could only speak, she would have told him in no uncertain terms what he might do with his insistence. She did not want Jenny, no. But even less did she wish her to be entertaining Leo rather than herself!

It was plain that Jenny did not feel equal to the task of withstanding Leo. Or perhaps she did not wish to? There came that smile again.

'I am sorry to give you the trouble of getting me home, Mr Wetheral. It is most kind of you. And I must of course abide by your wishes.'

Oh, indeed? And just what were his wishes? Timothia was not left long in doubt. Leo was returning the smile, with one of quite revolting condescension, as he crossed to the door and opened it.

'Perhaps you would care to walk in the grounds?'

'Thank you,' murmured the girl, although she cast a doubtful glance back to the bed before she moved. 'Perhaps I might return later and change the compress, Miss

Dulverton—if Mr Wetheral permits. But I will not wake you, if you should be asleep.'

'You are very good,' was all Timothia found herself able to utter. She forced the ghost of a smile, and watched the girl pass out of the room. To her dismay, Leo left the door open and came quickly back to the bed. Timothia schooled her countenance to an expression that she hoped might pass for satisfaction.

'Sleep!' he said softly. 'Believe me, it is what you need. You look altogether *distrait*.'

A moment later, Timothia was staring at the closed door, the emotions burgeoning in her bosom a compound of indignation and a strong desire to go into hysterics. *Distrait!* And why in the world did he suppose she looked so? Her cousin's capability was forgotten. Instead, Timothia railed against his arrogant, high-handed attitude.

What right had he to eject the girl from her chamber? Did he know better than the doctor? Oh, yes, he knew. So well that he had no need to enquire of her what she might be feeling. He was able to make his diagnosis at a glance! So convenient a diagnosis, too. Had he discovered Timothia sitting up in bed, and chatting in an animated way with Jenny, he might have found it a trifle difficult to lure her out of the room. A walk in the grounds! But how charming that he could devote himself to a chit of a girl when his cousin lay half at death's door in one of his spare bedchambers.

Here, the absurdity of her thoughts caught at her reason. She could hardly be described as being at death's door. She ought to be grateful for Leo's care of her situation. It was true that she'd had a terrible morning, and she ought to be tired. Why in the world was she so agitated? What was it to her if Leo preferred Jenny's company to her own?

To her increased distress, she found that tears were starting to her eyes. Oh, no. She had not even a handkerchief. She must not weep! But the perturbation of her soul would not give way to convenience. The tears continued to gather and fall, and she was obliged to blot them on the sheet, sniffing frantically.

The increased movement disturbed her foot, and the ache started up again. It was too much. Timothia gave way to sobs, pulling one of her pillows around her face and crying into it. Such was her condition that she barely took it in when a stealthy hand tucked a handkerchief into her fingers. Finding it there when the sobs abated, she made use of it, quite failing in the desolation of her spirits to wonder how it had come there.

She was past thinking, and it was not long before the accumulated pressures of the day took their toll, and she did indeed sink into slumber.

When Timothia emerged once more into wakefulness, she found her greatest friend sitting by her bed.

'Susan!'

'Dearest Timma, do not move, I beg of you!' came the breathy response as Susan started up from her chair.

Timothia sank back, briefly clasping the hand that was preventing her from further motion. 'But how came you here? I had not imagined that you could know of it.'

'Valentine came to the Rectory,' Susan told her, fussily straightening the bedclothes.

'Oh, I see.' She blinked a little on the remnants of sleep, and yawned, glancing towards the windows. 'It is daylight still? I feel as if I have slept for hours.'

'It must by now be close on three o'clock. Leo said he had left you to yourself some two hours since.'

Something of earlier events stirred in Timothia's memory. The image of Jenny Preseley came into her mind. Jenny—and Leo. Walking in the grounds.

'How are you feeling, dearest? Does the ankle pain you very much? Can I do anything to ease it?'

Timothia's gaze came back to the anxious one above her. She was not aware of more than a dull ache at the injury, which, she was just able to see, was still covered by a compress. She could not feel it to be cold any longer, although she dared say it might have been changed while she slept. But a separate problem was beginning to present itself.

'Not the ankle,' she said, shifting her torso and arms to liven the deadened muscles. 'That is troubling me very little. But I feel uncommonly stiff to one side.' She passed one hand down the right flank and over her shoulder, feeling her protesting upper arm. 'I must have fallen heavily.'

'Yes, indeed, and you are bound to feel it, poor Timma,' said Susan with ready sympathy. 'Shall I massage it a little for you?'

'Presently, perhaps.' Timothia yawned again, sighing out a heavy breath and shifting her head from side to side to ease the muscles of her neck. 'I was hot against Dr Preseley for confining me to bed, you know, but I confess I feel in no case to get up.'

'I should think not,' agreed her friend. 'In any event, Leo would not hear of it. Now, are you hungry?'

The question spoke straight to the most basic of needs, and over the top of a vague irritation at the idea that Leo commanded her movements Timothia realised that she was ravenous. She'd had nothing to eat since early this morning—a mere snack before her ride. It was her custom to take breakfast afterwards, to avoid indigestion. On the other hand, the thought of consuming a meal gave her a slight nausea.

'I suppose I ought to partake of something,' she said reluctantly. 'I am extremely hungry, but I have no strong appetite for eating, I must confess.'

'I know what you mean,' nodded Susan. 'One never does, when one is ill. But I am sure you will be the better for some food.' She added in a bracing tone, 'Besides, I have strict instructions from Leo that you are to be fed upon waking, so I shall ring the bell. I dare say Mrs Salcombe has it all arranged.'

Timothia watched her rise to the bell-pull at the side of the bed, torn between gratification at her cousin's concern for her welfare and burgeoning resentment that he should have taken over the ordering of her life. No doubt he had dictated the precise ingredients of her meal. Well, if she did not like what he had selected, she thought rebelliously, he might plead in vain. She would starve before she ate it!

But the likelihood of Leo's pleading anything at all very quickly vanished, for Susan told her that he had elected to accompany Valentine to Fenny House to fetch Mrs Hawnby.

'He has gone to my home?' she repeated blankly, beset by a sudden, and hideous, sense of desertion. It found expression in a trivial complaint. 'Pray, why could he not have waited to discover if there might be anything I particularly needed? If that is not a man all over!'

'Now, Timma,' uttered her friend in a chiding tone, reseating herself in the chair by the bed, 'that is not fair. After everything he has done, dearest, it is ungrateful in you to speak so.'

Timothia knew it. She had the grace to amend her words at least—if she could not bring herself to withdraw them. 'Well, I am grateful. It is good of him to take the trouble, I dare say.'

Only that Leo should leave her was a source of so much dissatisfaction that she could not help being shrewish. Yes, it was shrewish, Timothia Dulverton! What right had she to complain of neglect? Merely because he had left her to sleep while he disported himself with Jenny Preseley was no reason to object to his conduct in leaving her to the care of others, while he went off to fetch back her companion. So what, it suddenly occurred to her, had become of Jenny?

'Has Jenny gone home, then?' she asked.

Susan began fidgeting with the folds of her pink muslin walking-dress. 'Well, yes, I believe—yes, she has gone.'

Timothia eyed her friend with a growing feeling of unease. 'What is it, Susan? You may as well tell me at once, for you know you are useless at prevarication.'

'Oh, I know it!' exclaimed her friend in evident agitation. 'Only I did not wish to trouble you with my silly concerns at such a time.'

'Your concerns?' Timothia relaxed again. 'Susan, I am not incapacitated. At least, I am tied by the leg, but that is all.'

'Are you in pain?' asked Susan quickly, rising again. 'Shall I change the compress again?'

Timothia waved her down. 'Don't try to avoid the subject. What is it that you are not telling me?'

The pansy eyes gazed at her helplessly. 'Valentine has driven her home.' She reached out to clutch Timothia's hand. 'Oh, Timma, I am trying so hard not to mind it.'

'Well, don't mind it, for it means nothing at all,' said Timothia stoutly, and with a conviction that she was far from feeling. From what she now knew of Jenny Preseley's plans, she could not but feel that Valentine was no more safe than Leo. But it was a conjecture that she did not care to share with her best friend. Why worry Susan unnecessarily? Besides, she could not betray Jenny's confidence.

She became aware that the large brown eyes were swimming. 'Don't despair, dearest Susan!' she uttered, holding tightly to her friend's fingers. 'Pray don't cry!'

'Oh, no, no, I did not mean to,' said Susan huskily, hastily withdrawing her fingers and hunting in an inner recess of her gown for a handkerchief. She blew her nose, wiped her eyes, and adopted an air of determined cheerfulness.

'Pay no heed. I am being very silly.' She could not forbear a sigh, however, much to Timothia's concern. 'The thing is that I had such a dreadful argument with Valentine.'

Timothia stared. 'This is quite unprecedented. What in the world made you quarrel?'

To her surprise, a steely look came into her friend's eye. 'It was on account of your mishap. Oh, it had nothing to do with it directly; you must not feel that you are in any way to blame.'

'But what happened?' demanded Timothia impatiently.

Susan looked mutinous, clearly reliving the memory. 'You see, when Valentine came to see me, he had meant only to apprise me of your misfortune before driving on to Fenny House. But that would not do for me, I can tell you! I insisted that he bring me to you directly.'

'I am very glad of it,' said Timothia, for she infinitely preferred the company of Susan to that of the Preseley chit. 'But do you mean to say that he did not wish to do so?'

'No, for he was bent upon carrying out Leo's wishes. You must know they had been intending to go to Huntingdon to watch some hateful prizefight, and they were to go in Valentine's coach.'

'Expecting to come home foxed, of course,' put in Timothia sapiently. 'Else they would have gone in an open carriage.'

'I do not know,' said the less worldly-wise Susan. 'But, however it was, Leo thought with his coach so handy Valentine could fetch Mrs Hawnby. And he had agreed to it, and had come out of his way, taking the longer route, especially to inform me of your accident. He actually said that he had thought himself to be doing me a favour—and Leo a disservice thereby!—when he chose to interrupt his mission.'

'But what was his hurry? After all, I am unlikely to move from this spot before Edith arrives,' Timothia pointed out.

'Just what I told him,' agreed Susan. 'But, would you believe it, he turned it back upon me! What was my hurry? You may imagine how I felt. Why, you are my very best friend in the world! I asked him how he would feel if someone should prevent him from going immediately to Leo upon a similar occasion. Of course he had no answer!'

'Of course not,' agreed Timothia, fascinated by her friend's new warrior guise.

'So then,' went on Susan in triumph, 'I pointed out that it was a much shorter distance from Old Hurst to Wiggin than it was to Fenton, and would take him very little additional time. He could drive through Wood Hurst instead, after all, and get to Fenton all the quicker. I thought then that he must oblige me, but no. He offered instead to take me up on his way back from Fenny House.'

Indignation sparkled in the big eyes, and Timothia was obliged to exercise a degree of self-control to prevent herself from laughing. It was so very humorous and odd to see Susan out of charity with Valentine, of all people.

'What did you say then?'

The bravado collapsed. Susan looked mortified. 'I am afraid that I lost my temper. I cannot remember the half of the things I said—and to Valentine! I only know that I could not restrain myself, for I felt him to be so very disobliging and unkind that there was no bearing it.' She paused, biting her lip, and Timothia saw that she was again on the verge of tears.

'Susan, don't be distressed. You did very well. I wish you had hit him!'

'Oh, don't say so! It was quite bad enough as it was.'

'But you got your way, did you not?'

Her friend nodded. 'Oh, yes. He brought me here. But he was so f-furious with me that he s-said not one w-word to me the whole journey,' she disclosed dismally. 'And—and when Leo suggested that Jenny might go home since I had come Valentine *immediately* offered to take her up—just as if calling at the Preseley house before going on to Fenton would not inconvenience him, when he knows very well it is quite out of the way.'

'You should have hit him,' was Timothia's verdict. The doctor's residence was on the same road as Wood Hurst, but further south towards St Ives in the opposite direction. It would mean Valentine must double back. 'I never thought Valentine could be so childishly vengeful!'

To her surprise, Susan brightened. 'Do you indeed think that it might have been so? I did wonder if perhaps he was doing it to spite me. I own I could bear that more easily than that he should have been wishful for Jenny Preseley's company.'

Timothia could not blame her. It might even betoken a stronger feeling for Susan than Valentine was himself aware of. Though this she would not confide to her friend for fear of giving her false hope. Then she recalled the other odd feature of this affair.

'But I thought you said that Leo had gone with him?'

'Oh, yes. He decided to do so then, I believe. For he said he should go because he thought he could better deliver the evil tidings to Mrs Hawnby.' A rather watery giggle escaped her. 'He said she was such a dragon that Valentine might take fright, and make a muff of it.'

Timothia did not share her amusement. All interest in her friend's affairs had temporarily subsided. Why had she not thought of it at once? Leo had chosen to accompany Valentine only at the instant when his friend had offered to carry Jenny back to her home. Was he so taken with her that he must needs ensure that Valentine did not steal a march on him? And such a poor excuse!

But, try as she would to whip up a feeling of resentment, Timothia could do nothing to placate a dreadful hollow growing in her stomach. She was relieved when Mrs Salcombe entered the room, bearing a tray with covered dishes, for it enabled her to persuade herself that the hollow was only her hunger, growing too insistent to be ignored.

It took some minutes—and a deal of argumentative organisation—for her two would-be assistants to prepare her suitably to take her meal. Preoccupied, Timothia bore little part in the discussion until at length it penetrated her absorption, and she intervened.

'You will not move me without a resurgence of pain, so for pity's sake let us get it over with!'

She then sat up abruptly—provoking an outbreak of expostulation—and, gritting her teeth, lifted her leg as best she could from the confines of the bolster, and dragged herself backwards, wincing at the sudden onset of pain. Her whole frame protested, and she was glad to pause while the pillows were banked behind her. With a sigh, she relaxed into a sitting posture, and smiled at her attendants.

'There, that was not so difficult.'

'All very well, Miss Timma,' said the housekeeper severely, 'but you have disarranged your bolster.'

'And you hurt yourself, dearest.'

'Well, if you will renew the cold compress, I dare say I will soon cease to feel it.'

While Susan busied herself at this task, Mrs Salcombe attacked the bolster. 'I only hope I can remember how the doctor did it.'

Fortunately, it did not prove beyond her scope to reproduce Preseley's example. Timothia was just realising how very much more comfortable the doctor had in fact made her by placing the bolster there, when Mrs Salcombe brought the tray to the bed.

'It is all very simple fare,' she said, a note of apology in her voice, 'but that is what Mr Leo requested.'

Timothia fought off an impulse to reject the food. But as the covers were lifted she was obliged to concede that her cousin had gauged her requirements with uncanny accuracy. A few slices of tender chicken breast, accompanied by two or three braised potatoes and fresh young peas, were offered, along with a jug of barley water, which was to be left on the bedside table, and a compote of summer fruits.

Her appetite quickened as she began to eat, and she was able to finish nearly all of the meal. It did much to improve her spirits. She felt a deal better, and since her ankle was benefiting from the fresh compress, which had been wrung out in water still extremely cold from the melted ice, she began to contemplate the possibility of removing on the morrow.

This scheme, however, was frustrated immediately upon the arrival, an hour or so later, of Edith Hawnby, who had come equipped with so many bandboxes that Timothia wondered aloud how it had all fitted into Valentine's coach.

'With difficulty,' said her companion briefly. 'But it is of no use to cavil. Between us, Polly and I had a time of it. I've brought that girl with me, by the by. No wish to leave her alone with only two male servants in the house. I dare say she can make herself useful here.'

Timothia agreed to it, although there were servants enough in Leo's house. But Polly could certainly not be left with Bickley and Padstow. Not that she had not implicit trust in both, but a country girl could not trifle with her reputation. Besides, Polly would probably have a wonderful time, put to the blush and giggling, among a crew of virile young footmen.

'But what in the world have you brought?' she asked, returning to the main issue.

Edith told her. The recital lasted several minutes, and at the end of it Timothia gave it as her opinion that her companion had gone stark, staring crazy.

'You have brought sufficient for a month, I should think!'

'But, Timma,' cut in Susan in a voice of protest, 'it is likely that you will be here that long. You cannot hope to walk upon that foot for at least a week, and then you will only get about with help. I should guess that you will not go home for at least three weeks.'

Timothia was so much horrified by this suggestion that she fell into a mood of unrelieved gloom, which deepened as time went on and her cousin made no attempt to visit her. She had roused herself to bid farewell to Susan, who had hurried away on hearing that Valentine was waiting to drive her home.

'What in the world shall I say to him?' she had whispered in frantic haste as she'd bent to kiss Timothia's cheek.

'Say nothing beyond what civility dictates,' Timothia had advised in an undertone, for Edith had been busy directing Polly where to bestow the articles of clothing that had been brought for her mistress from Fenny House. 'Unless he should open the subject, which I think most unlikely if I know Valentine, you need not refer to it yourself.'

Slightly cheered, Susan had gone on her way, but Timothia knew that she trembled and felt for her deeply. She had been herself in a like case in a way, for she had dissipated so much energetic thought upon Leo's conduct that she could not help a trifle of apprehension at how she would receive him.

That she was not called upon to receive him appeared to have a deleterious effect upon her condition. A headache was added to the muscular stiffness on the side where she had fallen. The pain in her ankle became ever stronger as her leg grew tired and aching from remaining in the same place, and the cold compresses seemed no longer to afford relief. Every motion was an agony, and by the time darkness fell in the late evening she could no longer tolerate her position. She felt as if she had been lying in bed like this for days!

Turning with great difficulty, she lay on the side that had not been damaged in the accident, and for a short time found that the change lessened her sufferings. Even the ankle's agonies gave way to it. But it did not take long for her bones to settle, and the aches started up again, one by one, as it appeared to her tortured body. Timothia knew enough to realise that tossing and turning would only worsen her state, but it proved hard to resist this seeking after relief.

There was no turning on her other side, and in the end she was forced to return to her original position on her back. But the cradling bolster had become dislodged, and her attempts to retrieve it with her sound leg served only to make her lose it over the end of the bed.

'The devil!' she cried aloud, and, bracing herself, leaned out of the bed to tug at the bell-pull.

Edith had retired to dinner herself after feeding Timothia with a sustaining broth, and she had not yet returned. It must be well after nine. Surely dinner was over? And what ailed Leo that he could not even pay her the courtesy of a visit? Had Jenny Preseley's charms so affected him that he had utterly forgotten his cousin's presence in his house? Impossible. For he was dining with Edith. Had he perhaps had an engagement? No, it could not be that, for he was to have gone to Huntingdon that day and would not have expected to return until well into the night.

A knock at the door produced Polly, who hastened to replace the bolster, and revealed, upon enquiry, that Edith had dined in private in the bedchamber allotted to her. An item that further depressed Timothia's spirits, for it promised no news of Leo. Polly added that she was to keep watch through the night, and a truckle bed was being set up for her in the dressing-room next door. Edith, as Timothia learned, would be with her in a very few minutes.

Her companion duly arrived, and, having taken one look at her charge, delivered herself of a single word.

'Laudanum.'

'What?' said Timothia stupidly.

'I am giving you laudanum,' repeated that redoubtable dame, waddling purposefully to the dresser where she had earlier deposited a number of bottles and jars seized haphazardly from Timothia's bedchamber at home. Armed with a squat brown bottle and a large spoon, she obliged Timothia to take a liberal dose.

It had a rapid effect. Before she could rediscover the discomforts of her body, she slipped quietly into sleep. But it was a sleep punctuated with strange visions. She floated in mists, and the mists were peopled with shadows. One such seemed to sit in silhouette by one of the posts at the end of her bed. Its shape expanded, grew in volume looming over her, and then retreated again, shrinking back to its place.

The thing had stayed above her long enough for Timothia to recognise the face. It belonged to her cousin Leo.

# Chapter Eight

But Leo would not be sitting there, leaning against the post at the end of her bed. Not in the middle of the night. Besides, the curtains were open on that side, and she was sure that Polly must have shut them. She looked to the other side, and it seemed to her that the closed drapery there billowed outwards and in again. Outwards and in again.

Her gaze went back to the other side, where a faint source of light was formulating shadows about that part of the room which she could see. They shifted, growing and shrinking. She sought the strange one at the end of the bed. Yes, it was still there. The shape of a man. There would not be a man's shape on her bed—and who would open the drapes? It was undoubtedly a dream. Then what in the world had caused her to see that face?

'A hallucination,' she said aloud. 'It is undoubtedly a hallucination.'

'So you are awake,' said the hallucination.

Timothia started. Heavens, now she was hearing voices! She frowned at it in the darkness. 'I don't know,' she said cautiously. 'For one thing, if I were awake, I cannot imagine what you would be doing there. Edith would never allow it. Even cousins are not immune to the dictates of propriety. Besides, I cannot understand in the least why Leo should do such a thing, so I suppose I must be dreaming.'

'What if you are not dreaming?' it asked, and it did indeed appear to be Leo's voice coming at her out of the dark shape. Which was, of course, impossible.

'I suppose I should be obliged to order him from the room.' Only she would prefer to keep him—especially if the only way he was liable to visit her was in her dreams. She felt it imperative that she make this clear at once. 'But I must tell you that I don't in the least wish to do so, and I should prefer not to wake up, if you don't mind.'

'Not in the least,' came the low-voiced answer. 'Tell me something. Did the dragon give you a drug of some kind? Something to make you sleep?'

How foolish of it to ask that. 'But you know she did. At least I know it, which comes to the same thing. What was it she said?' Strangely, even in her dream she was able to recollect perfectly. 'Yes, laudanum.'

'I begin to understand,' said the hallucination. Then, soft-voiced, it asked, 'Will you tell me something else?'

'You are going to ask me why the curtains about the bed are billowing in a manner which is enough to make anyone seasick. Or why, indeed, they are open at all.'

'No, I know why.'

'You do? That is very strange, for I do not. If you know, then I ought to. It stands to reason.'

'Why don't you wish to order Leo from the room?' it asked abruptly.

'But you must know that,' objected Timothia. After all, if it was a product of her own mind, she would know the answer, so she need not ask the question of herself. She strained her eyes to see in the gloom the outline of the shape at the bedpost. 'I wish you will come closer. I cannot see you well at all in this half-light.'

Obligingly, the hallucination shifted, rising very tall, and sitting down again at a point so much more near at hand that she was just able to make out its features.

'Is that better?' it asked softly.

Timothia chuckled. 'It is grossly improper. Why, if I can command my imagination this easily, there may be no limits to what I might not do with you.'

A low laugh reached her. 'Dare I hazard a guess?'

'Don't be stupid. You are only in my mind, so you know perfectly well. Only it is quite wrong of me to be envisioning my cousin Leo kissing me, and useless besides. We both know well enough that he would not dream of—'

At this point, the hallucination moved swiftly and suddenly, cutting off her words with its lips. Startled, and not a little amazed at how very real the sensation seemed, Timothia did not react for a moment. The mouth upon hers was feather-light, the lips just brushing her own. A feeling of warmth began to invade her. Unable to help herself—and just as if it were really happening—her own mouth began to move under the imagined touch. It seemed that the lips and she performed a dance, touching and shifting, gentling each other in caresses tender as a breeze upon a delicate flower.

She thought she felt also the light touch of fingers that trembled on her cheek, ran down her neck and shoulder, and came to rest in a gentle pressure that encompassed her swelling breast. The warmth inside her spread downwards. Then the invasive lips pressed closer, hardened desperately for a brief moment that swept her through with a melting sensation. Then all was gone.

Timothia opened her eyes. The hallucination was still

there. Then the dream had not ended! Relieved, she brought a wavering hand from out of the bedclothes and reached out to try to touch it. The hand was seized in what seemed a strong clasp. She felt her fingers being kissed, one by one.

'That is a very romantic touch,' she said aloud. 'I wonder how I thought of it?'

'I would I could know just how vivid is your imagination!' said the hallucination, with just that teasing quality that she remembered from the Leo of an earlier time.

'Enough to think of bringing you into this bed with me,' she answered, and then gasped a little at her own daring. 'What in the world would Leo think if he could hear that? He does not even know that he arouses me.'

'He does now,' argued the hallucination.

'That cannot be.' An odd sensation of floating attacked her, and she ran her fingers down the hand that had hold of her own. 'I think this bed is in the clouds. Or is it the ocean?'

Her palm was pressed to a mouth, a kiss planted, and her fingers were closed over it into a fist. The hallucination held it so, warmly between its hands.

'You were right. This is grossly improper. I had better go, before I am driven to take unforgivable advantage of your condition.'

It moved to get up. Desperation gripped Timothia. Her fingers turned in his, seizing his hand.

'Don't go! I like this dream.'

'So do I—but I must not stay.'

'Why? What harm is there? Dear hallucination, don't leave me, I pray you,' she pleaded desperately. 'I have been so lonely!'

'Don't!' it begged, anguish in its voice. 'I promise you, at this moment, there is nothing I wish for more than to climb between the sheets with you—and take you, in a fashion long and lingering. But you are not yourself, dear one, and I must not do it.'

Timothia released her clutch on its hand. Was this the substance of her own imagination? She grew hot at the thought of the words she had put into its mouth. Hot with desire and embarrassment both, her heart melting at the endearment she had given to its tongue. Dared she allow her imagination full rein? The answer came without thought.

'I have to let you go, for I do not know how to imagine the rest.' She had to laugh. 'But this is bizarre. I cannot think that if you were really Leo you would be quite so chivalrous.'

It seemed to her that the shadow above her stiffened. Brusqueness sounded in its voice. 'Do you know me so little? I begin to wonder, Timma, if you are playing a trick upon me. You are really awake, are you not?'

A wave of disappointment flooded her, driving all her enjoyment away. That voice! That harsh comment! Both too like reality. She groaned in protest, and flailed helplessly against the changing vision.

'Oh, go away! I don't wish to dream you any longer. If you are going to turn into the hateful man who has been tormenting me so, then leave me at once. I don't want the real Leo! I don't want him near me.' She was crying, throwing her hands over her eyes. 'I will not see you any longer. Go away, go away, go away!'

Dry sobs racked her, and back came all the aching discomforts of her body that had not penetrated the dreams. She heard the bed-curtains rattle, as if an ill wind caught at them, and in her mind the bed tossed and swayed, battling a storm. It seemed a long time that it lasted, while images built in her head.

Oppressive visions, of Faithful neighing outside her window; of her ankle puffed to the size of a bolster; of red-haired, voluptuous maidens, wallowing in a huge bed that occupied another gusting cloud some distance from her own; and of Leo, sneering down at her as he threw document after document onto her bloodied sheets, bidding her see to them now that he had her secure.

Her wrists were grasped in fingers that felt altogether too strong to be a dream. Her hands were pulled from her eyes, and a face was bending over her.

'Wake up, Timothia! Wake up!'

Her eyelids were heavy, but she dragged them open. Edith's face hung above her, a nightcap tied under the chin in a bow. A grey light filtered through the half-open bed-curtains. The images receded. She tried to speak, and found that her tongue felt clogged. She managed a dry whisper.

'*Water.*'

Edith's face disappeared. Then Timothia's head was raised, and a glass was put to her lips.

'Come, child. Drink some water.'

Obediently, Timothia sipped at cool liquid. It tasted oddly, and she recalled the barley water that had been placed at her bedside. In a moment or two, the thick woolly sensation in her head began to dissipate a little.

The light increased, and she blinked upon the sight of young Polly—a sturdy wench, raw-boned and tall, possessed of a gaucheness that betrayed her extreme youth—who was engaged in drawing the bed-curtains fully aside.

'You were groaning in your sleep,' Edith told her, pouring out another measure of barley water, and obliging Timothia to drink again.

Timothia pushed away the glass. 'No more, thank you.'

She brought one hand up and passed it raggedly over her face.

'Polly woke me,' said her old governess tersely. 'Thought you were having a nightmare.'

'More than one,' Timothia muttered, looking uneasily about. But, to her relief, the room was still, and the bed no longer billowed and tossed. The substance of the dreams had receded almost out of her memory, but she knew that objects of the material world had kept changing shape.

'My fault,' Edith said. 'Probably gave you too big a dose of laudanum.'

'I think I did sleep like a log at first,' Timothia told her tiredly. She discovered that, although the offensive movement of her surroundings had ceased, there was no diminution of the ills of her flesh. Her body ached, seemingly all over, with a concentration in the muscles of her right side which felt too stiff to move at all.

'I feel terrible,' she said, sighing.

'You look it,' returned Edith. 'But we'll soon change that. Polly, open the drapes at the windows.'

Timothia turned her head on the pillow and blinked at the unsettled world beyond the window panes. So grey? It must be early.

'What time is it?' she asked of Edith, who had been bustling at a far table where a basin and ewer stood.

'Close on seven.' Her companion tutted, waddling back across the room. 'Which is why there is no hot water in that jug as yet.'

'I had thought it was dawn,' said Timothia, still gazing at the dullness outside.

Edith tugged at the bell-pull. 'No, it's just raining. A filthy day.' She bustled off to the chest of drawers. 'A good wash and a change of clothes. That is what you need.'

The thought of the effort involved made Timothia sag further into her bed. She could not move! It was too much to expect of her.

'How is the ankle?' asked her old governess, returning to the bedside armed with a clean nightgown.

'My ankle?' It was, Timothia discovered, the one area where pain had dulled rather than increased. 'It feels rather better.'

'That's one blessing, then.'

But it was not destined to remain so. As Polly and Edith set about the process of readying Timothia for the day, it became imperative that she leave the bed for a space. With reluctance, she allowed her two helpers to assist her to get up and hop to a chair. Polly remade the bed with the assistance of one of the Wiggin maids. She had come in answer to the bell, and was immediately despatched for the indispensable ewer of hot water.

Within a few moments of Timothia's leg being vertical, and the blood draining down to the ankle, the swelling returned along with the throbbing pain she had experienced in the early stages.

She had perforce to rely heavily on Edith to aid her to make her ablutions, and it was with intense relief that she was tenderly returned between her sheets at last. But she felt the better for the freshening wash, the feel of a brush untangling her pale yellow locks, and the cool touch of a clean nightgown. So much so that she dozed a little, in a much more relaxed fashion than in the fitful night, while she waited for Polly to bring her breakfast on a tray.

Timothia had protested when Edith had sent Polly off, believing that she felt too ill to eat. But her companion was brisk and adamant.

'You won't do yourself any good by rejecting food. You don't know it, but it is just what you need.'

She was found to be right, for in the event, after an initial difficulty, Timothia made a good meal, partaking of baked eggs together with several slices of bread and butter. But her aching limbs betrayed her halfway through her second cup of coffee, and she was obliged to fall back upon her bank of pillows.

The hour had by this time advanced beyond nine o'clock, as she discovered upon a somewhat agitated enquiry of Polly. She stopped the maid as she was taking away the tray, for Edith had gone down to breakfast herself once she saw that her charge was making the effort to eat.

Nine o'clock—and no visitors! Other than Edith, who did not count. Not that there was a selection of persons who might visit her at such an hour. Timothia could think of only one. Perhaps she should have asked Edith to convey a message to her cousin that she wanted to see him. Except that she felt quite oddly about seeing Leo—she could not think why. Was it perhaps because he had not visited her again yesterday? Surely he would not let another day go by without coming in to see how she did? It would not do! Aside from anything else, she was a guest in his house. He was guilty of incivility already—not having bothered to send so much as a message of goodwill. Nothing, indeed, since he had taken Jenny Preseley out for a walk in the grounds.

She was dwelling with dull resignation upon the conclusion that Leo really was forming an attachment to the doctor's daughter when Polly re-entered the room. She was bearing a folded note, the sight of which immediately threw Timothia into an incomprehensible fluster. She looked at it, but did not take it, gripping the edges of her sheet with tense fingers. Her heart was pounding. It must be from Leo! Why was he writing to her? What did he want?

'Don't you want it, Miss Timma?' asked the maid, looking surprised.

'No!' Timothia threw her hands over her face. Why she should be so agitated, she had no idea. 'Polly, give me a moment!'

The girl's voice came again, amazement in the tone. 'Why, whatever is the matter, Miss Timma? It's only a note.'

Only! Drawing a breath, Timothia brought her hands down and looked at the maid. 'Who is it from?'

Polly shrugged. 'I dunno, Miss Timma. It was Mister Crieff as give it to me.'

'I knew it!'

Feeling as if it did not belong to her, she forced her fingers to reach out and take the note. But one glance at the inscription of her name on the outside was enough to make her flatten it to the coverlet. It was Leo's hand, no doubt about it. She did not want to know what was inside. But at the same time she felt desperate for a sight of the contents.

She saw that the maid was still staring at her. Small wonder. She must suppose her mistress to have taken leave of her senses!

'Thank you, Polly. That will be all.'

The maid bobbed a curtsy. 'Can I get anything for you, Miss Timma, afore I go?'

'Nothing, thank you.' She watched the girl move to the door, and a thought seized her. 'Stay, Polly! Will you ask Mrs Salcombe if I may have a tisane, if you please? I have the wretchedest headache, and she made me something of the sort yesterday.'

Polly agreed with alacrity, and left the room. Timothia lifted her hand, and looked again at the offending note. The first upset had dissipated. She was at a loss to understand herself. What should take her to behave like a simpleton, all for a note from Leo? Yet still she hesitated to open it.

A glimmer of something slipped across her mind, but it was too swift to catch. A hazy memory, perhaps? Giving herself a mental shake, she sank into her pillows and picked up the note.

There was no seal, which seemed to indicate that whatever was inside had no matter in it that was particularly personal. The thought gave her courage. She spread the sheet open, and experienced an unaccountable drop in her already lowered spirits at the seemingly innocuous contents of the note.

There were but a few lines. A cryptic apology, without reference to its cause. 'I have only to beg your pardon.' Well, but for what? For not coming to see her, she must suppose. Then notice of an unavoidable absence from the house today—on business. Estate business? Perhaps some other business that he did not care to name, Timothia decided dejectedly. Business not unconnected with a certain red-headed female, she dared say. And what was this? 'I will do myself the honour of calling upon you on the morrow, if you wish, when we may discuss it.' Discuss what? Do himself the honour! What in the world did he mean by such formality? Then one final sentence, which only made sense if she had understood what he was talking of. 'Only send me word.'

It was signed with his name. No salutation, nothing to indicate within what sort of sentiment he held her. Puzzlement kept her from feeling anything very much for a short while. The note was extraordinary. Timothia read it over and over again, without arriving at any better understanding of her cousin's meaning. It was frustrating, for while she would have liked to send for him immediately she must suppose him to have already left the house. This, above all, penetrated. He had gone without even seeing her! Why could he not have given her this message in person?

A nagging doubt dragged at her heart. There was something about the note that rang a bell. But, for the life of her, she could not place it.

The arrival of Mrs Salcombe, bearing the requested tisane, was a welcome respite from thinking. And, she suddenly realised, an opportunity to gain information. She lifted the cup from the proffered tray.

'Where has Mr Wetheral gone this morning?' she asked, trying for a conversational note.

'I believe he was riding to the north wood, Miss Timma. Some matter which Mr Beauleigh requires him to look into.'

Timothia had yet to hear that her cousin would look into anything if he could get Beauleigh to do it for him! What in the world could take him to the north wood? It was, she knew, a deer park. About the only thing, in her own experience, that could require attention there would be damage after storms. She cast a glance through the window at the rain still misting down.

'He has gone out on horseback in weather such as this?'

Mrs Salcombe followed her glance. 'Yes, it seemed foolhardy to me, too. But Crieff says that Mr Leo was insistent.'

Dismay spread through Timothia's veins. There could be no doubt about it. Leo was avoiding her! The conviction grew that she was missing something vital. Oh, her wayward memory! Why could she not catch at that elusive clue? There was a cogent reason for the cryptic messages in Leo's note; she was sure of it. And she ought to know what it was!

She was obliged to allow Mrs Salcombe to depart about her business. She could have wished that the housekeeper had not seen fit to remind her that she should expect the doctor this morning. Not that she had any objection to seeing Preseley. But if he should once again bring his daughter—!

Time, however, brought instead Susan Hurst. Timothia was genuinely shocked at her friend's folly.

'What in the world made you come out in this?' she demanded, gesturing wildly at the windows. 'Of course I am only too delighted to see you, Susan, but you should not put your own health at risk.'

'Don't scold!' begged her friend, throwing off a woollen travelling cloak with a capacious hood, which she was wearing over a round gown of double muslin, made high to the throat with a standing ruff, and a vest of blue velvet over it. 'See how well wrapped up I have been?' She cast the voluminous garment upon a chair and came to the bedside. 'I could not reconcile it with my conscience if I had not ventured forth to see how you did.'

Timothia grasped her hand and drew her down to exchange a fond salute, but continued to protest. 'That is all very well, Susan, but I know your father has not a closed carriage. Do you tell me you have come here in the gig?'

'Oh, no. Claud was at home last night, and he was so kind as to allow James to drive me in his phaeton,' said Susan reassuringly.

'That is almost as bad,' objected Timothia, for she knew the phaeton belonging to the young Reverend Mr Hurst was an ancient vehicle, with a hood so rickety that it was prone to slip back at the slightest lurch. 'Your face is damp, and your hands are freezing!'

Susan had been rubbing her fingers together, but she desisted at once, and disclaimed. 'I assure you I don't feel at all cold, dearest. How could you think I would desert you, only for a little change in the weather?'

'I could wish you had done so,' said Timothia worriedly. 'You know how susceptible you are to colds. And why could not Claud drive you here himself?'

'He is working with Papa today—some sermon or other which he feels unequal to putting together without expert help—and besides, if he had come I would have had to ask for Leo's assistance to return home later. James is waiting for me, and so I may go at my leisure.'

Timothia was obliged to be satisfied. But the arrangements that Susan had made for her own conveyance reminded her of the quarrel with Valentine that had occurred on the previous day. She lost no time in asking what had occurred when he had driven her home.

Susan blushed. 'You will think me excessively poor-spirited, Timma, but I could not bear it.'

'What do you mean? What happened?'

The pansy eyes went down as Susan hung her head. 'I found myself apologising for my earlier bad temper.'

'You did not!'

'I did.' Her chin came up, a trifle of defiance in the gesture. 'And I am very glad I did so, to be truthful, for Valentine came down off his high ropes immediately.'

'Oh, did he? How magnanimous!'

'Timma! Now, you are not to say unkind things, for Valentine begged my pardon very prettily, and said that he was glad I had taken him to task because he is too apt to be thinking only of his own convenience, and that he had not realised until I became so very discomposed how important it was for me to come to you at once.'

Timothia stared at her. 'Valentine said all that?'

'Yes, indeed he did,' Susan assured her, nodding vigorously. 'You may imagine how astonished I felt, for I have never heard him express himself in such terms.'

No more had Timothia. The suspicion deepened that Valentine felt more for her friend than he knew. If only she had been upon terms with Leo, she might have questioned him on the subject. This thought brought back to her mind the vexed question of Leo's note, and she lost no time in acquainting her friend with its contents.

'How very odd, to be sure!' commented Susan, staring at the sheet. 'What can he mean by this?' Then Timothia saw her start, and the big eyes looked up, brimful of alarm. 'Do you suppose he can have got wind of the rumours?'

'What rumours?' asked Timothia, frowning.

Susan clapped a hand to her mouth, consternation swiftly succeeding the alarm. 'Oh! Oh, Timma, I had not meant to say anything of it! I did not want to worry you.'

A cold feeling crawled in Timothia's stomach. What now? Was there to be no peace? 'It is too late now. You may as well tell me at once. What is being said?'

'Oh, dear,' uttered her flustered friend. 'I only know what Claud told me. He had it from my aunt last evening before he came home.'

'I might have known your aunt Hurst would be at the back of it,' said Timothia resignedly. It was only what might have been expected. 'What did Claud say to you?'

'It is all on account of your mishap,' Susan began. 'You see—'

'Surely that has not swept around the countryside already?' interrupted Timothia, aghast. 'I know I feel as if

I have been in this bed for ever, but it was only yesterday that I fell from Faithful's back.'

'But, Timma,' protested her friend, 'you must know that is time enough for word to spread. Your accident happened in the morning, and you may be sure the Clents talked of it with their neighbours—'

'At the village inn at Wood Hurst, no doubt.'

'And Dr Preseley will have mentioned it at the Browns', for you said that Jenny spoke of his having gone there.'

Timothia groaned. 'A curse upon country people and their wagging tongues!'

'Yes,' agreed Susan mournfully. 'There is no stopping any interesting tidbit from making its way to the ears of every hostess around. Servants will talk!'

Not only servants. Timothia had no doubt at all that, if Valentine had been too busy on her behalf yesterday to add his mite to the tales doing the rounds, he would certainly be making up for it today. She did not say so to Susan, however. There had been dissension enough between the two. She recalled what Susan had first said that had spawned this upsetting dialogue.

'Yet I do not see how Leo could have heard about it. It cannot be that circumstance that made him quit the house on horseback in this horrid weather.'

'Is that what he did?' asked Susan, round-eyed.

'So I am led to believe. It is all on account of this note, I am certain of it. If I could only put my finger upon the chord that is floating somewhere at the back of my mind,' said Timothia fretfully.

'Well, I hope Leo may not hear of the stupid things people are saying,' said Susan. 'I fear there is little hope that he won't, especially if he has gone abroad in this fashion.'

Recalling that she had not yet been given the substance of the rumours, Timothia asked her friend just what Claud had related to her of Lady Hurst's comments. Susan was reluctant to open her lips further on the subject, but Timothia was insistent.

'Well, if you will press me to it, my aunt Hurst supposes that your staying in Leo's house will lead inevitably to scandalous consequences,' disclosed Susan.

Timothia frowned in puzzlement. 'What scandalous consequences? Surely no one could suppose that Edith would not have been summoned to protect my reputation?'

She saw, with rising dismay, that Susan looked altogether conscious, blushing and refusing to meet her eyes. She drew a breath, and spoke with all the determination at her command.

'Susan, if you love me, *tell* me!'

'Oh, Timma,' said her friend distressfully, 'I am so sorry, but my aunt Hurst says that Mrs Hawnby has proved such a poor chaperon—allowing you to go to parties alone, and not even troubling herself to remain with you when gentlemen visit at your house—that no one can possibly rely upon her to prevent the worst from happening.'

The worst? Well, how much imagination did it take to puzzle that one out? 'You mean, I dare say, that they think Leo may attempt to make love to me.'

Susan was nodding, but Timothia heard the echo of her own words with an abrupt shock of remembrance. An image sprang into her mind. Leo—in the darkness, a shadow seated on her bed. And—*kissing her.*

'Timma? Dearest—why, whatever is the matter? You have gone quite white!'

Timothia's heart had leapt into her mouth. That note!

But she had been dreaming. Surely she had been dreaming! The images came flooding back. Leo—or someone she had thought was he—had been in her room last night. She had spoken with him as if to a vision. Or she'd thought she had. The picture was hazy, mixed with strange movements of the room. Snatches of conversation came back to her. Words—unbelievable words—that she had said. Of desire. Of her need of him! Heavens, had she really invited him into her bed?

She sat bolt upright, reaching out to seize Susan's fingers in a frenzied grip. 'It was a dream! Pray tell me it was only a dream!'

'Timma! Dearest! Calm yourself!' burst from Susan, who leapt to her feet and pressed unavailingly at Timothia's shoulders. 'Lie back at once! You will hurt yourself.'

Indeed, Timothia could feel all down her side the wrench she had given herself. But what did that matter in the face of this appalling disaster? For it was nothing less. If that dreadful memory had been only a dream, then why had Leo written to her in such terms?

'Where is the note?' she uttered in agitated tones. 'Leo's note! Where did you put it, Susan?' She saw it lying upon the coverlet, and grabbed it up, tearing it open.

'I do wish you will lie down, dearest,' begged her friend, in accents of the utmost concern. 'What is wrong? Why do you want the note? What is all this about a dream?'

Timothia hardly heard her. Sinking back upon her pillows, she perused Leo's cryptic message once more, barely aware of speaking her thoughts aloud. 'He is begging my pardon, you see. For what other reason would he do so? I thought it strange at the time, and now I must perforce understand it, heaven help me! Discuss it? No, indeed, I had rather die! I should scarce know where to look! Can it truly have happened? Oh, if it did, then I am utterly undone!'

'But what has happened?' demanded Susan shrilly, justly discomposed.

In a few halting words, Timothia gave her to understand a general outline of the events that had happened—or that might have happened—the previous night.

'I had been drugged out of my mind, Susan,' she said raggedly. 'Edith gave me so much laudanum that I was visited by the most horrific dreams. I could not recall them, only that they were bad. Would I had not recalled this one either! Oh, could it have been but a dream?'

Her friend, to her dismay and horror both, appeared to delight in the possibility of its having been real. 'Only think how romantic if it were Leo himself!'

'Romantic? It is disastrous!'

'But why, dearest? There can be only one explanation. Leo loves you.'

A jolt struck at Timothia's heart. It was unlike anything she had ever experienced. She was obliged to gasp in air to get her breath. Her mind was numb. But after a moment or two the sheer absurdity of the suggestion began to penetrate. If the matter she recalled of Leo's words had any substance, then 'love' was not their portent. The feelings that the dream Leo had cherished were far other, having to do only with—let her face the word squarely!—*lust*.

'No, not that,' she managed to say, over the pulsing beat in her bosom that had succeeded the first shock.

If Susan had been about to protest it, she was forestalled by a knock at the door. Not without a certain relief, Timothia saw her companion peep round the door, and, having evidently satisfied herself that the time was appropriate, ushered Dr Preseley into the bedchamber.

* * *

Timothia was almost glad of the spasms of pain that smote her as the doctor re-examined her ankle. None but Susan might then take her pale-faced agitation for other than this cause. The pulsation at her breast was a good deal worse, she dared swear, than that at her foot!

'The swelling is reducing,' said Preseley in a satisfied tone, 'but there is still a good deal of inflammation. But I am pleased to see this little area of bruising, for it means that the blood is beginning to dissipate. That, you know—' with a smiling look up at his patient '—is a most important development.'

'Why?' demanded Edith, when Timothia failed to respond beyond a blank stare.

'Because we thus run no risk of gangrene, for the fluids have no opportunity to become infected from lack of movement. You may look to see a good deal of purpling all around the inflamed area.'

He looked at Timothia again, and she made an effort to rouse herself from the stupor of mind attendant upon her frayed nerves.

'You spoke of—you mentioned yesterday that the bone may be cracked.'

The doctor smiled his reassurance. 'I did, and I cannot entirely rule it out, though I now feel that it is unlikely. However, as a precautionary measure, I will strap it with a small splint. It should not make you uncomfortable, and indeed will be found to help you once you begin to get about again.'

There was matter enough in this to snap Timothia back to attention. She seized on the implication, driven by the riffle of panic that accompanied her perturbation.

'Then it may not be long before I can get up?'

'A few days, perhaps.'

A sigh escaped her. 'Then I can remove from here! I can go home.'

Preseley's brows rose, and he came around the bed to her side. 'Now I thought we had agreed, Miss Dulverton, that you were settled here for some little time.'

'No! At least, it was your notion. I never agreed with it.' Whatever she might have said yesterday had no longer any meaning. After last night she wanted only to escape from this house at the earliest possible moment. She tried to steady her voice, which she knew was uneven in its tenor. 'I should—I should like to go home as soon as possible. May I?'

The doctor looked regretful. 'I am sorry you should be so anxious for it, Miss Dulverton, for I truly cannot recommend it.' He threw up a restraining hand as Timothia opened her mouth to speak. 'No, no, only hear me out.'

'Quiet, child!' put in Edith quickly, with an admonitory look. Timothia compressed her lips on the babbling protests that were running through her head. She was not rational, she knew it. But how should she be?

The doctor resumed, both face and voice conveying a wealth of sympathy and understanding. 'I appreciate the awkwardness of your situation, my dear, but I cannot imagine that you would wish to retard your own recovery.'

'No, of course not, but—'

'My dear Miss Dulverton, trust me! You are a sensible woman, and an active one. You may not know it, but you will find difficulty in getting about even when you are able to put your foot to the floor. It is only sensible to recuperate where there is plenty of room to manoeuvre. Your cousin—'

The panic thrust through. 'Do not speak of my cousin! If you mean to keep me here on Leo's account, I—'

'Timothia!'

With difficulty, Timothia bit back the frantic expostulations that wanted to ripple off her tongue. The mere
mention of Leo, and she could willingly scream! Heaven
help her, but she knew she was driven by factors outside
her common sense. She must remember that Dr Preseley
only had her interests at heart.

'I beg your pardon,' she said with difficulty. 'I am behaving insufferably.'

Preseley smiled. 'Have no fear. I am quite used to receive abuse at the hands of my patients. Invalids are never
in their best humour.' He cleared his throat. 'Forgive me,
my dear. I do not mean to sound discourteous, but what
Mr Wetheral gave me to understand is that the rooms and
corridors of Fenny House are—'

'Poky!' finished Timothia. She was mortified. She
might have known that Leo would put a spoke in her
wheel!

'I should not have used the expression, but yes, I believe he did say that,' laughed Preseley. 'That being so—'

He was interrupted, much to Timothia's chagrin, by
Edith Hawnby.

'Say no more! Fenny House is clearly out of the question. And I am in a position to know. Don't put yourself
about, Dr Preseley. I shall see that she stays here until
you give her leave to go.'

Timothia threw an anguished glance at Susan, who grimaced and shrugged her shoulders. Would Edith have
been so complacent had she known about last night? She
would change her mind soon enough if Timothia were to
tell her about the rumours. Only she would not do that,
for Edith could only be hurt by the implication that she
had failed in her duty—and that people were talking of

it. Particularly since Edith's casual governance had just suited her own inclination.

She contented herself with animadverting bitterly upon the workings of fate, when once the doctor had left the room in search of a suitable splint.

'It is all a fiendish plot! It would not surprise me if Leo and providence between them had contrived the whole on purpose to undo me.'

'I have often observed,' said Edith prosaically, tidying the bedclothes about her ankle, 'that providence has a way of working things out to one's own secret desires.'

A remark which hit so accurately that Timothia was inevitably roused to rebellion. 'I have no secret desire to remain in this house, I assure you.'

She received one of her old governess's enigmatic looks. 'Haven't you? In that case, my observation must be inaccurate.'

Timothia bit her tongue on any further retort. Edith saw all too much, that was the trouble. She was grateful to Susan, who came over to the bed and gave her hand an understanding squeeze. But then she recalled her friend's ludicrous delusion about Leo's emotions, and concluded that neither of those closest to her had the least understanding of her relationship with her cousin.

The splinting and bandaging of her ankle proved so excessively uncomfortable that no thought of Leo—or indeed anything but the activities of Dr Preseley—had the power to hold her attention. When he had done, she felt so weak and ill that her well-wishers grew seriously concerned.

'I think I will give you a little syrup of poppies to make you sleep,' said the doctor. 'And then you should be left in peace.'

That did rouse Timothia. Syrup of poppies? After what

had occurred in her dreams? No, indeed. She made an effort to open her eyes.

'No, I thank you. I have had enough of the effects of opium, Dr Preseley.'

He looked frowningly down at her. 'I beg your pardon?'

This time she was glad of Edith's intervention. 'What she means is that I gave her too much laudanum. She had nightmares. I should think she had better not have any more.'

Preseley looked a little shocked. 'No, indeed! I do not recommend it except in extremes—and then only a very little will suffice. There are those who have become addicted through overdosing themselves.'

Timothia grunted. Overdosing? If she never touched the stuff again, it would be perfectly acceptable to her. 'Thank you, Doctor, but I had rather not be of their number.'

He laughed. 'Nor I count you so. Let us instead try a little herbal remedy.'

'Oh, not camomile!' groaned Timothia. 'I have already had some today, and it has done nothing to restore me.'

Preseley smiled. 'I was thinking rather of valerian. It is mild when fresh-picked, but has sedative properties and is soothing to the nerves.'

Timothia was moved to eye him with suspicion. Had he, then, noticed her agitation? She supposed he could hardly have missed it! She watched him moving to the door, where he paused with his fingers round the handle, and turned back.

'I will have Jenny collect up some valerian directly. I understand Mrs Salcombe keeps a well-stocked garden of herbs. Since Jenny is in the conservatory at this moment with Mr Wetheral, she may slip on her cloak and nip outside without incurring any ill effects from the rain.'

Upon which, he walked out of the room, leaving Timothia dumbfounded. She was unable to think beyond the unpalatable facts—and the protests that contradicted the possibility.

Leo was then here. He had not gone out. But he had written specifically to convey that intention. And he was with Jenny! Again? After last night? It could not be true. Or was it last night which had not been true? Then why had he written so to her? He had only to beg her pardon— but not for that. He might do so for lingering in the conservatory with Jenny Preseley. And Timothia would not forgive him that! How could he? After all he had said to her—here in her bedchamber. Only he had not said it, had he? She had imagined the whole. A curse upon the laudanum! And oh, that Jenny Preseley might be struck down with a plague!

She beat her fist unknowingly into the coverlet by her side, and it was immediately borne in upon her that Edith was eyeing her. With that look of a sphinx! Timothia turned her own eyes away, and was glad when her friend—evidently sensing her distress—spoke up for her.

'You see, Mrs Hawnby, we had thought Leo to have gone out. He was to have been away all day on business. He told Timma so in a note, this very morning.'

'Did he?' came the cool response. 'Well, I dare say that is what he intended.'

Drawn by something in her tone, Timothia looked back at her. 'What do you mean, Edith?' She could have cursed herself for the quiver in her voice. It did not appear that her companion noticed it—if one could tell anything from Edith's phlegmatic exterior.

'He set out, as I understand it, only to meet Dr Preseley and his daughter on the road. I gather that he turned back to accompany them, for they arrived all together.'

Timothia met her eyes fully, and knew that Edith penetrated her mind. She managed to maintain control until her companion, with one of her characteristic nods, waddled to the door and went out. Then she looked at her friend, and saw Susan's features sink into concern before they blurred in her vision.

'Oh, Timma, my love, don't,' she begged, running to the bedside. 'Oh, don't, my poor dearest Timma!'

But it was of no use. 'I c-can't h-help it,' uttered Timothia brokenly, stretching out her hand. 'He is s-smitten with her, S-Susan, I kn-know he is!'

Susan took her hand and all but climbed onto the bed. Timothia felt herself gathered into a close embrace, with her head in her best friend's lap. She gave herself up to helpless sobs, racked by a sensation of bitter hurt.

# Chapter Nine

Leo listened with only half an ear to what the Preseley chit was saying. He could not think why he had allowed himself to be lured into the conservatory. Lured? Perhaps that was too strong a word. But Jenny had undoubtedly drawn him hither, on the pretext of finding some flowers for Timma's room. It was his own fault, for had he not mentioned her liking of flowers only yesterday when he had sent the girl out to wander about the grounds? He had joined her there only to make sure that she kept away from his cousin.

Timma had looked so drawn, there was no bearing it! He'd had to obtain her some peace. He had found a pretext to leave Jenny after some time, and returned in stealth to Timma's room to check on her, and had found her asleep. It had only been by the most supreme act of will that he had torn himself away. Indeed, when Valentine had proved to have interrupted his errand to bring Susan back here, Leo had seized on the opportunity to take himself out of the vicinity, so strong was his compulsion to post himself by Timma's bedside. Which, as Valentine had pointed out, could only result in wrecking her reputation.

It might enforce her acquiescence in the future he had planned for them both. But, knowing Timma, it would certainly serve to divide him from her, driving a deeper wedge between them. And that, in the new knowledge that his wayward conduct had made him privy to, was too unbearable to be contemplated.

He had thought, after that night on the Fenns, that he had succeeded in ousting from his mind and will his obsession with marrying his cousin. Indeed, he had fought hard to overcome the tendency of his thoughts to contemplate nothing but roseate visions of Timma in his house. He had seen her everywhere! At his desk, in his parlours, in the stables. Flaxen locks awry, skin golden in the sun, the swell of her full bosom enticingly exposed, the beguiling smile curving her lips. And—most disturbing vision of all—flushed and radiant, in his bed.

Then, when he had all but won the battle over his baser self, had come her accident. Seeing her spread upon the ground, helpless and broken! All the instincts of their long and affectionate association had consumed him, sweeping away every remnant of the distresses of the latter days. Yet, after the first shock had abated, he had come in while she slept and watched her lying in that bed. She had looked so vulnerable, her hair splashing its pale gold sheen across the pillows, and he had been shaken with a powerful recurrence of desire.

He had felt acutely its intrusion at such a time. Was he a monster, to be subject to such inappropriate promptings? For two pins, he would have gathered her up into his arms and—

'A penny for them, Mr Wetheral.'

Leo started, horrified to have allowed his thoughts to wander thither. Jenny Preseley was standing between the two tall palms at the very end of the conservatory wall where a pair of French doors, tightly closed at present, gave onto the gardens. Leo drew a breath, pulling himself together.

'I beg your pardon. My mind was wandering.'

The girl smiled. 'So I saw. I expect you were thinking of Miss Dulverton.'

Leo felt himself redden, and moved away to stare through the rain-splashed glass at the green lawns outside. 'She is the chief subject of my present thoughts, yes.'

'You must be very worried.'

He turned to look at her, a frown in his eyes. What was the girl at? Had she brought him in here only to talk of Timma? If so, it was a tactic whose object was not immediately apparent.

'Miss Dulverton is my cousin,' he said evenly. 'We have ever been close.'

Jenny nodded, smiling. 'My father has told me. Like brother and sister?'

Leo was betrayed into a short laugh. 'It ought to have been so, I suppose.'

'But it was not, was it?'

There was a seriousness in the tone, but she was smiling still. If this was a ploy, its meaning escaped him. 'Why do you say that?'

Jenny chose not to answer this. Her smile increased, and instead she asked him as she moved across to a collection of plants, 'Do you think Miss Dulverton would care for these purple flowers? I believe they are called lilies of the Nile.'

Leo allowed himself to be drawn into a discussion of which of the many exotic blooms were likely to appeal to Timma. He could not think what he was doing here. He cursed himself for abandoning this morning's intention to escape from the house. He had only himself to blame for running his head into a noose! But that made it no easier. He did not know how he was to re-establish himself with Timma. Instinct had dictated that he ought to give her time. Hence his decision to avoid her.

Only, when he had run into Preseley, he had suddenly recalled the doctor's warning yesterday, after he had examined Timma's injury, that he suspected cracks in the bones. All else had faded in the anxiety to hear Preseley's further diagnosis. Only when he had arrived home had he recalled the awkwardness that must attend any encounter with his cousin. He had resolved to await the doctor's verdict—without making any attempt to see Timma—and then resume his mission.

Not that he had the slightest desire to ride through the wetlands of the forest in search of Beauleigh's infuriating oak. And in this rain. But anything was better than the direful prospect of facing Timma again! At least, not yet.

Was it by design or accident that he had found himself instead in Jenny Preseley's company? He had been so preoccupied that he could not tell how it had happened. She seemed innocent enough, but he could not be impervious to the broad hints that had been dropped by the Baguley matron. Years of London society had inured him to the wiles of matchmakers, and he had learned not to trust even the most ingenuous of feminine creatures. One did so at one's peril! Even Valentine, who was not noted for his perception, had an ingrained instinct of self-preservation when it came to designing débutantes.

But Jenny Preseley had all the advantage of an apparent artless charm. Wasted on himself—if that was her intention. He regretted having been betrayed by his annoyance with Timma into encouraging her that night at Somersham. He was reaping the harvest of it now. Unless the chit's anxious solicitude over Timma was genuine.

He discovered that Jenny had stopped speaking again, and was regarding him in mute question over the top of a row of potted orchids on a stone table. He drew a breath, and forced a laugh.

'I am sorry, Miss Preseley. I was miles away again.'

'It makes no matter.' She was giving him a bright smile. 'Orchids, do you think?'

'No, she would disapprove of their being taken from this habitat,' he responded automatically. He grimaced, shifting to converse with her across the stone table. 'I should have told you before, but I did not like to dampen your kind intention. The truth is that Timma believes one should not cut flowers. They should be left, she says, to live out their natural term. She would accept roses, I think, in these especial circumstances. But it is too wet, and the blooms are already on the decline.'

Jenny was silent for a space, looking at him with, he thought, speculation in her eyes. What in the world was the chit up to now? He was not left wondering for long.

'You know Miss Dulverton so very well, Mr Wetheral,' she commented in a tone that gave nothing away.

'Necessarily,' he replied shortly. 'We have spent a good deal of time in each other's company.'

'You are going to be married, are you not?'

The question took him so much unawares that he knew not what to say. He stared at her blankly. How should he reply? She could not know of the dissension that had attended that very question. Or no, perhaps she could know it. Had not the world been discussing the matter for some little while?

'You have been listening to gossip, Miss Preseley,' he said flatly.

She blushed and looked away. 'I beg your pardon, sir. It was impertinent.' Then her eyes came back to his, and there was trouble in them. 'I only asked because—because I wanted to be able to say something that might protect Miss Dulverton. Oh, not to you! But—oh, dear, this is excessively awkward!'

Leo's frown grew as he watched her move away from him. But the implication in her words hung heavy. What had caused her to bring this up? He moved around the table to her and grasped her shoulder, turning her to face him.

'Miss Preseley, if there is aught you have to tell me, I beg you will do so—and without roundaboutation. Believe me, where Miss Dulverton is concerned, I have as much interest in protection as you—more, I dare say.'

'Yes, of course,' said Jenny, looking up at him with evident concern in her face. 'To tell you the truth, it was for that very purpose that I suggested we should come in here. Only I did not know how to bring up the subject.'

The relief that Leo felt on learning that she had no designs upon him was overwhelmed by the instant anxiety that attacked him at the idea that some danger threatened Timma.

'Well, now that you have broached it, pray don't hesitate to give me a round tale. What is the matter?'

Thus adjured, Jenny appeared to relax a little, and her air became confiding. 'You see, a letter was brought over to me from Mrs Baguley this morning. She is hot for news from this house. Indeed,' she added, with a rising indignation that did more to endear her to Leo than anything she said, 'she had the effrontery to bid me snoop out any little tidbit that I could, for she had heard that my father is attending Miss Dulverton.'

'Oh, the deuce!' burst from Leo. 'Do you say that the gossips are already at it?'

Jenny nodded. 'I am afraid they are. If you will forgive my speaking blunt—'

'Miss Preseley, I will welcome it.'

'Well, they are making something disgraceful out of Miss Dulverton's staying in your house,' Jenny said frankly.

'But surely they must realise—if they have not also heard it—that Mrs Hawnby is come here.'

Jenny shook her head. 'They do not place any faith in her ability to prevent anything from happening.'

'Devil take it!' Leo swore, taking a sharp turn about the room. He could not very well blame anyone for taking this point of view. He knew it to be true. Not that it excused his own conduct. But he was perfectly aware that nothing but his own honour had prevented events last night from being pursued to their logical conclusion. Despite the fact that the dragon Hawnby had been two doors away, and Timma's own housemaid in the dressing-room next door.

He saw that Jenny Preseley was looking rueful, and drew in his breath against the building anger. 'There is more?'

She nodded. 'I pledged myself to tell you it all, Mr Wetheral, though it pains me to say this. Mrs Baguley has even dared to suppose that there is no serious injury, and it is but an excuse to continue a liaison which must have been going on for several years.'

Leo stared sightlessly at her face. How dared they? How dared they impute such base conduct to Timma? For himself, he cared not a straw. Let them say what they would of him. But what had Timma ever done to deserve that slur?

'That is why,' came the voice of the Preseley chit, jabbing into his thoughts, 'I asked if you were going to be married. For you have only to announce your betrothal, and they will be silenced.'

Announce his betrothal? The devil! How little the girl knew of Timma! He might readily give in to such pressures—only to spare her any further humiliation. But if Jenny supposed Timma would allow herself to be coerced into marriage by such idle gossip-mongering she was mightily mistaken.

'What will you do?'

Leo looked at the girl. 'I do not know, but if you are wishful to be of service to Miss Dulverton you may write back to that—to Mrs Baguley that you are more often in the sickroom than I. Not to mention Miss Hurst, Mrs Salcombe, and I don't know how many maids—let alone the dragon Hawnby!'

Jenny nodded seriously. 'Yes, that is very true. But will you not—?'

'I will not ask Miss Dulverton to kowtow to a parcel of busybodies, no,' he answered swiftly, out of a sudden rise of passion in his chest, and hardly conscious of what he said, or to whom he was speaking. 'You do not know her, Miss Preseley, but I do. Timma would die first! And since I am extremely desirous of marrying her I will do nothing to jeopardise my chances.'

A beaming smile swept across Jenny's face. 'I knew it! Oh, I am so glad I have not been mistaken. You are in love with her, are you not, Mr Wetheral?'

Timothia's expression of despair was over. Her natural resilience reasserted itself before long, and after speaking her mind—in a rather watery fashion, and with renewed recourse to a sodden handkerchief—on the subject of designing hussies who hid a vixenish soul under an innocent front she straightened up against her bank of pillows and allowed Susan to run a comb through her tangled hair.

'Are my eyes red and puffy?' she demanded uneasily.

'You could not expect that it would be otherwise, dearest,' pointed out her friend, making a thorough examination. 'But the effects are already wearing off. In a moment or two, no one who sees you will suspect a thing.'

Relieved, Timothia shifted into a more comfortable position, cautiously moving the bandaged foot. The initial agonies attendant upon having it splinted had reduced considerably, although she was still very conscious of the ankle. Her other physical ailments had eased a little with moving the muscles, and the bout of tears had done a great deal to lessen the tension of her nerves.

'I don't think I require Dr Preseley's valerian, after all. Which may please Jenny, for I am sure she is much more pleasurably occupied!'

'Dearest, don't say so. And I think you should drink the brew in any event, for you look peaky still. There are shadows beneath your eyes.'

Timothia sighed. 'It is well that I have no mirror by me, then, for I am sure I should crack it.'

'That is silly.' Susan placed the comb back upon the dresser, and returned to the bed, sitting down beside it with an air of great importance. 'Now, Timma, I want to talk seriously to you.'

The ghost of a smile crossed Timothia's features. 'Are you going to treat me to one of your "elder sister" lectures?'

'Yes,' said Susan resolutely, and then frowned. 'At least, no—I wish you will not try to turn the subject.'

'Very well,' said Timothia meekly, folding her hands together and relaxing into the pillows. 'Go on.'

'Timma, you cannot continue in this way.'

'In what way?'

Susan waved agitated hands. 'In this dreadful state of depression and nerves!' She drew a determined breath, and uttered tensely, 'You must speak to Leo.'

At once, a tattoo started up in Timothia's breast. Speak to Leo? No, she could not! 'Susan, it is useless to tell me that. What in the world do you suppose I might say to him?'

'The truth, of course,' pursued Susan doggedly.

The truth! About last night? But she had no idea what was the truth. And besides, it was hardly a subject she could bring herself to discuss with Leo. She saw that Susan's pansy eyes were fixed upon her face.

'Susan, how can I? Suppose it never happened—why, I should feel doubly conscious. Especially now, when I have every reason to suppose that he is fixing his interest with Jenny Preseley.'

But Susan was not to be put off. 'You do not know that. And after his manner to you yesterday, when he was so very concerned for you, it is ridiculous to suppose that he does not care for you.'

Timothia shifted her shoulders in a gesture of discontent. 'It does not mean anything. He fell automatically back into the bond of friendship that we have ever shared, that is all. I would have been as distressed as he had our positions been reversed, I assure you.'

'You have no need to assure me of it,' said Susan breathily. 'How could it be otherwise, when you are completely in love with Leo?'

A stone lodged in Timothia's chest. She tried to speak—and failed. It was not true. It could not be true. If that were the substance of her feelings towards him, she would have known it! She would have felt it long ago. This was not love! This agonising, hideous state of indecision and despair. It was not possible. Love was tender, and sweet. If she were in love, she would not be so critical of Leo. Love would have made her gentle towards him, not fierce and venomous as she had been. No, whatever it was that had ruined the bond of friendship between them, it was not love.

'You are mistaken,' she said, and could only ascribe the husky quality of her voice to the grief that had entered her soul. 'I do not regard Leo in such a rosy light. How could I, when I know him through and through? No, Susan, it has naught to do with love.'

'What, then, do you call it?' asked her friend, and Timothia could not remember ever having heard such a sceptical note in Susan's voice.

'You do not believe me, but that must be because of your own feelings towards Valentine. I could not swoon over Leo! I admit that I find myself attracted to his manly quality, but that does not betoken anything more romantic than lust.'

'Timma, how can you?' protested Susan in shocked tones.

'For pity's sake, let us call a spade a spade! I am not a schoolroom miss, and nor are you.'

'Very well,' agreed her friend, 'but then why are you jealous of Jenny Preseley?'

'I am not jealous!' objected Timothia. 'It is not that, I assure you. I do not deny that the thought of Leo falling—*succumbing* to her wiles—' she corrected herself rather hastily '—is galling to me.'

'Because you cannot bear the thought of his marrying anyone else!' said Susan bluntly.

'I do not deny it,' Timothia uttered strongly. 'It is hard for me to release myself from the too strong bond of friendship. I thought I had done so, but to my shame I find I cannot. It hurts me dreadfully! And I know that it affects Leo too. But,' she added with fierce determination, 'it is not—it cannot possibly be!—love.'

And nothing was going to move her from this standpoint! Susan looked as if she would have argued further, but they were interrupted at this moment by Edith, who came in with tidings that were not altogether welcome.

'Dr Preseley has gone, and Jenny is running out to fetch this herb. She is going to prepare the drink herself, and bring it to you. Mrs Salcombe wishes to know if you are staying for luncheon, Susan. You may have it in here with Timothia, if you wish.'

While she listened to her friend accepting the invitation, Timothia was willing herself not to enquire after Leo. Edith did not volunteer any information about him, and she was obliged to bite down on the question. She would not lower herself to ask! But when her companion left the room she was slightly cheered by a decision of Susan's.

'Dearest, I have just thought what I may do for you.'

'You are not thinking of talking to Leo on my behalf!' exclaimed Timothia, seized with a sudden fear.

'Of course I will do no such thing. I might have spoken to Valentine, however, but perhaps I may not see him.'

'I am glad!' said Timothia with emphasis.

'In any event, it is not that,' said Susan. 'What I was thinking, Timma, is that I will go after luncheon, and offer to take Jenny up in my carriage. Once she is removed, and if I am no longer here, Leo will feel himself obliged to visit you.'

For a moment, Timothia's spirits lightened. But then she recalled the embarrassment that must be attendant upon a meeting with Leo. 'Not unless I ask him. Remember that he said in his note that I should send him word.'

'Then ask him!'

Timothia looked at her. 'What have I been saying to you? Besides, I do not wish him to visit me only because he feels obliged to do so.'

Susan leaned forward and gripped her fingers. 'Dearest Timma, you do not wish to remain upon distant terms with him; you know you do not.'

'No, but—'

'Then take this opportunity, I beg of you!'

There was time for no more, for Polly and two maids entered with the promised luncheon trays, which they busily served. It was a light meal without frills, such as Timothia could readily eat, and they had barely started on it when Jenny Preseley entered the room, armed with the drink made from valerian. Timothia schooled herself to receive the girl with every evidence of pleasure, and found the drink to be acceptably tasty.

'It is sweetened with honey,' Jenny told her. 'I think you will find that it will make you sleep soundly.'

Whether it was due to the drink, or to the stresses of the day, in the event Timothia did drop off to sleep, about a half-hour later. The last thing she remembered was Edith summoning Jenny to the luncheon parlour, and Susan whispering to her that she would follow to persuade Jenny to remove with her after she had eaten.

She awoke to the sound of heavy rain, and wind rattling strands of ivy on the panes. A storm! Timothia started up, her friend's final words leaping to her mind. She only hoped that Susan had reached home before it broke. Her glance caught at the chair by the head of the bed. Edith was dozing there.

Timothia blinked away the mists of sleep, and lay back among her cushions, her gaze idly sweeping the room. It halted, transfixed. Her heart jerked. Leo was standing by the far window, looking out.

He had evidently not yet noticed that she had woken. Almost holding her breath for fear that its unsteadiness would give her away, Timothia regarded his profile, trying to stem the tide of warmth and consciousness that flooded her at his presence. Oh, this was so excessively uncomfortable! This was *Leo*. Her lifelong companion and friend. How was it possible that she should experience such a degree of inner tumult at the mere sight of him?

He looked excessively attractive, despite the forbidding set of his jawline. His hair had grown, one unruly lock of it now falling across his brow. She could not see much of his eyes at this angle, but the line of both nose and chin carried strength and purpose. His hands were clasped behind his back, his shoulders taut, and the power of his muscle showed even in the relaxed pose of his buckskin-clad thigh. Timothia could not think what had possessed her to refuse him.

Leo must have felt her watching him, for his head turned and their eyes met. For a brief moment of silence, Timothia could not look away from that startling blue gaze. Then the sombre quality of it penetrated, and consciousness returned. Her own eyes dropped, and she made a play of shifting her position in the bed.

Leo glanced at the Hawnby dragon and saw her still sleeping. It afforded an excuse to remain silent for some moments longer. As well, for he knew not what to say. He had come in on impulse, abandoning his earlier intentions—driven by so intense a need that he could not resist. And then he had spent the last ten minutes standing here, rehearsing speeches in his head. But that look had changed everything! Nothing that he had intended to say seemed an adequate response. All his attention had been on redeeming himself somehow—for last night had convinced him that Timma could not forgive his wanton destruction of their earlier relationship. But what he had seen in her eyes this moment past was a message altogether different. Unless he had misread it?

Anxiety gnawed at him. But the silence was becoming oppressive. Bracing himself, he started softly across the room towards the bed. She looked up, alarm in her face, and he halted. For want of anything else—for no more intelligent an idea occurred to him—he put a finger to his lips and indicated the sleeping companion. As if that could explain his silence!

Timothia looked across at Edith, and then back to Leo. He was moving again! Oh, heavens, what to do? What did he mean to say to her? In a state of unnerving trepidation, she watched him pick up a chair and approach to the opposite side of the bed from where Edith sat. The business of setting it down quietly and taking his seat took time, but insufficient for Timothia to compose herself. But something had to be said! Whispering, she found herself stating the obvious.

'You have not, then, gone off to the north wood?'

Leo seized the subject with alacrity, delivering, in a lowered tone, quite as inane a reply. 'I decided against it, on the score of the weather.'

'Yes,' murmured Timothia. 'It is quite a storm, is it not?'

'It has become worse through the day.'

To Timothia's dismay, this remark appeared to have exhausted the topic of the present climate. She could think of nothing else to say on the subject. Dreading another silence, she sought for some other, equally harmless. She found it.

'Has Bickley come for Faithful?'

'I told him to leave the horse resting here for a day or two, and I would send to him.'

'But is he fretting?'

'Bickley?' asked Leo unthinkingly.

'Faithful.'

'No, no. He has settled very well. He cannot return now to Fenny House until the weather improves.'

Which left Timothia with no further questions. She thought frantically. Oh, of course. Leo's excursion to the north wood.

'What—what business had you?'

Leo almost started, realising that he had been on the point of expressing a hope that the storm would not last out the night—almost as stupid as his reference to Timma's groom! Her question threw him completely. What was she talking of?

'Business?'

'In the north wood.'

'Ah, yes.' Eagerly, he embraced a topic that might prove fruitful. 'Beauleigh is putting up some fencing there, and he wished me to—'

'Fencing!' interrupted Timothia, all her managerial instincts aroused. 'But the north wood is a deer park!'

'Yes, I know, but—'

'Leo, you cannot allow him to fence it!' All else was forgotten. Embarrassment slipped away, ousted by an imperative need to make her cousin see sense. 'Deer must be allowed to roam free if they are to survive. If you fence them in, you will have every poacher for miles around stalking your lands, and killing off the fawns!'

'No, no, Timma, you mistake,' Leo uttered, slightly irritated. 'There is no question of fencing off the deer park. The thing is, there is a blasted oak.'

'Oh, I see.' She frowned. 'Is it merely withering, or do you have a blight?'

Leo shifted his shoulders in a helpless shrug. 'That is

just what we do not know. Beauleigh wished me to see for myself, for he is in favour of cutting it down.'

'If there is a blight, you must do so, of course,' agreed Timothia. 'And burn the trunk, too.' Then her eyes widened as a thought occurred. 'It is not the ancient oak that sits in a clearing by itself? I remember my uncle saying that the roots had spread so far that nothing else can grow around it.'

'Did he?' Leo could not remember his father ever having spoken to him on the subject. But then he had not shown the slightest interest in anything to do with the estate lands. He sighed. 'Timma, I have no idea which oak it may be. You know I am no hand at matters such as this.'

She caught his tone, and recognised in it the old despair at his own failings in administering the lands. The root cause of their estrangement shot back into her mind, and she remembered, all too clearly, why she had refused him. Embarrassment returned, and she stumbled over her words.

'I only meant—it was only that—if that was the—the tree, then there is hope that it may be only withering,' she said, finishing in something of a rush. 'Close fencing would probably answer.'

Leo said nothing for a moment. If his interest in the blasted oak in his north wood had before been tepid, it was now utterly defunct. Nothing could have been more unfortunate than to remind Timma of what had prompted him to offer for her. Especially, he abruptly realised, since it had no longer the same importance. Not that her value in that area was any the less. On the contrary, she had just proved how very much more able she was than he to make judgements upon such matters. Only he no longer cared for that! Would Timma believe him?

'Timma—'

She cut across him, low-voiced and tense. 'That note, Leo.'

The devil! Must she bring that up? His chest hollowed out. 'It does not matter.'

Her gaze came up to his. 'Does it not?'

The wistful note pierced him. He leaned forward. 'Timma, I never meant—it was outrageous of me to…' He petered out, unable to continue against the expression in her face.

'Then it did happen,' she said in a horrified whisper, a tremor in her lips. 'It was not a dream!'

Appalled, Leo watched her throw her hands over her face. What could he say? How to ease her embarrassment when he felt it as acutely as she?

'The things I said!'

He heard it only muffled through her fingers, and wished fervently that he might reach out and quiet them. 'Forget it, pray! I assure you I do not regard it—can hardly recall—'

He broke off, for a grunt from the other side of the bed informed him that the dragon Hawnby was stirring. Leo watched her yawn herself awake, unable to decide whether he was glad or sorry. For Timma's sake, since he had proved himself to have little self-control when she was so distressingly vulnerable, he supposed he must welcome the necessary curb.

Timothia had no such doubts. Relief flooded her, for there must be an end to this disastrous tête-à-tête! She withdrew her hands from her face, and turned gratefully to her companion. 'I believe you have slept longer than I did, Edith. Look, Leo is here.'

The old governess directed a stare across the bed, and grunted. 'I see him.' She heaved herself up from the chair, and began waddling round the bed. 'I dare say you will like to be private together.'

Two voices struck in unison before she could reach the door.

'Mrs Hawnby, no!'

'Edith, stop!'

The companion halted, turning to look at them in surprise. Timothia felt herself go hot, and she could not look at Leo. She had called out from panic at the thought of being alone with him. The reason why he had done so became obvious a second later—and none too welcome.

'Mrs Hawnby,' he uttered urgently, rising from his chair, 'you must not leave the room, if you please. It is imperative that Timma is not left unchaperoned while I am here.'

Timothia was convinced that a flush was staining her cheeks. He could not have made her more conscious if he had spoken outright of last night's appalling occurrence. Heaven help her, but she could have no lingering hope that it had been a dream. He had as good as admitted the whole!

Her companion moved back into the room, and directed her all-seeing eye at Leo. 'It has never seemed to trouble you before.'

Leo's cheek darkened, and he crossed to the window, avoiding the woman's formidable gaze. 'The case was different then. In my house, Timma is more vulnerable.'

To his dismay, the dragon chose to take this up. 'More vulnerable to what, Mr Wetheral?'

Heavens, let him not say it! Timothia sought hastily for some other explanation—and found it. 'Gossip, Edith. Leo is right. People are already talking.'

Leo's eyes turned swiftly towards her. 'You have heard that too?'

'Susan told me.'

'I had it from the Preseley chit.'

It was like a douche of cold water. Where else would he have heard it? Timothia looked away to hide the instant distress. She had almost forgotten! Now she saw why he wanted to dismiss last night as being of no account. And Jenny must have found the gossip most inconvenient. She could not wish to have Leo compromised by Timothia's presence in his house, when she wanted him for herself.

Edith's matter-of-fact tones intruded on her thoughts. 'Won't make a particle of difference whether I'm here or not. People are bound to talk. They always do. As long as you are inhabiting the same house, nothing will serve to stop tongues wagging.'

'Then we must not inhabit the same house!' Leo said, snapping uncontrollably. He could not have Timma compromised, whatever it took!

'Timothia can scarce remove,' Mrs Hawnby pointed out.

'I can—in a day or so at least.' And she would, for it was evident that Leo did not want a repetition of her ill-fated drug-induced dreams, whatever she might wish!

'You know very well what Dr Preseley said, this very morning,' Edith reminded her.

'What did he say?' demanded Leo. 'He told me only that the ankle was healing as it should, and that he had splinted it with a bandage.'

It occurred to him all at once that he had not even enquired after Timma's state. Coming to the bed, he tried to remedy this lapse, but in his dispersed state of mind succeeded only in firing questions without giving her time to answer them.

'I have not asked you—is the ankle still paining you? Are you feeling more the thing today? You don't look as if you slept at all well. Devil take it, there are rings under your eyes, Timma! What more did Preseley tell you? Have you cracked the bone? He did not say. I wanted to ask, but you were sleeping when I came in, and—'

'Mr Wetheral!'

He stopped in mid-stride, his glance flying to the dragon's face, and then back to Timothia. A faint glimpse of her provocative smile was playing about her lips. He sighed out his breath, and threw up his hands.

'I beg your pardon!'

Timothia let out a tiny laugh. Her heart was heavy, but she could still find Leo's tempestuous outburst endearing. 'Never mind it. I am better. The pain is much less, and Preseley does not believe that I have cracked any bones. The splinting is only precautionary.'

'Thank the Lord for that! But you cannot possibly remove. Surely Preseley cannot have given you permission to walk on it?'

It was Edith Hawnby who answered. 'By no means. He is of the opinion that she should recuperate here, since there is no room to move at Fenny House.'

'Yes, but that does not mean—' began Timothia.

'Don't even say it!' Leo threw at her angrily. 'You will stay here for as long as it takes. If need be, I will myself go and live in Fenny House!'

Timothia was obliged to laugh. 'I wish I might see you!' She saw the grin appear in his face, and felt her constraint lessen. 'But you need not carry on in this autocratic fashion. I can be just as stubborn as you. If there is to be any question of your removing from your own house, merely because of a pack of gossip-hungry vultures, then you may take it that I will have myself carried out of here the very moment that your back is turned.' She saw him glance frowningly at her companion, and added quickly, 'Don't look to Edith to support you! You must know perfectly well that nothing she can say would stop me, once I made up my mind to it.'

Leo was all too aware of it. Why in the world he wanted to saddle himself with so pigheaded a female, he could not think! Well, so be it. If she did become compromised through her own folly, then she would discover that he could be as adamant as she. If need be, he would force her to the altar! After—well, that could take care of itself. He had rather not think about that just at this moment.

'Very well,' he said evenly, meeting the bright rebellion of his cousin's gaze with steely determination. 'Let it be as you wish. But from this moment I do not set foot in this room as long as you are in the house.'

The night had been filled with unquiet dreams. Not, to Timothia's relief, the stuff of drug-induced nightmare. Thankfully, she could not remember the substance. But she knew that a certain pretty redhead had featured strongly, and she thought there had been a laughing chase on horseback through the confines of Leo's north wood. For the rest, there were snippets of motion, and the suspicion of some heat-laden tangle with a strong-limbed torso of unknown origin.

At least Timothia was loath to guess at its identity, and could only be grateful for the merciful blanket of forgetfulness. It had been a long day besides, and she did not wish to remember that either. Knowing that Leo was in the house—and determined not to present himself in her bedchamber—had prevented her from thinking of anything else. She had lain in bed, staring dully at the grey drizzle that continued long after the lashing rain had died away.

Edith, with a belated recognition of her duty, had seen to it that either herself or Polly had remained in the room at all times. A development that Timothia had found acutely restrictive. Not that she would have done anything other than lie there had she been alone. But the continued presence of another person had seemed to set a barrier even upon her thoughts. She had sunk into a slough of despondency that had followed her into sleep.

This morning, however, she felt the curb more on her energies than on her thoughts. Her physical condition had improved with the enforced rest. The ankle no longer ached as incessantly, starting up only with motion. The bruising at her right side had subsided considerably, with but a twinge or two if she made an incautious move. Timothia began to fret at the necessity of remaining abed, and wondered if Dr Preseley might sanction some exercise.

While she waited perforce for his dictum, once having been readied for the day, Timothia called for more pillows so that she might sit more upright, and obliged Polly to bunch two under her knee to give her further support than the bolster provided. This so much improved her comfort that she began to wish for something to do.

'A book?' suggested Edith. 'Would you wish me to hunt through Mr Wetheral's library? No doubt your aunt will have left some suitable volumes.'

Timothia approved this plan, and could not but be gratified when Edith returned some time later, armed with a stack of reading matter which, she said, had been picked out for her by her cousin.

'Leo chose them?' she asked, looking over the titles of the leather-bound volumes. Warmth invaded her breast as she took them in. How well Leo knew her tastes! There were her favourite poets, and a copy of *Tristram Shandy* to laugh over. Oh, and here was a Smollett that she had not read. She smiled to see that Leo had not omitted to include two thick tomes that he supposed must appeal to her—one on agriculture, another on the farming of pigs! She turned over the last book, a slim little folio of rather dilapidated appearance. It was evidently very old.

*The History of the Tales of the Fairies,* she read. Oh, Leo! She opened the book, and discovered a brief note inside. 'A touch of the will-o'-the-wisp.' It was signed only with the letter 'L'.

Tears started to Timothia's eyes. That he had remembered was infinitely precious. Had he sought for it, recalling that Madame D'Aulnoy's tales were on his library shelves? Or had he come across it by chance, and sent it to her for a jest? However it might have been, Timothia was touched by his thoughtfulness. He was once again the Leo of her childhood. Oh, if he could but have remained so! She would not then be in danger of losing him to a hateful wretch who would only use him to further her own ends.

Sighing, she placed the rest of the books upon her bedside table, and spent a pleasant hour browsing through those long- forgotten stories that had enchanted her early years.

She was roused from her absorption by the arrival of a note from Susan, bearing ill tidings. To her consternation, she learned that her friend had been soaked to the skin on her return journey, the downpour to which Timothia had woken yesterday afternoon having begun immediately after Susan had set down Jenny Preseley at her home. Not surprisingly, Susan had succumbed to a chill. 'But, though I am subject to fits of sneezing and Mama has confined me to my bed, be assured, dearest Timma, that it is nothing but a cold in the head.'

Her friend was the more troubled by her inability now

to pursue her vigilant aim to keep Jenny Preseley away from Leo. In a burst of self-sacrifice, Susan offered to stifle her own hopes and send Valentine to Wiggin to steal the girl away. 'For you will not deny that Valentine is even more eligible than Leo, and must inevitably attract her interest.'

Timothia was both touched and exasperated by this effusion, and immediately rang for paper and ink that she might send back an instant reply by the footman who was waiting. She had just completed a brief note imploring her friend to stop being stupid and concentrate on getting well, when Jenny Preseley herself was ushered into the room.

'Miss Dulverton, I am come in place of my father, who is trusting me to take back a report of your ankle. Oh, do not fear me! I am pledged not to touch his bandaging, but only to enquire how you feel, and to look where the bruising has reached.'

Submitting, with inward reluctance, to the girl's admittedly gentle examination, Timothia could yet not prevent herself from awaiting her verdict with interest.

'It is just as Papa told me to expect,' she said at last, in a satisfied tone. 'There is a bruise all the way down to your toes, and it looks to be creeping up your leg above the bandage.'

'Is that good?' demanded Edith blankly.

'Excellent. The more it bruises, the better it is healing.' Replacing the covers, Jenny came around to the side of the bed and smiled at Timothia. 'And now I am obliged to say what I had rather not. Dear Miss Dulverton, I am sorry to tell you that I will not be able to visit you again for some few days.'

Suppressing an inclination to cheer, Timothia spoke

with an assumed expression of regret. 'Oh, why not, Jenny?'

'Mrs Baguley has invited me to go with her to a house party at Great Gidding, and Papa will not have me refuse on account of her kindness to me.'

Timothia was startled—and delighted. 'At the Marquis of Rockingham's home? I should hope you would not refuse!'

A sentiment which appeared to relieve Jenny's mind. 'I had hoped to see you once more, but since tomorrow is Sunday we are to travel today, for everyone is supposed to be there for an excursion early on Monday morning.'

Timothia was able to say all that was suitable with heartfelt enthusiasm. But she was less satisfied later, when she received from Edith the news that Leo was also going away. A horrid suspicion leapt into her mind.

'Not to Rockingham's seat?'

'No use asking me,' said her companion. 'All I know is that he and that fool, Lord Pentre, are to go together. Some house party or other, I understand.'

# Chapter Ten

Timothia's bosom heaved. 'Leo has forgotten, then, that I said I would remove the moment he left the house!'

She had supposed that she had run the gamut of emotions concerning Leo, but she found she was mistaken. She was seething. She had not thought that he would really leave. But then, it had not occurred to her that there would be an invitation to some horrid house party where red-headed hussies would be scheming to get him to themselves. Besides, it was one thing to quit the house in order to spare his cousin from unpleasant talk. It was quite another to go off pleasuring when his invalid guest was obliged to keep her bed!

When a note from Leo was brought to her, she regarded it for some time in a silence laced with tension, ready to erupt. She did not open it until she had settled in her mind the letter that she would immediately despatch to Bickley and Padstow, bidding them come instantly to fetch her back to Fenny House.

Her cousin appeared to have read her mind.

'Pray don't take an affront into your head,' Leo began in his note. 'I had decided not to attend this shooting party at Waresley. But in the circumstances I think it better to go. Valentine accompanies me. Timma, do not attempt to leave my house in my absence, on pain of dire consequences!'

The burgeoning fury dropped out. Elation took its place. Waresley? But that was in entirely the opposite direction to Great Gidding! Then he would not be in company with Jenny Preseley. And it was a shooting party. There would be no females there at all. So much for the Preseley chit and her abominable scheming!

Only one circumstance remained to cloud her triumph. She did not know how long Leo might be away. She did not want to find herself anticipating his return. Better to fix her mind upon a definite period—then one could not be disappointed.

Timothia caught herself up. What in the world did she mean by such a calculation? As long as Jenny Preseley was not in question, what did it matter to her how lengthy a stay Leo made at Waresley? It was not as if she would miss him.

A disquieting feeling of emptiness accompanied this thought. Then another notion hit her—deepening the sensation into a distinct discontent. Waresley was but a few miles from St Neots. Leo was bound to take the opportunity to visit his sister Barbara at their uncle Herbert's house. He might be detained there for several days! Unless he planned to stay with the uncle throughout? No, he would not do that, for they would be up at dawn for their sport from Waresley.

Try as she would to overcome them through the next two days, Timothia could not shake off the feelings associated with the thought of Leo's being absent for any length of time. They were all too familiar. When she at length identified them, she discovered that she was experiencing a similar loneliness to that which had attacked her after that last encounter on the evening of the party at Somersham. A loneliness that had led directly to her accident.

It persisted this time, despite the alternating presence of Edith and Mrs Salcombe. Despite endless games of backgammon and cribbage; through two volumes of *Humphrey Clinker*; without cease during a whole morning of playing solitaire with an aged pack of cards unearthed from a trunk by the housekeeper; and with no diminution of its power for hour upon dreary hour of staring out of the window at the intransigent face of summer, which had remained grey and cloudy. Nothing served to lessen the sensation. Until Timothia was ready to scream!

She had not felt remotely this bad during the endless days of boredom during her year of mourning. Had she thought of Leo from one day to the next? No, she had not. Had it occurred to her to wonder from moment to moment what he might be doing, or how he might look? Most certainly it had not. Then how had all this started? What had changed that she must needs be pining for a sight of him?

Pining? Was it so indeed? This was so alien an idea that Timothia was obliged to re-examine her entire relationship with her cousin—from the point of his bizarre proposal. But when she tried to recall how she had felt when he had offered for her she could not do it. Were he to renew his offer now, what would she reply? The question set her pulses racing. But Leo had no intention of renewing his offer—had he? She could not entirely rule out the possibility that he might wish to wed elsewhere. Although she could be pardoned for thinking he might still have marriage to his cousin in mind after what he had said that night of her hallucinatory dreams.

But then, would he not have offered again—had he

meant to?—when he heard that there were rumours abroad? It would have been a perfect opportunity. But would she have accepted him on those terms? Timothia did not know.

She was still in an undecided frame of mind by Wednesday, the fourth day of Leo's absence, when Dr Preseley finally pronounced the swelling on her ankle to have reduced sufficiently for her to risk putting her foot to the floor.

'Only for very limited excursions, if you please,' he warned. 'And do not attempt to walk without help.'

Timothia bit her lip, and then grimaced. 'You will scold me, I fear, Dr Preseley, but I am obliged to confess that I have already tried walking.'

The doctor eyed her somewhat narrowly. 'Indeed? And how far have you progressed?'

She was obliged to smile. 'Not far. In fact, it is quite impossible for me to go more than a step or two without leaning heavily upon Polly's arm.'

'Ah, so your companion does not know your guilty secret,' said Preseley.

Timothia saw him look across at Edith, and endured her old governess's eye with rueful humour. 'I did not tell her, but I shall confess myself astonished if she does not know.'

Edith snorted. 'Do you take me for a fool?' She turned to the doctor. 'I thought the only way for her to realise that she should not be doing it was by letting her try. If I had thought she was overtaxing herself, I would have stopped it.'

'There now, you see, Dr Preseley,' laughed Timothia. 'I am well guarded.'

'I could wish you had been tied to the bed!' returned the doctor, somewhat exasperated. 'We can only trust that you have not seriously put your recovery back. I ought to insist upon your remaining in bed another day or so, but—'

'Oh, no!' groaned Timothia. 'No, I beg of you, pray don't. Why, I have been here for almost a week. I will be good, I promise. I am heartily sick of lying in bed. And I hardly feel the ankle at all now.'

'That, my dear Miss Dulverton, is because you have been resting it. You will feel it very rapidly, I assure you, if you begin to use it to excess.'

Timothia subsided, sighing deeply. 'Forgive me. I am the wretchedest patient, am I not?'

Relenting, the doctor smiled at her. 'Yes, you were ever a rebellious spirit, as I recall. Never mind. I will find means to ensure your obedience.'

'You behold me utterly penitent,' said Timothia, that provocative lilt on her lips. 'Tell me what I must do. But do not order me to stay in bed!'

Preseley laughed, and complied. 'You may get up, then. But only walk for a few minutes at a time, perhaps twice or thrice a day at first. Do not stand about on the leg, and when you are sitting keep it raised. High, if you please. Not upon a footstool, but upon a chair. And no stairs.'

'Very well,' agreed Timothia. 'And when may I walk for longer periods?'

'When you are able to do so without any other support than a walking-stick. You do not want to be reduced to using a crutch for several weeks, which is only too likely, if you do not abide by my instructions.'

Timothia was so delighted to be allowed out of her bed that she was ready to promise anything. She could hardly wait for the departure of the doctor before instructing Polly to find her something to wear. But it was Edith who selected a plain muslin gown of apple-green, made high to the throat, with half-sleeves, the raised waistline that had become established in fashion over the last eighteen months, and a quantity of diaphanous petticoats in which she might comfortably move, over a more modestly opaque underdress.

It took some time for Timothia to be arrayed in these garments, for she found that she had perforce to do as the doctor ordered for she could not stand without help. She was obliged to be dressed while sitting on the end of the bed, and to lean on Edith as she stood so that Polly could quickly arrange her petticoats about her. She then had to sit down again, while Edith combed and dressed her hair, which felt oddly when it was confined once more in her habitual single plait, after being worn loose for so long.

Polly put a flat-heeled slipper on her good foot, and observed that the other, still in its splinted bandage, must remain bare. Timothia accepted this, and bade her run to open the door.

'I am ready now, Edith.'

But no sooner had the maid started to pull the door open than it was seized from her hand and thrust fully open from the other side. Indeed so forcefully that it banged against the wall, startling Timothia into looking up. Her cousin Leo was standing in the aperture.

'So!' he said, a wealth of meaning in the one word.

'Leo!' gasped Timothia faintly.

He strolled forward, a steely glint in his eye. 'Yes, it is I. And not a moment too soon, I apprehend.'

Timothia stared at him, the blood pounding so forcefully in her bosom that she was unable to utter a sound. Where had he sprung from? No one had told her he had returned!

'It is my understanding,' he continued, in a tone that warned her that he was about to become autocratic and inflexible, 'that you are behaving in a manner that is both pigheaded and stupid. I have therefore given my word to Preseley that I will personally ensure that you do nothing further to retard your progress. Do I make myself clear?'

The initial shock receded, to be succeeded by amazement. If the past three days of inertia had done nothing else, they had, by improving her physical condition, strengthened her spirit. She retaliated without hesitation.

'I beg your pardon? Do you imagine you have the right to come marching into my bedchamber—without, I may add, so much as a by-your-leave—and lay down the law to me in this intolerably high-handed fashion?'

'Yes!' he said coolly.

Then, before she had an inkling of what he meant to do, he bent down, and swept her up bodily as if she weighed no more than a feather.

'What in the world are you doing?' she demanded, hastily flinging one arm up about his neck for support.

Leo grinned suddenly. 'Carrying you to the saloon.'

He was moving on the words, and Timothia immediately found herself at a disadvantage, for his proximity had the most unsettling effect upon her pulse and breathing. Quite dreadful palpitations hammered through her veins, and it was as much as she could do to prevent his becoming aware of this unsettling state of affairs.

'P-put me d-down!' she cried plaintively.

'By no means,' he responded, turning sideways so that he could get her through the door.

'Leo, for pity's s-sake! I can very well walk. Indeed, Dr Preseley t-told me to do so.'

'For a very few minutes only. Don't fret! I have the whole programme from his own lips, and I intend to see that you stick to it—to the letter.'

'Very well,' she protested desperately, 'but I do not need to be carried!'

But Leo paid no attention, and she was obliged to endure the most uncomfortable sensations for the length of the gallery, and into the informal upstairs yellow saloon. It was so called not from its furnishings—which had in fact been re-covered a number of times, as Timothia knew, and were at this present time done out in strawberry with simple white walls—but from having ever been the sunniest room in the house. There was today scant evidence of this, bar a brightening feel behind the clouds as the mist was beginning to lift.

Timothia was all but breathless when she was at length deposited—with extreme gentleness, as she was quick to note—in an easy chair placed close to the window.

'There,' said Leo, removing his arms from under her. 'And the leg must be up. Valentine! That stool, if you please. No, the large one.'

Bewildered, Timothia took in not only that Valentine was in the room, but her friend also. 'Susan! You are better! Oh, Valentine, thank you,' she added as he brought a stool of chair height. 'Leo, I can very well manage—'

But her cousin paid no heed, lifting her leg without ceremony—much to her embarrassment—and placing a cushion hastily brought by Susan upon the stool before he lowered her ankle to rest upon it.

'But why did no one tell me that you were all here?' Timothia was demanding, when her eye fell upon a fourth occupant of the saloon. Her heart dropped.

'Jenny!' She paused, fought to control her features, and forced a smile. 'You are back already. How do you do?'

'Never mind me!' exclaimed the other girl, clapping her hands. 'How wonderful it is to see you emerge from your sickroom! We are all here expressly for the purpose, you know, by way of celebration, for Mr Wetheral would not let any of us make our presence known.'

Timothia frowned up at Leo, who was still standing over her, looking down at the leg. 'You need not remain there like a gaoler! I am scarce likely to run away.'

Leo laughed and shifted to the window. 'I would not put it past you.'

'For shame, Leo!' protested Susan, leaping to her friend's defence, a slight crack in her voice the only evidence remaining of her recent head cold. 'Poor Timma can barely move. It is horrid of you to tease her so.'

'She may count herself fortunate if teasing is all,' declared Leo trenchantly, 'for I assure you I intend to become a deal more "horrid" if she does not do as she is told!'

'If I had known you would come home only to be tyrannical, Leo,' said Timothia crossly, 'I should have taken myself off while you were away.'

Valentine burst out laughing. 'We have only to hear from Leo that he would have fetched you back again without delay, and the illusion of being in the schoolroom will be complete!'

He was leaning on the curved backrest of a chair. It stood opposite the sofa on which Jenny Preseley was placed alongside Susan. The whole seating arrangement created a cosy bower that took advantage of the wide window while in no way diminishing the large proportions of the room.

'It is very true,' Susan remarked to the other girl. 'You must know that these two were forever quarrelling when we were all children together.'

'I am not quarrelling with Timma,' Leo pointed out. 'She is quarrelling with me.'

'Is there a difference?' asked Jenny, laughing.

Brought up short by the girl's question, Timothia curbed her tongue on a fresh retort. If Leo chose to behave like a child, that was his affair. She did not wish to expose herself further before Jenny Preseley! This put her in mind of her surprise at the girl's presence.

'How is it that you are back so soon? I had imagined you would be at Great Gidding for at least a week.'

'Oh, the party broke up early,' said Jenny airily, 'for the weather was so bad that no one could go out of doors. They had to cancel a picnic, and all the rides they had planned.'

'Don't tell me!' put in Valentine in a disgruntled tone. 'We had to give up all attempts to go out with our guns for the whole of the forest was waterlogged.'

'Oh, what a disappointment for you!' cried Susan.

'Yes, but at least Leo was able to see Babs, so it was not quite wasted.'

Timothia looked at Leo. 'I had thought you might go to Uncle Herbert. How is Barbara?'

'Very importunate about her come-out,' said her cousin.

The moment the words were out of his mouth, he regretted them, for Timma flushed, turning instantly away. Devil take it! To remind her of that was the last thing he had meant to do. Now she would retreat from him again. And he had been succeeding so well! Treating Timma in the old way had done much to ease the tension between them. Useless to hope that she would not hold that clause of his offer against him. He could not think, now, why he had introduced the problem of Babs at all. Lord, but he had been clumsy! Small wonder Timma had rejected him.

He felt unequal to continue this farce. He looked at his friend. 'Valentine, shall we go?'

Timothia's heart jumped. 'Go?' she uttered involuntarily, her eyes flying to his face. 'But you have only just come!'

'Be back in time for dinner,' Valentine said, moving out of the circle towards the saloon door. 'Must take advantage while the rain holds off.'

Leo had already moved to join him, for he could not bear the reproach in Timma's eyes. Well might she complain! But he was pledged to show himself abroad, in the expectation of lessening loose talk. He had already set it about that he was hardly ever in the house while Timma stayed there. Now he was going to make it his business to call upon various neighbours to allay suspicion and encourage some at least to counter the rumours. If he had been seen so much abroad, no one would suppose him to be dancing attendance upon his cousin. The logical thinking beyond this was that they could not be lovers. At least, so he hoped.

'We have one or two calls to make in the neighbourhood,' he said shortly.

A moment later, the two gentlemen had said their farewells and were gone. Timothia's intense disappointment found expression in a wash of invective.

'But how extremely flattering! I am but just out of bed, and the wretch storms into my chamber, drags me forth in the most high-handed fashion, and delivers me here without even bothering to consult my wishes. And, not content with throwing me down as if I were a sack of potatoes, he walks out of the place two seconds later— just as if I had nothing more to wish for! Of all the autocratic, uncivil, selfish, abominable—'

'Oh, pray don't, Miss Dulverton!' pleaded Jenny. 'Don't speak of him so hardly. I know you do not mean it.'

'Of course I mean it! And I shall speak of him just as I choose, the hateful—'

'Timma, do stop!' Susan rose from her chair and crossed to the window, looking out. 'I wonder if I may see them depart from here?' She turned her head to her friend. 'I know just how you feel, dearest, but carping will not mend matters.'

Timothia subsided, but her eyes smouldered still. To think that she had wasted so much of her time in thinking about him! She had supposed herself to be missing him. Now she saw how little worthy he was of such attention. How could he treat her so shabbily? Well, she knew after all how she would answer him, if he dared to renew his offer. The Preseley chit was welcome to him!

Lost in her own discomfiting frustration, Timothia forgot discretion and spoke without thinking.

'I am done with him, Jenny. You may have him with my goodwill!'

There was a gasp from Susan at the window, and an expression of shocked dismay spread over the features of Jenny Preseley. Realising what she had said, Timothia threw a hand to her brow, and cursed, borrowing from Leo's store.

'The devil! I did not mean to say that. Pray do not regard it!'

But there did not appear to be any hope of the girl's being able to disregard it. Timothia saw her eyes cloud over, and a quiver at her lower lip. She was instantly struck by remorse. But who knew if the threatening tears were genuine? She felt movement, and saw that Susan had come to stand beside her chair. To her surprise, her friend did not immediately dash to Jenny's defence.

'Perhaps it is as well, Timma, that you said it,' she

uttered unexpectedly, placing a hand on Timothia's shoulder.

Looking round at her, Timothia saw that she had her gaze fixed upon Jenny Preseley's face. The other girl met the unusually hard look in Susan's eyes, but did not speak.

Timothia watched her swallow, press her lips tightly together, blink several times, and then clear her throat. It struck Timothia that she was making a valiant effort to hold back the tears. Was she innocent after all?

'I am—I am sorry you should think so badly of me,' she said, her voice a trifle husky. 'When I t-told you of my schemes, I never thought—'

'What schemes?' interrupted Susan, looking from one to the other.

'I did not betray your confidence, Jenny,' Timothia said. 'Susan knows nothing about it.'

Jenny drew an audible breath. 'But she believes me to be scheming, nevertheless.'

'Well, you are on the catch for a husband,' said Susan, a trifle huffily, moving to the other chair with a defiant swirl of her pink muslin petticoats, and sitting down.

'But not for a man who is clearly destined for someone else,' Jenny protested, a spurt of anger sounding in her voice. 'Why, what a creature you must think me!'

'Why should we suppose otherwise?' returned Susan, in an unusually catty way. 'You are in a string with Mrs Baguley, and my aunt Hurst has made it all too clear that your patroness considers all eligible males around these parts to be fair game. You have not been slow either to partake of Leo's company. Dare you deny it?'

'Yes, I do deny it,' answered Jenny, in a dignified manner that drew Timothia's reluctant admiration. 'Upon what occasion am I supposed to have done so?'

'You walked with him in the grounds on the very first day of Timma's accident,' Susan reminded her.

Jenny looked blank for a moment. Then her eyes went to Timothia. 'You surely do not think…?'

She faded out, and Timothia waited. She saw Susan offer to speak and held up a hand. 'No, Susan. Let Jenny have a fair hearing.' She was beginning to suspect that she had misjudged the girl. Either that, or Jenny was a very good actress. She was playing the innocent with conviction.

'Go on, Jenny.'

The girl's eyes reproached her. 'You do think it! How could you suppose I would try to steal him from you? Or even that I could, had I wanted to. Do you wish to know what happened that day?'

'Yes!' came from Susan, her tone belligerent.

'If you please,' said Timothia, more moderately.

'Having got me out of your chamber, Mr Wetheral told me he had done so only so that you might rest. He bid me amuse myself in the gardens, and went off to his library.' She hung her head. 'I am afraid I did not do as he asked—at least, not immediately.'

Timothia frowned. 'What do you mean?'

Jenny turned rueful eyes upon her. 'I crept back to your room, Miss Dulverton. Forgive me, but it seemed to me that you were utterly cast down as we left, and—you will hate me for saying this!—I had heard certain rumours…'

'Go on,' said Timothia again, a trifle grimly.

'Well, I wondered if perhaps your being obliged to stay in Mr Wetheral's house was causing you concern, and…'

'For pity's sake, Jenny, say what you wish to, and stop trying to be tactful!' uttered Timothia, exasperated.

'Tactful!' echoed Susan sceptically.

'Be quiet, Susan! Let the girl talk.'

Her friend subsided, and Timothia watched Jenny Preseley draw a determined breath. 'I guessed that your accident had aggravated some sort of quarrel. When I came in, I found you weeping, Miss Dulverton.'

'Heavens!' cried Timothia, caught by a sudden memory. 'Was it you who gave me that handkerchief?'

Jenny nodded. 'I did not stay. I could not feel that we were well enough acquainted for me to interfere. So I stole away again, and—most fortunately, as it chanced—went into the grounds as I had been bidden. There Mr Wetheral found me. I believe he came out for no other purpose than to make certain that I had not been up to disturb you.'

There was silence for a space. Then Susan spoke rather grudgingly. 'All very well, but why should you continue to come here, day after day? What motive had you?'

'I came here with a wish of helping Miss Dulverton, if I might. And,' she added with a sudden surge of anger, 'I beg you will not accuse me of setting my cap at your precious Lord Pentre!'

'How do you know he is my precious Lord Pentre?' demanded Susan furiously, leaping to her feet.

Jenny let out a short laugh. 'I am not blind, Miss Hurst. Anyone must suppose it who sees you making sheep's eyes at the man every time he comes within your vicinity.'

'How dare you?' screeched Susan.

The two of them would come to blows in a moment! Unable to intervene physically, Timothia was forced to use the most authoritative voice she could command, for Jenny had also risen to her feet, and the exchange was becoming ever more heated.

'Enough! Susan, be quiet! You too, Jenny! That will do, both of you!'

It was several moments before she succeeded in persuading the two young ladies to desist. But, at length, they both reseated themselves, glowering at each other in high dudgeon. Timothia was hard put to it to refrain from laughing. And Susan was a revelation! It struck her all at once that her friend's attitude might possibly spring more from a fear that she might lose Timma to Jenny Preseley than from any real concern for Valentine's safely remaining a bachelor.

'I think we must acquit Jenny of having any designs upon Valentine, Susan,' she said coolly. She held up a warning finger as both females started up as if they would speak. 'No, be silent! As for Leo—' She sighed. 'Jenny, I believe I owe you an apology.'

'How could you imagine that I would betray you, Miss Dulverton?' cried Jenny in a tone of real hurt. 'After I had given you my confidence!'

'I know.' Timothia smiled wryly. 'It was nothing you did. The truth is that my association with Leo has been reduced to such a shambles that I no longer know what either of us feels about the other—least of all myself!'

'But why should you—?'

'Because of my uncertainties, Jenny.' She was betrayed into a laugh. 'Your very confidence served to work upon those fears within me that were throwing me out of common sense. And my injuries did nothing to help!'

Jenny leapt up from her chair, and came quickly over to drop on her knees beside Timothia's chair. She seized her hands. 'I would have been set down even if I had tried to wean Mr Wetheral's affection away. Dear Miss Dulverton, he can talk of nothing but you!'

Timothia's pulses stirred, and her voice was not quite steady. 'Is that true?'

'I swear it! I know that he still wants to marry you, for he told me so when I warned him of the gossip that was circulating.'

She released Timothia's hands, and got up, moving to Susan. In a daze of elation, Timothia watched her making peace with her friend. She hardly heard what was said, for her mind was in ferment. Then Leo did mean to offer for her again! Oh, this time she would give him a different answer. All doubts were set at rest. They would be married, and she might live in this house with him, and help him—just as he had asked!—to manage his estates. And see now, Barbara was anxious for her come-out. It was all falling into place. There were no barriers any longer, for the very thought of what must occur to fulfil the rest of the bargain was enough to send warmth in shivers down her veins. Yes, Leo might have his heir!

Awaking from a light doze, Timothia opened her eyes to a bright blue sky, and a resurgence of the exultant blissful feeling that had filled her bosom these several days. She was relaxing on a chaise longue of cushioned wickerwork that had been placed for her under the spreading branches of an aged tree. There were rugs and cushions scattered about, upon which Susan and Jenny had earlier sat, squabbling over who should fetch Timothia's book.

Jenny had argued that she ought to do it, since Susan was kind enough to offer to carry her home in her carriage. Not to be outdone in self-sacrifice, Susan had insisted that she knew the volume in question and could more readily lay her hand upon it. Tiring of yet another pointless dispute between them, displacing the real cause of their dissension—for it had become a point of honour not to seem actually to quarrel—Timothia had urged Susan to fetch the book and requested Jenny instead to ask Polly to bring her a cup of coffee. She had been relieved to see them go at length. Not that she resented their petty wrangling. They might skirmish all they wished, except that it interfered with the dreamy contentment of her mood.

Everything had changed. Even the weather was smiling so that she was comfortable only in her simple blue muslin. She had been reunited briefly with Faithful, the day Bickley came over to fetch him home after the rains had ceased and the ground had dried. The stallion had greeted her with almost as great an air of scolding as had her groom, and then yielded as quickly to his fondness for his mistress.

Her ankle was healing just as it should, to Dr Preseley's satisfaction as well as her own. He had been very happy with her last Saturday when he'd visited, for the swelling was so much reduced that he'd had to change the bandage. He had insisted on renewing the splint as well, but Timothia hoped he might remove it when he came tomorrow. She was sure she no longer needed the additional support. She was able to walk quite far already—had Leo permitted it!

He reminded Timothia of a mother hen, fussing and fretting over the exact amount of time she might spend exercising the ankle. The moment he felt she was overtaxing herself, he would scoop her up and carry her to whatever destination she required. Even when he allowed her to use her own feet, his arm was firmly about her waist, supporting her from the right side.

Timothia had suggested once or twice, with a deliberately provocative allure in her smile that she knew affected him not a little, that she might with advantage make use of a crutch.

'I will have one made for you, if you wish for it,' he had said, glinting down at her as he paused in the corridor. His voice had lowered, and his hand at her waist had moved slightly in a tempting caress. 'Do you wish for it?'

Timothia had been obliged to draw in her breath rather sharply, for even that slight pressure had shot added warmth through her, heating blood already inflamed.

'You know I don't,' she had answered, adding with mock venom, 'Wretch!'

Leo had laughed, and they had gone on their way. It had been but one of several increasingly daring encounters between them—ever since the night of her emergence from her bed, when all four friends, with the addition of Edith and Jenny, had dined in an atmosphere of rising gaiety.

Timothia had been acutely conscious of Leo throughout the meal. He had caught her watching him, and from that moment Timothia knew that he had been unable to keep his eyes off her. Try as she would to avoid his glance, she had found herself mesmerised, returning again and again to meet the hot need she had sensed in him. Images had chased one another through her mind, and she knew she had dreamed them often and often in the nights of her incarceration.

He had bid her goodnight in the curtest of tones, but Timothia, aware of the cause, had been elated rather than hurt. She'd lain in bed, drenched with yearning, willing Leo to throw off all notions of chivalry that could keep him from coming to her. He had not come, and Timothia had hated him for it!

But in the succeeding days there had been such licence to proximity provided by the excuse of her disability that she'd found herself unable—and unwilling!—to make any further effort at concealment. She knew it to be useless. Leo was, she knew well, as certain of the intensity of her reaction to his maleness as she was of his desire for her. Why should she hide it? She wanted him, and being wanted by him had sent her into a species of delirium.

Or so she thought of it. She was in a state of constant exhilaration. Her ankle did not trouble her, for even when she walked she felt as if she were several feet above the ground! She was every day in the expectation of Leo renewing his offer, and she had every intention of accepting him. She could only suppose that his hesitation sprang from a chivalrous determination—wholly misplaced!— not to put her at a disadvantage. Was he waiting for her to be fully recovered?

She glanced towards the mansion. Leo's library window fronted the lawn, but it was too far away for her to see into the room. Besides, he must be at his desk, working. A sudden flush of warmth swept through her. Oh, but she wanted to see him! It had been at least two hours since luncheon. He had helped her to walk out here, and then left her, saying that he had letters to write.

The image of him sitting at the large table in the library came to her—head bent, that rakish look of his unruly hair throwing his neatness out. She pictured his lean countenance, the bright blue of his eyes, and the mulish set of his stubborn jaw as he fought with her for supremacy. An abrupt weakness took Timothia unawares. It was as if her whole being melted.

Thought left her. She rose up from the chaise longue, a trifle of unsteadiness in her legs. Reaching for the cane that had been provided for her use, she made purposefully for the house, limping with automatic care. She was driven by a deep-seated need that took no account of reason.

It took her some time to cross the lawn, and she was obliged to halt for some minutes when she reached the house, holding on to the wall. She could feel the pressure on her ankle, and knew that she ought not to be walking so far. But she must go on! She could slip in a side door and so save herself some of the distance.

Leo had left the desk by the time she reached the library. She halted in the doorway, her searching glance sweeping the room, while a staccato beat of anticipation pounded in her heart. Then she saw him at the window.

A small sound alerted him, and he turned. 'The devil, Timma, you startled me!' He frowned, staring at her pale face. He had just thrown the window up, and had been looking out to find her, for she had not been in the chaise longue when he had come from his desk to check if she was all right. She must have walked all the way from the garden!

'What the deuce are you doing?' he demanded, coming quickly forward. Something in her expression halted him. In a very different tone, he asked, 'Timma, what is it?'

Timothia looked away, and back again. The sight of him filled her with the oddest sensation. She felt light-headed, and her breath caught in her throat. The strangest thought floated through her mind. Leo—through all her life, and infinitely dear.

'Nothing,' she said, smiling at him. 'Nothing is the matter.'

He gave a short laugh. 'Your behaviour is very peculiar.'

'Is it?' She heaved a deep breath, as if she was so overcharged that she could no longer contain it. Not knowing what to say or do, she cast around the room for inspiration. The desk! There must be something there to hand. She limped towards it.

Leo started forward again. He reached her, but Timothia warded him off. 'I can manage.'

He dropped back, watching her. Puzzled, he saw her look over the piles of papers. Without thinking, he excused the mess, moving to the other side of the desk. 'I cannot keep it neat the way you used to do at Dulverton.'

Timothia looked across at him, and smiled again. 'Perhaps I can help. You should not feel reticent about asking me.'

Leo shook his head in a gesture of impatience. 'I don't wish you to be spending your time slaving away for me.'

'That is not what you said before.'

'Things are different now.'

Oh, so very different! The knowledge of what he meant flurried her senses. She could no longer look at him as openly. Unseeingly, she lifted a stack of papers with her free hand, and let them fall so that they slid awry and out of place. A tiny laugh escaped her as she saw what she had done.

'Your way, Leo.'

He frowned across at her. 'Timma, I am at a loss to understand you. You are acting very strangely. Are you sure you are yourself?'

She did not dare to look at him. She thought she would burst, for the pressure in her breast was almost unendurable. She wanted to laugh aloud! Dance round the room! He would think her mad. She felt him watching her, and gave in to the compulsion to look up.

Leo met her eyes. Why she was acting thus he could not tell. It was endearing, and yet it made him wary. Was she up to some trick? Then he saw her lips part and the tip of her tongue just moistened them. There was nothing deliberate about it, but it was uncannily erotic. His pulse-rate shot up.

The blue gaze grew hot, and heat sprang up in Timothia's veins. It seemed an age that they stood there thus, eyes on eyes, throbbingly still, across the intervening expanse of the desk. She knew not if she moved. Nor whether Leo did. She knew not what became of her supporting cane. She knew only that they were there, standing face to face, only inches apart.

And then he reached for her. She felt his lips, and her own trembled under them. She could not breathe, yet his arms about her—so close about her—were not tight. They were gently supportive. His body barely brushed against hers, but the touch of him burned. A tiny sound escaped her—of longing.

Leo flamed. He drew her into him, and his mouth pressed demandingly into hers. She jellied, sagging against him, and he lost all power to think.

Timothia was liquid heat. Her will was no longer her own. What he asked of her, she gave him. Her lips were his, her curves and hollows open to his touch. She would die in his arms if he desired it.

His mouth dragged at her own, and she groaned in an agony of passion. A tempest raged in her bones, twisting and tumbling. She moaned softly, and sank down, quivering in every limb, as he pulled away.

Leo's hands were under her shoulders, supporting her, and she opened her eyes to find herself seated in the chair at his desk, half fainting, the room dizzying round her. She looked into Leo's face, bent down towards her, and saw the same ravaged look that mirrored her own devastation.

'Deuce take it, Timma,' he uttered hoarsely, 'you have drained me! I have never wanted anyone so much in my life—and yet I could not do it!'

Timothia was unable to speak. She took one of his hands as he slipped them from her shoulders—and held it to her cheek. Then she let it go. Leo was frowning as he drew the hand away. He took a few paces from her, and she saw, with tenderness, that he was still catching his breath. It gave her a glow of pleasure to know that her love was this powerful.

It took some moments for the explosive results of that passionate caress to begin to subside. When Leo turned again to look at her, Timothia felt abruptly shy. A novel, and extraordinary, experience. She did not know what to say to him. It was all too new, too bewildering. The real-isation had crept up on her so suddenly that it had all but taken her breath away. And then to be kissed at the moment of discovery! How could she not have given herself wholly into the embrace of the man who had ever had her heart? She must have loved him for years—and not known it.

And then all at once he began to laugh. 'Oh, Timma! You cannot now dare tell me that you want a platonic relationship.'

A riffle of unease shadowed the blanketing happiness in which she was enwrapped. Need he say that? What had it to do with their present circumstances? She smiled a little, uncertain why he laughed.

'You must know I do not.'

He grew serious again, and Timothia was conscious of relief as he came back to the desk. She waited, a shade of expectation—apprehension?—holding her breath sus-pended. Why was he frowning down at her?

'I was not going to say this until you had left the house. But then I had no intention even of kissing you until I might do so with no possibility of your being hurt by gossip.'

'I see,' she said carefully, eyeing him with a brow that was slowly clouding over. Her heart grew wary, and the radiance dimmed a little more.

Leo was regarding her with—yes, a speculative look in

his eye. Why? It should all have been so simple now. She could not have been mistaken—could she?

'Timma, surely there can be no further barrier to our marriage?'

'Barrier?' She could barely say it.

His voice was eager. 'You cannot deny your attraction for me, can you?'

The veriest pinprick, but it hurt. The words slipped out before she could control them. 'Need you ask?'

Leo drew a taut breath. 'I have to be sure! Your previous objection cannot stand. There can be no question of our not becoming bedfellows.'

Timothia gazed up at him, mute. She waited again, and it seemed to her that every particle inside her grew hushed also. But Leo did not say the words she needed to hear, and the silence lengthened. Slowly it filled. With a building pressure. With an inner cry that took root in Timothia's heart—and stayed there.

'You do not answer me,' Leo said at last, and his voice was heavy. 'Timma, I am asking you again to marry me.'

And that was all! The answer came—etched in fire. There would be no marriage, for Leo did not return her love.

# Chapter Eleven

The sofa was wretchedly uncomfortable, and the footstool upon which her leg rested was in quite the wrong position. The hideously dark third parlour, which Timothia had taken over for her sole use these last few days, felt unbearably stuffy. Its wood-panelled walls were unrelieved by anything more attractive than a portrait of Mama, who so much resembled her nephew Leo that Timothia could hardly bear to look at it. The weather—typically in this never-ending excuse for a summer—was too inclement to permit of opening the paned casements more than an inch or two. And the view was so dull that there was little point in having had Padstow turn the sofa to face the window. How she hated Fenny House! It was ugly, inconvenient, and—with savage emphasis—*poky*.

Susan's entry, bearing a vase in which she had arranged the roses she had brought with her, did little to lighten Timothia's mood. For her friend, she knew, would only reopen the argument that had served only to depress her.

'There, dearest,' said Susan, placing the vase of blooms upon the small table set in a corner of the room. 'They will serve to cheer the place up a little. And you need not complain of their having been cut, for Papa was but pruning the rose bushes, and I seized them from him.'

She crossed to take her place next to Timothia on the sofa, which was the only seating accommodation that could fit into the room along the inner wall, aside from a couple of straight-backed chairs at either side of the fireplace.

'Now, where were we?'

Timothia sighed. 'Pray do not start over again, Susan.'

Her friend's wide brown eyes fixed themselves upon Timothia's face. 'I must, dearest Timma. I could not reconcile it with my conscience not to pursue the matter. Tell me, what exactly did Leo say?'

'I have told you. He asked me again to marry him.'

'Yes, but what did he *say*?' demanded Susan insistently.

Timothia threw back her head in frustration. 'I cannot remember it exactly. Suffice it that he did not say what I had expected.' She caught Susan's glance, and emitted a mew of protest, bursting out, 'Very well, if you must have it, he said that I might not now object to our becoming bedfellows. Are you content?' She added, on a note of morbid satisfaction, 'I knew you would be shocked.'

'I am not shocked,' objected Susan. 'At least, I am, but not more than usual at the things you say, Timma.'

Timothia heaved another sigh, and reached out for her friend's hand, pressing it briefly. 'Susan, it was one of the points of dissension between us, when I first refused him. While I was staying in his house, I realised that it was no longer a barrier with me. Leo knew it. That is all he meant.'

'And yet you refused him again,' stated Susan flatly.

Unable to meet her eyes, Timothia looked out at the garden and the dull sky, a view necessarily broken up into squares by the leaded panes. But she did not see them, for her mind dwelled these days with obstinate insistence upon Leo's face—at the moment when she had told him she would not marry him.

'He was shocked—hurt, I think,' she said aloud, reliving the sensation of pain she had herself felt at inflicting it. But she'd had no choice. '*Insulted*—that was what he said.'

'After you had kissed him in such a fashion, I should think he might be,' declared Susan with unusual asperity. 'It was most improper.'

'It was not that. Leo didn't care for that.'

'What, then?'

The now familiar ache at Timothia's heart started up. 'He said that I had led him to believe that he might receive a very different answer. And I had, Susan. Only I could not marry him. I couldn't!'

Susan eyed her sombrely. 'And that is why you left Wiggin Hall?'

Timothia nodded. 'Leo made no objection. I was going to send immediately for Bickley, but Crieff told me that Leo had arranged for me to go in his coach.' She stared dull-eyed at her friend. 'He would not even come to say goodbye.'

She saw Susan's ready sympathy was stirred, but felt no inclination to weep. She had cried all her tears out. There were none left to match the desolation in her breast.

'That is most unlike Leo. He must have been very distressed, dearest. Indeed, I think we all were. I know that Jenny could scarce believe it.'

This piece of information did nothing to ease Timothia's discomforts. She had already sustained a visit from the doctor's daughter, who had come with her father when he had attended his patient on Tuesday, the day following

her departure from Wiggin—having looked in vain for her
there. Timothia had endured a pithy condemnation of her
foolhardiness in setting forth at all, let alone putting herself in danger of a relapse by returning to the confined
spaces of Fenny House. She had responded with less than
the truth, saying that she had ample space to exercise the
ankle to his instructions, and pointing out that Bickley was
able to carry her upstairs if the need arose, or Padstow to
assist her to walk as might be necessary to her comfort.
That she missed intolerably the more pleasurable ministrations of her cousin was a matter she had kept to herself.

Dr Preseley had grunted his dissatisfaction, and spoken
his mind at some length on the recalcitrance of difficult
patients. Timothia had been indebted to his daughter for
bringing his catalogue of complaints to an abrupt halt,
breaking in upon him without ceremony.

'Papa, you are distressing Miss Dulverton! I am sure
she is sufficiently scolded now. Do be kind to her again.'

Brought up short, the doctor had looked surprised, and
then rueful. 'Forgive me, my dear. Jenny is quite right. I
cannot think why I am running on in this grumbling way.'

He had rapidly resumed his usual cheerful demeanour,
offering some sound advice on the best methods of managing in the restricted environment. It had been Jenny,
however, whispering brief words into her ear as she bent
over her to say farewell, who had pierced Timothia's ar-
mour.

'I do hope, Miss Dulverton, that it is not a serious
breach between you and Mr Wetheral. He did look to be
uncommonly afflicted.'

Which piece of information had afflicted its recipient
to no little extent. That Leo might be suffering was almost
worse than her own despair. But as she could not ease

him without putting herself into a lifelong cage of anguish and unrest she was helpless.

To be reminded of it was of little use, and she told Susan as much. 'Pray do not tell me anything that you and Jenny may have discussed. I know it for myself, I thank you.'

Susan frowned. 'Timma, this is all so nonsensical. Can you deny that you are in a state of woe?'

Timothia could not deny it, but she refused to say so. 'What else can you expect? My ankle is still troubling me. And this house is driving me insane!'

She found herself the subject of one of her friend's more direct looks. 'You have always maintained that Fenny House is perfectly adequate.'

'Not for an invalid. Besides, I only said so because you would all condemn it so. I hate the place!'

'You need not dissemble,' said Susan, with an air of complete scepticism. 'You do not hate it at all. Your real complaint against Fenny House is that it does not contain Leo.'

Timothia uttered a cry of despair, throwing her hands over her face. 'Oh, don't, Susan! What is the use of tormenting me?' She brought her hands down, and fairly glared at her friend. 'What do you want me to say? That you were right—that I love Leo? Well, then, know it for the truth! Yes, I love him. I have no doubt that I have always loved him. Would to heaven that I had never found it out!'

To her annoyance, Susan was looking both smug and delighted. 'I knew it all along. But what in the world should stop you from telling him I am at a loss to make out.'

Timothia stared at her. 'Have you taken leave of your senses? Tell Leo that I love him! How could I possibly do so? Had he returned my affections he would have told me so when he renewed his offer. But he does not, Susan. Oh, he cares for me a great deal. But not like *this*.'

To her astonishment, Susan leapt from her seat and faced her, pansy eyes blazing. 'What is the matter with you, Timma? Must everything always be perfect? For my part, I would endure tortures for a tithe of the feeling from Valentine that Leo bears towards you!'

'Then why in the world,' demanded Timothia with heat, 'have you never told Valentine that you love him? It is all very well for you to ring a peal over me, Susan. At least I have but just discovered my feelings for Leo. You have never wavered in your love for Valentine, and you have known it for ever. Yet you would have died before you told him of it!'

Her friend looked thunderstruck, all trace of fury vanished. Timothia frowned as Susan continued silent for a space. Remorse began to creep into her breast.

'Susan, I—'

'No, don't say any more!' interrupted Susan in a flurried sort of way. 'You are perfectly right. I am quite as foolish as you, and even more to be censured.'

'Susan, pray don't—'

'No, no, be quiet! Don't spoil it, or my resolution may fail.' Timothia watched in puzzlement as her friend drew an enormous breath, and nodded with great determination. 'It is time and past that I took my courage in my hands!' She bent quickly to kiss Timothia's cheek. 'Goodbye, dearest Timma. I will leave you to brood in solitude for the moment, but in the hope that presently you may profit by my example.'

With which cryptic utterance, she tripped quickly from the room, leaving Timothia utterly mystified.

* * *

'Do you tell me,' she was asking Valentine some few hours later, 'that Susan actually confessed her feelings to you?'

'Bold as brass!' Valentine said, grinning. 'I have but just come from the Rectory. Old Hurst gave his permission without any trouble, I'm glad to say.'

Timothia did not doubt it. Susan's father must have blessed his good fortune. To have his daughter off his hands at last, and to the one man whom she most desired to wed. Lost for words, she looked across the dining-table to where Edith sat, signalling with frantic eyes for help. Mrs Hawnby shrugged in response, and plied the guest with more wine.

'We'll drink health to the happy couple,' she said, raising her own glass. 'Usual procedure, I think.'

Valentine had walked in upon them in the middle of dinner to announce his news, saying that Sue had begged him to tell Timma immediately. Amazed, she had demanded to know how it had come about, recalling with some unease her friend's words that morning. Susan had, it appeared, done just what she had told her friend to do, and informed Valentine that she loved him. Lord Pentre, it transpired, had promptly offered for her.

'I wish you very happy,' she said, lifting her glass. 'But, Valentine, I must tell you that I am barely satisfied.'

'Dash it, why not?' he demanded. 'I'm a good catch, aren't I?'

'You are an excellent catch,' Timothia conceded, 'but that is not the point.'

Edith laid down her glass. 'No sense in beating about the bush.' She turned to face Valentine who had taken a seat to one side of her. 'Thing is, my young buck, that you could have offered for the girl any time these five years. But you didn't. Now you walk in here, saying that she'd only to say she loved you, and you popped the question.'

'Just so,' said Timothia, grateful for her companion's bluntness.

'Well, what else could I do?' asked Valentine, raising his brows. 'I mean to say, this is Sue we're talking about. You couldn't expect me to do anything else—not with those spaniel eyes looking at me!'

'Yes, I know the look,' agreed Timothia. And she supposed he was right. What was a gentleman to do when a lady told him that he had her heart? Only, could he be satisfied with such a union? 'But do you truly want to marry her?'

'I do now,' he said cheerfully. 'Mean to say, I don't have any choice.'

Timothia caught Edith looking at her with that knowing eye. Did her companion understand her deep dissatisfaction? Could poor Susan possibly be happy with a man who had married her only because he could not do anything else? Somewhat to her relief, Edith chose to absent herself from any further discussion. Bidding Valentine not to keep Timothia there too long, for she ought to have the leg raised, she left them.

Valentine got up and took a chair closer to Timothia. He drew the wine bottle towards him as he spoke. 'Glad she's gone. Never could speak freely before that dragon of yours.'

'I wish you would speak freely, Valentine,' Timothia said forcefully. 'Edith was right, you know. It is of no use to pretend that you wish for this match, for you could have thought of it for yourself a long time ago.'

'Yes, but I didn't know Sue was that way about me,' objected Valentine. He tossed off his wine and set it down again, frowning at Timothia. 'What I want to know is why you didn't tell me, Timma. Mean to say, you're her best friend. Dash it, you should have told me!'

Timothia smiled. 'I suppose it would not occur to you that I would not tell you because I am her best friend. You had as well ask Leo the same. He and the whole county have been aware of Susan's feelings towards you, Valentine. Only you have failed to notice it.'

He looked utterly taken aback. 'Good Lord! Is it so indeed? Dash it, I'd have done something about it long ago, if I'd known.'

'Would you?'

'Well, of course I would. Haven't found anyone I'd rather be riveted to. Just didn't think of Sue, that's all.'

Concern for her friend grew. He was taking it all far too lightly. 'Valentine, do you love her?' she demanded bluntly.

He stared at her, then at the red liquid with which he had refilled his glass. He sighed a little. 'To tell you the truth, Timma, I don't know. I'm fond of her, but—love?'

Fond… Was it enough? Timothia recalled his quarrel with Susan. She had thought then that his feeling for her ran deeper than he knew. But then Leo was *fond* of her. And it had not been enough!

'You would know if you truly loved her, Valentine,' she uttered in a burst of sudden passion. 'Believe me, you would know it!'

Valentine's eyes came back to her, and he regarded her with an intent look that rather unnerved Timothia. She hurried into speech again.

'If you value my advice, Valentine, you will not marry Susan unless you can love her with your whole heart. She loves you so very desperately. It is unfair to her to marry her when you cannot return her love.'

He was obviously rattled by the remark, for he set his

glass down with something of a snap. 'Nothing to be done about it now. I can't hedge off.'

'Susan can, though.'

'Dash it, I don't want her to!' said Valentine irascibly. 'Apart from making me look like a chucklehead, I'm not at all sure it ain't just what I wish for—to marry her, I mean.'

Timothia thought she detected a sort of wistful look in his face. She was sorry for her earlier words, and looked for something positive to say. She found it.

'At least Susan will not disgrace you, despite it being an unequal match. She has such a flair for fashion, she always looks well.'

Valentine visibly brightened. 'That's right. She does, don't she? Taking little thing, Sue. Dash it, I am attached to her! And she needs protecting.'

'Which you may do for her, even if you cannot love her,' she said, before she could stop herself.

To her consternation, she came once again under that disconcerting intensity as he stared at her. 'Set a deal of store by that, don't you, Timma?'

She flushed, and drew a painful breath. 'If—if I loved a man the—the way Susan loves you, Valentine, I could not marry him without knowing that he returned my affections—at least as much.'

It was a moment or two before he answered. Timothia felt him eyeing her, and for want of something to do reached out for her glass, only to discover that it was empty. Noticing it, Valentine went to refill it for her.

'No more, I thank you,' she said, putting her hand over it before he could pour the wine.

He put down the bottle. 'Sue ain't like you, Timma. I don't want to sound like a coxcomb, mind. Thing is, when

I asked her to marry me, she said she knew I didn't love her.'

'She said that?'

He nodded. 'What's more, she said she didn't mind it. Said she was more miserable without me than with me. And I'm not sure she ain't in the right of it. I'd not go so far as to have called myself miserable before, but I can tell you this. The thought of marrying Sue is dashed pleasant!'

Timothia smiled and held out her hand to him. 'Then I must be satisfied. I do wish you very happy, Valentine.' In a rare moment of gallantry, Valentine kissed her hand and thanked her. A chuckle escaped her. 'And if nothing else you will have the satisfaction of having made Lady Hurst as mad as fire.'

Valentine let out a roar of laughter. 'That's enough to have reconciled me, even if I didn't wish to marry Sue!'

Which statement reassured Timothia somewhat. She could not be entirely satisfied until she had spoken with Susan herself, and she could not help wondering what Leo might make of it. But it was evident that Valentine was so rapidly accustoming himself to the idea that she thought it would not be long before he had persuaded himself that it had come out of his own head!

Susan responded with alacrity to her letter of felicitation and question, driving over to see her next day. Timothia greeted her with half a mind to dissuade her from what she still considered a hazardous step. But her friend's happiness was so transparent that she had not the heart to say one word against the marriage. In the event, Susan saved her the trouble.

'Dearest Timma, you must not fret for me—though I know you will! It is true that Valentine does not love me as I love him. But he has some affection for me, and perhaps it will deepen with time.'

'Is it enough for you, Susan?' she was unable to help asking.

Susan's radiance answered her. 'Half a loaf is better than none, Timma—especially if you have had no bread for years and years!'

It was not a sentiment with which Timothia could bring herself to agree. But she listened with every evidence of interest to her friend's plans for her wedding, and her expectation of much enjoyment in confounding such ill-disposed matrons as her aunt Hurst and Mrs Baguley. Susan's bubbling enthusiasm was infectious, and she was beginning to derive real enjoyment from her friend's art-less chatter when they suffered an interruption.

Padstow entered the parlour given over to Timothia's use. After one significant glance cast at his mistress, which she had no chance to interpret, he announced in a voice devoid of all feeling, 'Mr Wetheral to see you, Miss Timma.'

Timothia jumped in her seat, and Susan's tongue stopped dead. Padstow stood aside, and Leo walked into the room.

He stopped short when he saw that she was not alone. 'Susan! I didn't know. I—'

'No, pray come in, Leo,' said Susan, with what Timothia considered quite unlooked-for presence of mind. For no consideration in the world would she have had Leo turn around and walk out again! Although her heart was beating so fast that she was afraid of choking if she tried to speak.

Leo looked across at her briefly, but his eyes came back to Susan. 'I understand felicitations are in order.'

'Yes, thank you,' Susan said, beaming.

'I wish you happy, Susan, though I believe there is small need. I have seen Valentine. His head is quite in the clouds. I have no doubt that you will deal delightfully together.'

Timothia heard these words with a mixture of shock and confusion. Could he be in earnest? But why not? Leo had been himself willing to compound for marriage on a much lesser scale of affection! He would never see the matter in the same light as she did herself. She made an effort to pay attention, for Susan was relating the anticipated reaction of her relatives.

'I have sworn Claud to secrecy, for I am determined to tell my aunt Hurst for myself. I cannot wait to see her face!'

Leo smiled—a little mechanically, Timothia thought. 'I wish I might be present. She will likely go off in an apoplexy.'

'Oh, no! I dislike her amazingly, but I could not wish that upon her.'

'No, you are a good girl, Susan,' he said, and, pulling her quickly to him, gave her a peck on the cheek. 'You deserve your fortune, and Valentine is not worthy of you.'

But this Susan would by no means allow. Leo endured her protestations for a few moments, but his eye strayed constantly to Timma. She had said nothing since he had entered the room, and her silence was torture. He could hardly bear the drawn look in her cheeks—after she had been glowing with health on that fateful day. It had been but three days—and it felt like a lifetime. Unable to tolerate any further delay, he broke in on Susan's effusions.

'Give me leave, Susan! I beg your pardon, but I must speak with Timma alone.'

Timothia's heart jerked violently, and hammered in her breast. She saw her friend glance at her with a sudden dawning of hope and expectation. Susan turned back to Leo.

'Yes, of course. I was just leaving, in any event.'

She sped swiftly to Timothia, bending over her to kiss her cheek, and whispering, 'Send me word at once! I will be waiting to hear.'

Timothia had no chance to respond to this. It seemed that she had hardly wished her friend farewell than Leo was bowing her from the room, and shutting the door behind her. He turned, and Timothia met his eyes.

For a moment, he did not speak. She thought he was about to, but he appeared to change his mind, turning away and moving a few steps to the window.

'How have you been?' he asked, without turning round to look at her.

'Well enough,' she replied, low-voiced.

'You are managing all right here?'

'It is not easy. But yes, I am managing.'

Another silence fell. Leo was conscious of a severe constriction about his chest. How in the world could he broach the thing? It had seemed too obviously easy when he had set out. But in the presence of Timma his determination was fast deserting him. They could not go on like this for much longer. He found something with which to procrastinate.

'I came to talk of this betrothal.'

Disappointment dropped like a stone into Timothia's breast. So that was why he had come. She had been a fool to suppose anything else. To dare to hope. But she must not sit here mumchance. She had to say something.

'Susan is ecstatic.'

'Valentine likewise,' he replied, still keeping his gaze upon the garden outside.

Timothia followed suit, looking emptily upon the

brightness that had at last come out, as if the weather was in tune with Susan's happiness—as it had before been with her misery.

'Do you approve of it?' he asked.

She sighed. 'I did not at first.'

Leo turned at last to look at her. 'Why not?'

Timothia caught his glance and looked away again. That were quite impossible to answer. Heavens, what could she say?

'Why not, Timma?'

The repetition was made in that harsh tone that characterised Leo at his most bitter. It thrust straight into Timothia's heart. Huskily, she answered him.

'Valentine does not love her.'

'You don't know that,' he said, still in the same brusque way. 'How can you know that?'

She kept her gaze lowered. 'He told me so.'

'Did he? Did he say that he did not love her?'

Timothia shifted uncomfortably. 'He said that he did not know.'

'Ah! That is a very different thing.' He moved a step or two towards her. 'Look at me, Timma!'

She did so, and found his bright blue gaze fixed on her face, such a blaze of intense passion in it that she could not look away. Her heart thumped unbearably.

'Valentine did not know,' he said curtly. 'But he is in a fair way to knowing now. He is luckier than I was, for he had not to throw himself into the fiery furnace before he found it out!'

Timothia gripped her hands together in her lap. She could not mistake the tenor of this speech. Abruptly, she recalled her conversation with Valentine. He had seen it! Seen her feelings—and he had told Leo! Was she to be thrown a bone as Susan had been? No, by heaven, it was to insult her! Indignation blazed up in her chest, and her voice cracked.

'Don't dare to tell me lies, Leo! If you have only false protestations, make them elsewhere!'

A heavy frown descended on his brow. 'The devil! I have not even said it and you profess to disbelieve me!'

'I don't want to hear it,' she uttered throatily. 'Oh, Leo, don't do this, I pray you. I know what has happened. Valentine has given me away.'

Leo came quickly up, seating himself beside her, in the place vacated by Susan. His hand covered both of hers where they were clenched one inside the other. 'Timma, if you love me, for God's sake, make an end! I can endure no more.'

Timothia closed her eyes tight shut, willing herself not to give in. Oh, she wanted so much to believe in this—but she dared not!

'If you are going to ask me again to marry you—'

'I am! And I will ask you again and again and again, if need be—until you see sense! You idiotic woman, can't you see that I am so much in love with you that it is killing me?'

Her heart contracted so tightly that she thought it must burst. She had no idea as she turned to him that her eyes were tragic under a luminous sheen. Leo cursed. Next instant, Timothia was crushed in an embrace so violent that she could only just breathe. Leo's lips were hard as they found her mouth, and the intensity of his kiss quite drowned her senses.

He released her so suddenly that she fell back against the cushioned seat of the sofa, gasping for air. She felt her fingers seized, her hand drawn to his lips to be kissed, and kissed again with feverish haste. Then he all but threw her hand down again into her lap, rose up from the sofa,

and strode restlessly about the tight confines of the parlour
for several moments. Timothia watched him, mute, catching at her breath. But there was nothing she could do
about the bumping pressure of her chest, and the only
thought that kept reiterating in her head was that her
cousin had run totally mad!

Leo at length fetched up against the door, leaning at it
like a solid mass, his folded arms thrust one into the other
with fierce determination, as if he dared not leave them
free for fear of some wild intent on their part that he might
not control. The dynamic orbs gazed with belligerence
across at Timothia.

'Well?' he shot at her grimly.

'What do you mean, *well*?' she demanded.

'Do I love you, or don't I?'

Resentment welled up. With near careless haste, Timothia lifted her leg off the footstool, and thrust herself to
her feet. Leo took a frowning pace forward, but she threw
up a hand to stay him.

'Don't you dare come near me! I can stand perfectly
well. And if you have any thought of mauling me again
in that perfectly ill-bred fashion I shall—'

'Do what? Decide fast, because I have every intention
of repeating myself—'

'—strike you with a blunt instrument, Leo!'

'—as many times as it takes to drum some sense into
that pigheaded brain of yours!'

She glared at him as he overrode her, eyes snapping.
When he had done, she drew a breath, and spoke with
dangerous emphasis. 'If you hope to persuade me by this
means that you are fallen in love with me, let me assure
you that nothing will induce me to believe it.'

Leo let out a bark of rude laughter. 'Simpleton! There
is no question of my having *fallen* in love with you. I

have been in love with you since I don't know when, the more fool I! Merely because I have but just discovered it—'

'Aha!' cried Timothia, pouncing on this. 'You have but just discovered it! Very convenient, Leo, to have made this famous discovery the very moment that Valentine tells you that I am in love with you.'

'How do you know when I discovered it?' countered Leo furiously. 'I will lay you any odds that I knew my mind before ever you knew yours.'

Timothia was ready to scream. 'Leo, I don't wish you to do this! I am not a silly débutante whom you are obliged to cozen with false protestations of affection. Pray stop it!'

Leo threw his hands in the air in a gesture of utter helplessness, unable to find words as he stared at her.

'You will drive me demented,' he managed raggedly at last.

'Then you will be well served for lying to me!'

He let out a cry like a demon. Then his fingers clutched at his hair, dragging through it and wholly disarranging the already unruly locks, his eyes wildly roving her countenance.

'I don't know what to say to you,' he declared frustratedly. 'What must I do? Blow my brains out? Deuce take it, Timma, I swear if I did not love you so much I would strangle you!'

He shook his head in a gesture of confused disbelief, and Timothia felt suddenly and acutely conscience-stricken. Had she been taken at fault? Was she wronging him? Leo would not lie—would he? Not to his cousin. Not about something as vital as this. The righteous indignation that had been driving her dropped right out. Uncertainty filled her heart. And abruptly—breathless, holding her hushed and still—hope.

Leo saw the change, and a quiver of emotion ran through him. Oh, Timma. How vulnerable she was, after all! He felt her dilemma as if it were his own. Just so had he experienced it after that explosive kiss in his library. Unable, for the intensity of his own feelings, to dare to hope they were reciprocated. For fear her passion had betokened nothing more than his own had seemed to do, when first he realised his desire for her. Foolishly, he had held off from speaking his heart—afraid that if he did so he must lose her. In the event, his very reticence had done it for him. His thoughts led him directly into speech.

'I should have told you that day,' he said jerkily. 'I had known it then for—oh, since your accident. Though it was the Preseley chit who brought it to a head. Unwittingly. She said it outright. I recall it so clearly. ''You are in love with her, are you not, Mr Wetheral?''.'

He paused, and Timothia waited—a world of promise almost within reach. The bewildered disorder at his eyes made her heart turn over. Just so had she felt at the instant of finding out her own feelings.

'I said yes.'

The simplicity of this declaration did what all the earlier violent outpourings had failed to do. Acceptance melted her bones. She swayed a little. Next instant she was in his arms, and he was gentling her against his chest.

'Timma, my love, my darling friend—there could never have been any woman but you.'

'Nor any man but you,' she uttered huskily, and was obliged to choke back her tears as he kissed her with the utmost tenderness.

It was some time before Timothia was in any case to talk again with a modicum of her usual assurance. She found herself reseated, with her leg raised as before, having been swept literally off her feet in a flurry of petticoats and laughter as Leo's kisses became ever more demanding. He was obliged at length to pause for breath, and ended with one arm firmly about her, while in the other he held her fingers, playing with them like a child with a new toy.

'I cannot tell you how glad I am that you refused me,' he told her lovingly.

'The first time?' she said, with the smile that she was unable to halt for an instant.

'I shudder to think of that life I had proposed to you. The horror of the bloodless image I had conjured absolutely haunts me.'

'Yes, it haunted me at the time,' Timothia told him frankly.

Leo's arm tightened about her. 'With reason. I was deservedly set down.'

She shot him a provocative gleam. 'What? Do you tell me that you have abandoned your scheme to have me run everything while you disport yourself with guns and such?'

'By no means,' he responded on a teasing note. 'I am not willing to relinquish all my pleasures merely because I love you. And since you are of all females the most docile and obedient I cannot doubt but that you will quietly settle to your tasks in my absence.'

'Indeed? You have heard, I presume, of the warrior skills of a certain sisterhood among whom you are wont to name me. I believe that they dealt short shrift to errant husbands.'

Leo laughed and nuzzled her neck. 'Almost you tempt me to wander, my Amazon delight.' He tugged at her plait, loosening strands of her flaxen mane as he drove his fingers within it, pulling her head back. Passion throbbed in his voice. 'Would that I could carry you back to Wiggin Hall this very day!'

'You may, with my goodwill,' Timothia said, returning his kiss with matching violence.

'I hate to admit it,' she added when she was able, 'but you were so right about this house. Poky precisely describes it! I have missed Wiggin Hall.' She added with a lilt of her lips, 'As well as its owner.'

'Not, I dare swear, as much as I have missed your presence there. But lest I forget what is due to your honour, my love, I daren't take you back until we are safely wed.' Of a sudden, he tugged her head round so that she faced him, and frowned. 'Speaking of which, do you realise that you have not in fact responded to this latest of my many offers?'

Timothia raised her brows. 'So far as I am aware, you have not in fact made me an offer today.'

'Have I not? How very remiss.' He leaned in to kiss her again, lingeringly. 'Will you marry me?' Then, before she could answer, he put a finger to her lips, and his eyes grew sombre. 'Wait!'

Her heart stilled, and she seized his hand, drawing the finger away. 'Oh, what is it? Don't hurt me, dear heart; I couldn't bear it!'

Quickly Leo shook his head, gripping her fingers. 'No, no, nothing like that! Only—' there was an intensity in his lowered voice that caught at the depths of her love '—marry me, Timma! Not for our mutual advantage. Nor for my heir, nor to care for Babs. Nor to exercise your undoubted talents upon my estate. For none of the things I put to you with such barbarous insensitivity.' He drew her fingers to his lips and cherished them, drawing her closer. 'Marry me for affection, for companionship. And, most of all, for love.'

His features blurred in Timothia's vision. 'For all of that—and more. For a lifetime of friendship, Leo.'

Leo's smile came, and he traced the wetness under her eye with one finger. 'But you still don't say the word. Will you marry me?'

'With all my heart—yes.'

And for some little while there was no further need of words. But presently the most appalling presentiment struck Leo, and he raised his head abruptly.

'The devil!'

Timothia frowned in quick consternation. 'What in the world is the matter?'

Leo eyed her in some alarm. 'Would you place any odds against the chance that Valentine and Susan will wish to make a double wedding of it?'

Her eyes widened. 'I had not thought of that! Shall we elope?'

'Elope!' he scoffed. 'How could we possibly do so? You can scarce walk, let alone travel all the way to Scotland.'

'But we need not go to Scotland,' argued Timothia. 'We are both of age. There is nothing to stop us marrying anywhere at all, if we can but obtain a special licence.'

'If you imagine I intend to marry you in such a scrambling way, Timma, you must have windmills in your head,' Leo told her. 'In any event, you are in no case to be doing anything other than resting that ankle for a good few weeks yet.'

'Don't be stupid, Leo. I am perfectly well able to walk now. In fact, I am thinking of riding, for my right leg will not be needed, and—'

'If you dare to attempt anything so foolhardy—'

'Leo, for pity's sake, don't start to get boorish and autocratic all over again, for I tell you now that—'

The words were stifled in her throat, for Leo, recognising the futility of the argument, put an end to it by kissing her. By the time he finally released her mouth, after a shattering assault that left her breathless with yearning, she had but one thought in her head.

'Leo.'

'Yes, dear one?'

'I will marry you by any means you choose—but let it be soon!' A sentiment with which her betrothed found himself to be in the most complete agreement.

\*     \*     \*     \*     \*

# MILLS & BOON®

*Makes any time special*™

## Mills & Boon publish 29 new titles every month. Select from...

Modern Romance™  Tender Romance™

Sensual Romance™

Medical Romance™  Historical Romance™

## 2 FREE books and a surprise gift!

We would like to take this opportunity to thank you for reading this Mills & Boon® book by offering you the chance to take TWO more specially selected titles from the Historical Romance™ series absolutely FREE! We're also making this offer to introduce you to the benefits of the Reader Service™—

★ FREE home delivery
★ FREE gifts and competitions
★ FREE monthly Newsletter
★ Exclusive Reader Service discounts
★ Books available before they're in the shops

Accepting these FREE books and gift places you under no obligation to buy, you may cancel at any time, even after receiving your free shipment. Simply complete your details below and return the entire page to the address below. ***You don't even need a stamp!***

**YES!** Please send me 2 free Historical Romance books and a surprise gift. I understand that unless you hear from me, I will receive 4 superb new titles every month for just £2.99 each, postage and packing free. I am under no obligation to purchase any books and may cancel my subscription at any time. The free books and gift will be mine to keep in any case.

H0ZEA

Ms/Mrs/Miss/Mr .............................Initials..............................
BLOCK CAPITALS PLEASE

Surname ........................................................................................

Address ........................................................................................

....................................................................................................

....................................................Postcode..............................

**Send this whole page to:**
**UK: FREEPOST CN81, Croydon, CR9 3WZ**
**EIRE: PO Box 4546, Kilcock, County Kildare (stamp required)**